SEAL MY DESTINY

SEAL Brotherhood

Book 6

SHARON HAMILTON

SHARON HAMILTON'S BOOK LIST

SEAL BROTHERHOOD SERIES

Accidental SEAL (Book 1)
Fallen SEAL Legacy (Book 2)
SEAL Under Covers (Book 3)
SEAL The Deal (Book 4)
Cruisin' For A SEAL (Book 5)
SEAL My Destiny (Book 6)
SEAL Of My Heart (Book 7)
Fredo's Dream (Book 8)
SEAL My Love (Book 9)
SEAL Brotherhood Box Set 1 (Accidental SEAL & Prequel)
SEAL Brotherhood Box Set 2 (Fallen SEAL & Prequel)
Ultimate SEAL Collection Vol. 1 (Books 1-4 / 2 Prequels)
Ultimate SEAL Collection Vol. 2 (Books 5-7)

BAD BOYS OF SEAL TEAM 3 SERIES

SEAL's Promise (Book 1)
SEAL My Home (Book 2)
SEAL's Code (Book 3)
Big Bad Boys Bundle (Books 1-3 of Bad Boys)

BAND OF BACHELORS SERIES

Lucas (Book 1)
Alex (Book 2)
Jake (Book 3)
Jake 2 (Book 4)
Big Band of Bachelors Bundle

TRUE BLUE SEALS SERIES

True Navy Blue (prequel to Zak)
Zak (Includes novella above)

NASHVILLE SEAL SERIES

Nashville SEAL (Book 1)
Nashville SEAL: Jameson (Books 1 & 2 combined)

SILVER SEALS

SEAL Love's Legacy

SLEEPER SEALS

Bachelor SEAL

STAND ALONE SEALS

SEAL's Goal: The Beautiful Game

Love Me Tender, Love You Hard

BONE FROG BROTHERHOOD SERIES

New Year's SEAL Dream (Book 1)

SEALed At The Altar (Book 2)

SEALed Forever (Book 3)

PARADISE SERIES

Paradise: In Search of Love

STANDALONE NOVELLAS

SEAL You In My Dreams (Magnolias and Moonshine)

SEAL Of Time (Trident Legacy)

FALL FROM GRACE SERIES (PARANORMAL)

Gideon: Heavenly Fall

GOLDEN VAMPIRES OF TUSCANY SERIES (PARANORMAL)

Honeymoon Bite (Book 1)

Mortal Bite (Book 2)

Christmas Bite (Book 3)

Midnight Bite (Book 4 Coming Summer 2019)

THE GUARDIANS (PARANORMAL)

Heavenly Lover (Book 1)

Underworld Lover (Book 2)

Underworld Queen (Book 3)

AUDIOBOOKS

Sharon Hamilton's books are available as audiobooks narrated by J.D. Hart.

ABOUT THE BOOK

Navy SEAL Luke Paulsen, on the verge of PTSD stemming from the death of his fiancée and a brutal tour overseas, knows he is damaged goods and unsuitable for relationships. While paying respects to a fallen comrade, he is unprepared for the chemical attraction he feels for the carefree dark-haired beauty playing in the surf one evening.

Julie Christensen befriends the troubled SEAL, motivated by her yearning to soothe the young man's troubled soul. Fueled by intense mutual desire, they succumb to one night of mind-numbing passion. Afterwards, he is unable to shed the memory of his lost love and disappears.

When they meet again at a wedding that will forever bring their two families together, their passion and longing for one another forces them to confront their pasts in order to find a future together.

But soon the trauma of his service separates them. Julie goes back to teaching and Luke deploys for North Africa with SEAL Team 3. Upon his return, he receives a frantic call that Julie's life is in danger. Will he make it in time to save the woman he now knows he wants to marry and spend the rest of his life with?

AUTHOR'S NOTE

I always dedicate my SEAL Brotherhood books to the brave men and women who defend our shores and keep us safe. Without their sacrifice, and that of their families—because a warrior's fight always includes his or her family—I wouldn't have the freedom and opportunity to make a living writing these stories. They sometimes pay the ultimate price so we can debate, argue, go have coffee with friends, raise our children and see them have children of their own.

One of my favorite tributes to warriors resides on many memorials, including one I saw honoring the fallen of WWII on an island in the Pacific:

"When you go home
Tell them of us, and say
For your tomorrow,
We gave our today."

These are my stories created out of my own imagination. Anything that is inaccurately portrayed is either my mistake, or done intentionally to disguise something I might have overheard over a beer or in the corner of one of the hangouts along the Coronado Strand.

I support two main charities. Navy SEAL/UDT Museum operates in Ft. Pierce, Florida. Please learn about this wonderful museum, all run by active and former SEALs and their friends and families, and who rely on public support, not that of the U.S. Government.
www.navysealmuseum.org

I also support Wounded Warriors, who tirelessly bring together the warrior as well as the family members who are just learning to deal with their soldier's condition and have nowhere to turn. It is a long path to becoming well, but I've seen first-hand what this organization does for its warriors and the families who love them. Please give what your heart tells you is right. If you cannot give, volunteer at one of the many service centers all over the United States. Get involved. Do something meaningful for someone who gave so much of themselves, to families who have paid the price for your freedom. You'll find a family there unlike any other on the planet.
www.woundedwarriorproject.org

The video trailer for SEAL My Destiny is available on YouTube.

youtube.com/watch?v=M5l6SObygH8

CHAPTER 1

NAVY SEAL LUKE Paulsen had that dream again.

Her red lips felt like succulent pillows against his cool mouth. Though he was huddled in his Afghan dugout bunk, he could feel the delicate vibration of her moan as her lust for him whispered things. Unmentionable things. No matter how hard he tried, he couldn't recall her words. He could only remember the heat washing over him while she breathed life into him. Again. Like she did every night.

A sharp crack of gunfire forced him to open his eyes. He caught a glimpse of Carson's frightened face in profile just before the young Marine caught a round in the chest, ripping through him between his shoulder blades. In a graceful dance Luke had seen all too often, Carson fell into his arms, and he watched the youngster's life bleed out onto the sandy pit and all over his boots. He held Carson's clear blue gaze and, without saying a word, told him he'd see him again one day while he witnessed the young Marine's passage from his arms into the arms of death. The boy's eyes remained open and fixed after his soul had departed.

A split second later, Luke remembered who he was and why he was here. A day's ride by donkey from anywhere. He lifted the tiny mirror on a wire, the sun to his back.

Still clutching the body of the lifeless Marine, he traced the trajectory of the round that had killed his young apprentice and caught the glint of dark blue steel disappearing into a blackened doorway. Laying the Marine down gently, he picked up his H&K MP5, counted to five while he clicked the safety once. Before he saw the barrel of the ragman's rifle again, he fired off several rounds which landed exactly ten inches above the protuberance, and then saw the red spray of a kill.

Was it wrong that the color of the spray reminded him of her crimson lips? That he died a thousand little deaths with each of her kisses?

His dreams were stealing his present.

A WEEK LATER, SO Luke Paulsen watched the sun pour itself into the horizon from one of San Diego's white sand beaches. The afterglow felt good. So did the flush on his face from the three beers. He usually drank with the rest of his SEAL Team 3. But this last DT, Dissociative Tour, in Afghanistan had teamed him with cadres of young Marines eager to prove themselves, including Carson, the medic-in-training.

But Carson had drawn a different card and had taken the short flight to heaven while his body took the long flight home. Luke raised his long-necked IPA to the sunset and toasted the kid.

"To all the young hearts you won't break," he whispered to the soothing waves and the sunset.

It was a damned shame. Carson would have made an excellent doctor.

Luke heard laughter as two lovelies in shorts ran past him to splash in the surf. Slender, tanned legs kicked droplets of white foam into the air. He loved watching the girls' carefree spirit, just being goofy and lacking an ounce of self-consciousness. He couldn't help but smile.

The dark-haired girl, the one with the cut off, inside-out sweatshirt that showed her muscled midriff, stopped and turned to face Luke. Her brown eyes were set wide apart over a thin nose that led to full, bright red lips. She licked those lips and pushed her mahogany brown hair from her forehead, exposing a delicious ridge of little worry lines on an otherwise smooth and flawless forehead. She cocked her head at a tiny angle and waved in that embarrassed way her mother must have told her never to do. Especially to a strange sailor sitting alone on the beach with empty beer bottles at his feet.

Luke waved back, using the same twiddled fingers she used, sending his communication off with a shy smile. He imitated the angle of her head and felt the dangerous curiosity and wonder of their chance meeting.

He wanted her in the worst way.

The blonde was pulling her friend, gesturing to a spot down the beach, but the dark-haired girl wasn't having any of it. Luke's unspoken message clearly had reached her, and the golden tethers of his thoughts drew her to him, just as if he had special powers. It was lovely when that happened. He could almost believe in the supernatural, like those paranormal guys his sister read about in her romance novels.

The exquisite young thing with the well-defined legs came to within striking distance. If he wanted to—and hell, yes, he wanted to—he could reach out and bring her into his arms. And he could tell she wouldn't resist. But it would be so much better if he showed a little restraint.

Those who wait? What was that saying?

No matter. Luke felt the confusing enchantment, like vamps did in those books. It was a pleasant fantasy. Let her have her way with him. *Yes.* He could tell she believed she had a date with destiny.

I can be your destiny for one night, darlin'.

She disposed of her friend with a sharp command and, alone now, stepped closer to Luke. "You look like you could use some company," she said as she swung her upper torso from side to side. Her feet were planted in the sand and he watched her pink nail polish peek out from beneath the grains.

Lady, you have lovely toes.

But she'd asked a question that needed an answer.

"That depends." He was stunned at the joy it gave him let his eyes walk slowly up her body, every lovely inch, heightened by the knowledge that she let him. He watched the tops of her breasts quiver under the cotton sweatshirt.

He'd learned to assess subtle changes in body language and heart rate. He noticed the blush in her cheeks and the red blotches on her chest just below the delicate V at the top of her breastbone. His eyes roamed over her quivering chest again, and he smiled. He couldn't wait to hear her response.

"Depends on what?" she asked. Her brown eyes mirrored truths he wasn't sure he'd divulged to himself.

"If it's complicated," he said. "I like *un*complicated." He was telling her something he was trying to convince himself he believed.

She took a sudden brief inhale, her gaze quickly

diverted to the ocean, giving him a full-pour look at her upper torso, every curve and dip, until he thought perhaps he could even taste her skin. What Luke saw in profile was a strong, handsome woman with a body made for hard loving, and who was unafraid.

Then she turned back and faced him fully. She sunk to her knees in front of him so quickly he thought perhaps she'd suddenly gotten ill. "I don't do uncomplicated," she whispered. "I like it *complicated* and rich. I like entangled. I like feeling everything and being sorely missed when I'm gone."

She didn't physically touch him, but she had mated with a part of his body that was rarely visited.

His soul.

The next few minutes flew in a blur of erotic fantasy, his body working on autopilot. He asked her the question without speaking a word. Keeping her eyes on his, but raising an eyebrow, she smiled softly, waiting for his response and then focused on his mouth. He stood, held out his hand, and they raced for the parking area.

He walked around the front of his red Mustang, watching her squirm to get comfortable, crossing those impossible legs on his leather front seat. His pants were tight from things springing to life. Yup. He had the brass band, the pom-poms, and the whole fucking cheering section working on him now. It was going to be an effort to take it slow.

He realized he wasn't going to be in charge when he opened the driver's door and tucked his stiff torso carefully around the steering wheel. When he looked at her face, she was staring at his lap.

So much for secrets.

Now that she knew he knew that she knew, it was going to be fucking impossible to move any slower than the speed of a bullet train.

"I'm between places..." he began by way of an apology.

"I have a roommate, and she's home tonight," she said as she frowned. "But I'm okay with a motel."

They were magic words. He leaned across the center console and planted a long, languid kiss against her hungry lips, lips just like the girl in his dream. She wore her perfume subtly, somewhere behind her ears or between her breasts, because the mild fragrance hooked his chest until he found himself with his arms wrapped around her, pressing her into him, feeling those firm, perfect breasts.

Her delicate fingers slid down his thigh and traveled over his erection. She squeezed him, and his package stiffened to full attention. He didn't want her to stop, but he'd make a mess right there in the front seat of his Mustang if they didn't get to a motel quick.

He managed to separate himself but held her fingers in his right hand while he turned the ignition with his left. After the car roared to life, his fingers began seriously having their way with her smooth skin and the dimples above her bottom, just inside her waistband, working down. She leaned forward to allow him access to anything he wanted. His forefinger had just discovered the warm cleft at the top of her derriere. She inhaled and leaned back onto his hand. Her voice was ragged as she whispered, "Hurry."

He clumsily shifted into drive, again with his left hand, and drove one-armed, with his dick stiff enough to handle the steering wheel all by itself. The Pink Slipper Cottage motel came into view just in time.

He thought about saying something like, "I wish I could take you some place nicer," but that would draw too much attention to his meager military salary. Maybe she didn't like sailors. And saying something like 'You're probably used to more expensive places' might indicate he thought she slept around a lot.

Fuck. No, it was safest to just say nothing.

She was all over him while he signed the guest register. The college kid with thick, round glasses tried hard not to notice, except he kept clearing his throat and swallowing hard. She slid a hand down the front of Luke's pants, which made him do a reverse whistle with his mouth.

"Luggage?" the clerk asked and then snapped his

eyes shut after stealing a look at her. The young man was in pain and couldn't control his shaking.

"I'll get it later," Luke answered.

Room 428 was tiny, not that it mattered. As soon as the door closed behind him she was removing his shirt, her hands riding up the muscular ridges of his chest. The feel of her warm flesh against his, her hair brushing gently against the underside of his chin, the way she shimmied herself out of her shorts with the help of both his hands, were driving him wild with anticipation. He couldn't get them properly naked fast enough.

She stepped back and sat on the bed, allowing him a full-length view of her nakedness, her shaved pussy, and the lips of her sex dipping down like his thirsty tongue. She propped herself on one hand, her knees spread, as she let him come to her, while she twirled a bit of her dark hair around the fingers of her right hand. It was his turn to drop to his knees.

He looked up at her while his hands reached out and touched her, barely at first, then with a lazy forefinger that circled her nub and slid up and down her moist passage. He loved looking at the fire building in her eyes when he made her wetness coat first one finger, then the other one, then a third until she accepted him fully. She leaned back enough so that he had all the room he needed, in case he might want to bring his face to her peach and drink.

Which of course he did. Happy to oblige. He saw the pink flesh of her lips parted as his tongue darted around the little button that made her jerk while he sucked the lovely, tangy moisture from her like he needed it to survive, while his fingers smoothed over her ass and tested a slight press against her anus. She didn't shy away. His cock got so stiff he had to adjust himself with his other hand. And he let her see it.

He was feeling more alive than he had in days. He'd held death, but now he was holding the promise of an evening of spilled seed, sweat, and anything else they could think of. She waited for him to taste his fill, her long hair falling down to touch the tops of her buttocks as she arched back and moaned.

He took his time with her, which he knew was what she wanted. She said she liked entangled. Complicated. Well, hell, he'd give her intense, then he'd worry about the entangled later. Right now it was all about keeping himself in check long enough to keep from exploding all over his knees.

Finally, he stood, looking down at her, cupping her face between his hands. With his fingers reaching into the mahogany strands behind her ears, he brought her to his mouth, still wet with her arousal. Before they could meet, she closed the distance, pressed against his hunger, and fed from his lips. His tongue found hers and caressed it as she plunged deep.

Slowly she wrapped one leg around his and slid her wet sex against his thigh. Her breathing was ragged, telling him she couldn't press hard enough, couldn't get enough. He lifted her with both hands seated below her butt cheeks, and slid her over his erection until her opening got snagged on him.

At this she tensed. Out of nowhere she produced a foil packet. He didn't want to set her down, but she was determined he wear something, so he obliged her. He let her lead him over to the bed, where she pushed him down, climbed on top, and slowly ripped the upper edge of the foil packet. It was one of those fancy pink gizmos with ridges.

Holy Goats, how am I going to last?

As if she heard him, she smiled. She pulled on his hand where it rested under his head on the starched white pillow and made him help her. Used his fingers to lubricate her opening, then lubricate him, and then cover him with the pink latex. In tandem, they massaged his rock-hard cock up and then down slowly.

Two of his fingers were still inside her when his cock entered her and she took a quick, deep inhale, and then settled herself down on him, laying her legs back and to the side for full penetration. God, he was deep.

They began a rhythmic pattern. She rode him, and she raised herself and then crushed into him while her muscles contracted around him and he started to feel a loss of control.

He'd been clutching one of her butt cheeks so hard while he rammed up into her, he felt welts on her skin. She removed his hand and showed him she wanted to change positions. She rolled to her side, then on her stomach, raising her sweet little derriere.

He got to his knees behind her as if in worship. He could fully enjoy her little nude opening, the red glistening folds that beckoned to be touched, kissed, pressed to move aside.

He kissed her there, from behind, tilted his head and watched his fingers dip into her again. She closed her eyes, and then turned her face into the pillow, arching up even further. He tucked one of the pillows under her belly and smoothed his fingers over her ass, massaging the cleft between her cheeks. With one finger on her anus button, he positioned himself, ready to enter from behind. He rooted at her opening. His granite cock had no trouble navigating the lubricated soft tissues of her sex. He plunged deep again, deliciously burying himself to the hilt.

He was locked in her tangle of arms and legs, loving the smell of her arousal and the sound of her breath. He felt her soft flesh against his thighs, against his chest while he hovered over her, digging deep and having as much of her as he could. He couldn't stop long enough right now to properly take his time and explore. That would have to come later. Now it was all about having her or he'd die trying. Or explode like an IED.

She turned her face in profile to him while he continued to pump her from behind. Her lips pursed in an 'O' of heightened arousal, and when he saw goose bumps wash up her arms, he couldn't resist leaning over to kiss her bunched-up lips. Her eyes grew wide in reaction while he filled her, needed her more than he would ever be able to say. He kissed her through her moans, claimed her mouth, all of her.

She rose up on her knees, arched her back, pushing her butt into his groin, begging him to go deeper still. She threw her head back onto his shoulder, panting, pulling him into her with her fingers clutching his butt cheeks. He wanted to ram so far in he'd be blinded to everything else in the room.

Her spasms tightened around him. She held her breath, then shuddered and groaned into her release. And he was right there with her, thrusting from behind and then holding firm until he could pump out every drop.

This was the part when he always got uncomfortable. Several heartbeats later, he wanted to say something. Something other than 'thanks' or 'that was great.' But again, it was prudent not to say anything at all. He continued to taste and kiss and rub himself against her, every bit of her he could feel. This had been way too fast. He hoped she wasn't disappointed.

She didn't look like she minded. Besides, he had a plan for making it up to her.

He delicately flipped her over on her back, kissed the salty hollow between her shoulder and neck, and she groaned again when he re-entered her. Her skin was like silk. His tongue easily traced a path down over both her nipples, suckling them slowly, first the right and then the left. Her fingers sifted through his scalp. She traced the arch of his ears, then pulled his face to hers and begged for a deep, penetrating kiss, and he was only too glad to provide.

He'd fuck her until the moon rose and set, and then fuck her again at dawn and through breakfast if she would let him.

Fuck breakfast. Fuck lunch. Fuck dinner.

He'd found her. He'd finally found her, that woman from his dreams. He'd watched her walk with that tall, confident gait only the right woman for him could have. She was someone he could love and love hard. She could love all the sand and dust and death off him. She would let him show her how much he needed this connection.

And she wouldn't run away.

He was caught, entangled, willingly dying those thousand little deaths as she kissed him. His real flesh and blood dream woman breathing life into him.

Again.

And he would never let her go.

Well, at least not until tomorrow or the next day.

CHAPTER 2

JULIE WOKE UP to the feel of his lips on her chest. His gentle touch didn't startle her. He was leading her from sleep to the pleasure of his morning, and even though her dreams had been wonderful, this was better, much better.

She hadn't seen his face clearly last night in the dark, but her hands had traveled over his body hungrily, and she felt she knew him, all of him. As he looked up at her, she saw he was more handsome than she'd imagined. Clear, icy-blue eyes and dark brown hair, dark stubble on his cheeks and around full, sensual lips, his bare shoulders revealing powerful, muscles rippling under satiny skin.

"Good morning," he said.

"It kinda is a good morning, isn't it?" She traced his bottom lip with her forefinger. The weight of his chest against her breasts was delicious. She could feel his heartbeat and hear the rumble of his steady inhale and exhale. She liked him even better in the light of day.

She could tell he wanted to ask her things, talk to her, and she liked that about him. Their lovemaking had been fierce and consuming. He played her body like he'd done it for years. She wondered how he'd managed to do that.

He's an experienced lover. That must be the answer. The little niggling of doubt crept in, wondering if she'd satisfied him. Seeing his gentle smile and feeling the way his thumbs tenderly caressed her forehead, the way he brushed the backs of his fingers against her cheek, sent her the message he'd been pleased. Wanted more, but didn't want to show it. Was waiting for her move, and boy, that was sexy as hell.

"What are you thinking, beautiful?" he asked.

"I was thinking about you. Wondering where you'd come from, and what brought you to the beach last night, how come we crossed paths," she swallowed, "like we did." She blushed and saw his lips arch up at the corners while his eyes laughed.

"We did. We certainly did, didn't we?"

She tried not to grin. He was making her hot for him all over again.

"I think we both needed something," she said, and immediately regretted it.

He lowered himself to whisper to her lips, "I certainly did, and you certainly delivered."

Wow. Just holy fuckin' wow. Did he just say that? She rolled it around in her mind. It was okay that a hookup could be beautiful. That she would be left wanting more. But she'd never done this before, jumped into bed with someone so quickly. Recognized the need within her own body and found that missing piece in the arms of another. She'd always thought of herself as a cautious girl, and even a little afraid of love. What had made her say the things she'd said, do the things she'd done?

It was like some part of her had been revealed, a part she'd had no idea existed.

The familiar panic of second thoughts set in, and she caught herself reconsidering choices and decisions she normally made so carefully. She'd thrown caution to the wind, and had found something that was deep and in need of roots to grow. But it came with huge risks. She could get hurt.

He could too. She took out her internal disclosure statement, and, yup, she'd signed it and printed her name underneath in blood. That statement had prepared her for all the negative things that could happen, had saved her from the heartache of never getting that phone call the next day, the next week.

Or worse, thinking he could be somebody he wasn't, like the young Navy recruit she'd met last year in San Diego, who told her he loved her; only it turned out he was a serial liar and had girls lined up in every port all over the world. Either way, her internal disclosure was supposed to protect her from falling for the wrong guy.

He was too handsome, too beautiful as a lover, to be wandering around unattached.

"Where'd you go, darlin'?" He had a slight southern accent she'd just picked up on.

"Where are you from?"

"Here."

"No, I mean where did you grow up?"

"In a house, with my mom and dad and little sister. All over the U.S."

Little alarm bells began to flash. He was being secretive. Didn't want her to know personal details. It was not a good sign.

"You?" he asked.

"California native. I grew up in the North Bay area."

"Ah! She reveals herself." He kissed her gently. "Never been there, but I've had friends tell me it's a beautiful part of paradise."

"It is. My folks still live there." She was hoping that might spur him on to tell her more about him. But that wasn't going to happen.

He was watching the rise and fall of her chest. Was he making fun of her? Why had he answered so vaguely? She decided to be a little more direct. "Explain what 'everywhere' means, please."

He kissed her just under her right ear, right where it made her sex ache for him all over again. He'd found several of her spots. Holy cow, the guy was a sex machine.

He kept kissing her. "There's not much to tell. We lived all over the place. My dad was military." His knee rubbed over her thigh, moving up slowly on the bed until her wet peach was resting right on it. He moved back and forth until she was so hot for him he could probably feel the vibration coming from between her legs as he stroked her.

She was getting dizzy with desire.

She fingered his tats. He had a Celtic band across his bicep. A Fear/Faith scripted tat over his heart. What looked like maybe frog prints from his wrist to his elbow. The number 5326 on his other bicep. She'd seen the large skull tat on his back with something written under it in Latin. That one she could go look up later. So she chose the 5326 and brushed her fingers over it.

"Tell me about his one."

"It's the prime directive."

His face was deadly serious. She was looking for some hint, some help, so she could understand him. The number meant something.

"Directive for what?" she finally asked. That made

him grin, showing blindingly white teeth. He licked his lips.

"All beautiful women must be made love to as often as possible. The directive to stay in bed all day. Not to eat. Not to sleep."

"*All*? All day?" She sounded like a teenager for a second. Did he notice?

He nodded. God, how she loved those honest blue eyes.

"And how many of those do you claim? I mean, do you do this often?" She hoped it didn't sound jealous, but right now, lying underneath him, she didn't want anyone else in the picture. There certainly wasn't anyone else in hers.

"You caught me at a good time. I'm completely alone. And I've just come back from overseas." He was not smiling.

"So does 5326 specify what I'm supposed to do?" She softened her question by lifting her head and meeting his lips gently and then lying back to watch him take it all in.

He was moving his callused palms over her shoulders, splaying his fingers up the side of her neck and into her hair, clutching, drawing her up to meet his lips again. Into her ear, he said, "How long can you go without food?"

CHAPTER 3

A KNOCK ON the door followed by a key card woke him up. He'd forgotten about the checkout time for the room…it'd been lost somewhere between their lovemaking and his need for sleep to regenerate. He didn't want to wake her, so eased out of bed and was headed to the door to lock it when the maid opened it wide and shrieked at the sight of him standing there fully naked.

Luke grabbed a towel from the bathroom and wrapped it around his waist.

Of course, she hadn't slept through the little drama at the front door. She was smiling up at him, angling her head.

"Forgot about housekeeping," he said with a shrug.

"I'll bet you made her day."

Okay, he liked that. "I'm sure she's seen worse," he said honestly.

She sat up, pulling the sheet up over her chest, and

he figured it was because he'd covered himself up with the towel.

"Are you hungry?" he asked.

She twisted her long hair, brought her knees to her chest under the covers and closed her eyes. "Starved."

"Shower?"

"Love to." She uncovered, showing the flat tummy and abundant breasts that were more than a handful, but just right. She had hips and a nice ass but narrow waist. She wasn't overly buff or cut, but well toned, and had the softest skin he'd ever known. His package was coming to life while she walked in front of him, and when she allowed her hip to touch his member ever so slightly, it jacked his libido into a bonfire.

She got as far as the shower curtain before he could grab her arm and draw her tight against his chest. He got lost in the deep kiss he urgently initiated. His hand fisted in the back of her hair, and her little mewling sounds drove him to pull her tighter.

She melted against him, all her curves and valleys blending to complement his hardness. He was breathless, his heart slamming against his ribcage. He wondered if they should consider not going out, but willed himself to separate from her and search her face.

He didn't even know her name. He suddenly didn't want to ask her. That was such bad form. Wasn't the guy supposed to ask all those questions *before* having getting busy? He couldn't remember ever screwing up this way, and what would she think if he asked her now?

He decided just to kiss her again and forget about it until later.

She initiated the sex in the shower. He decided he'd try to pretend it was a welcome surprise, but it was secretly what he'd been wishing for ever since the maid woke them up. What a perfect way to begin a Saturday morning.

HE WAITED UNTIL their coffee arrived before he asked her.

"I'm a little embarrassed about this, but I don't even know your name."

He was relieved to see she smiled without appearing to take offense. "I was just thinking the same thing."

He sorted through all the things they'd done in less than twenty-four hours, and then had to look down at his coffee mug or he'd do a very unmanly thing: blush.

She reached across the little Formica table. "Hi. My name is Julie."

He took her hand. "And I'm Luke."

"Nice to meet you, Luke."

"Likewise."

She placed her hand back in her lap, took a deep

breath and let it all out again. Picking up her cappuccino, she said, "Well, that's better then."

He was thinking it was a little backwards, but he wasn't going to complain. "So, Julie, what do you do?"

"I'm a teacher."

He nearly spit out his coffee. "No way."

He could see she didn't particularly like his reaction. "Sorry." He softened his gaze, enjoying the way her curls framed her beautiful face. And then nerves crashed in on his blissful morning.

"You don't think teachers like to have a little fun?"

"Not the teachers I had." *Don't want to think about the teachers I knew.*

"Well it's not like we watch porn in the classroom." She tilted her head, watching him out of the corners of her eyes.

"You watch porn, too—when you're not in the classroom, that is?"

"No, silly. But I do like erotic films, you know."

Well...all righty, then. He wondered what those films were. But instead of going there, his need to get his bearings kicked in and he asked, "So you teach high school, college level?"

She laughed. "No. Second grade."

That did make him spit out his coffee. He was quick to cover his mouth with a napkin.

Damn. Just my damned luck.

"I'm sorry, but why is this a problem for you?" she asked. She was not smiling.

"It's not a problem for me. It's just that—" He didn't want to tell her that his last girlfriend had been a teacher. And that relationship had ended badly, tragically. He searched for something she could buy that would keep her from digging any further. "I don't get along very well with teachers. Even when I was a student I didn't."

"Apparently that's not true."

Her eyes danced when she smiled. He loved that part of her, but his insides were thickening and getting dark. He felt it coming on. He tried to sound casual, tried not to show it.

Please drop the subject, Julie. Please.

"I thought we got along very well last night," she said with a smile wiggling her eyebrows up and down.

He had to agree. The sex had been fantastic. But that was before he learned she was a teacher.

"You have kids?" she asked.

He winced. Why couldn't she stop with the questions? "No. I'm not even married."

"That has nothing to do with having kids."

That was true, but it pissed him off that she'd asked.

Don't go there. Remember your boundaries.

One of the men on SEAL Team 3 had five children

out of wedlock with three different mothers. "The answers are no and no." He could feel his defenses spring to life. That protective shell was slamming into place around his heart, placing armor all around it. He could almost hear the hinges squeaking from disuse. It was automatic. Nothing he could do to stop it.

"So, what do *you* do?"

Well darn it, there it was again. Luke wasn't in the habit of telling people he was a SEAL, or even that he was in the Navy, since they wouldn't believe him anyway, due to his longer than military-grade haircut. He gave her the line he told most women, "I'm a Fed Ex driver." He was hoping she'd buy it and then just drop all the questions.

"No way you're a FedEx Driver."

"I still can't believe you're a teacher." Her instincts were good, he thought. But there was no way in hell he was going to tell her he was a SEAL.

"Why is that so hard for you to believe? Didn't you think teachers like to have fun?"

He tried to deliver his response so she'd just leave it all alone. He sucked it up and answered, "Just doesn't fit the image. And I've dated a few teachers. And they definitely weren't into having sex on the beach." After he'd said it, he wondered if it had been a smart move. Maybe he was showing too much of his callused, damaged side. "Julie, look, I'm sorry. That sounded, um…"

The waitress appeared at the table and took their

order.

After she left, Julie was smiling down at her coffee. "You know, we didn't have sex on the beach. You took me to a motel, remember?"

"Well, yes."

So far so good. Maybe we can still weather this conversation.

"Okay, so architects and FedEx Drivers can meet a girl and want to have sex with her. Doctors can do it. Coeds, maybe military types," she looked up at him and grinned, "those tats, by the way, look oddly suspicious—all these people can hook up on the beach, but a teacher can't? Don't you see what's wrong with that picture?"

She had a point, but he wished she'd stop using that word *teacher.* "Okay, I agree with you. Maybe I do have some preconceived ideas, and maybe that's unfair of me. Concerning t—" He couldn't even say the word now. His mind raced to find something else they could talk about. "Now, librarians—"

"Grow up, get married, have sex and have babies. Just like everybody else."

He kind of liked her smart mouth and the fact that he couldn't talk her down, even though he'd given her all the signs. Even though he was getting uneasy. "Julie, I apologize."

"Accepted." She toyed with the rim of her coffee

cup with one forefinger. "So you've dated teachers, then. I assume we're talking dating and not just anonymous sex at the beach."

Damn it. Would you just stop it?

"I don't do anonymous sex at the beach." He worked to keep all the emotion out of his voice.

"Right." She grinned. Her dark eyes flashed him a knowing smile that would have interested his libido earlier this morning. But not now. The dark side had taken over.

She was twisting everything around. Everything she said annoyed him. "I think we need to take a couple of steps back, here, sweetheart."

She blinked twice and waited for him to continue, so he did.

"I mean you no disrespect, but I warned you last night. I don't do complicated."

"Talking is complicated?"

The talking wasn't complicated, he thought, it was the revealing his inner demons that had him concerned. No, that wasn't right. It had him scared to death. He'd had enough. The wall had been breached.

So much for building a relationship on trust and honesty.

But then he remembered he wasn't interested in a relationship with anyone. *Especially* not with a teacher.

CHAPTER 4

JULIE KNEW BETTER than to ask him if anything was wrong as they drove back to her apartment. He wasn't going to reveal anything about himself.

If she dug hard for answers, she might get stories and half-truths, just like the story about him not being in the military. She not only recognized the tats, she recognized some of the patterns of behavior. And that was beginning to send off warning signals.

It wasn't for her to judge, although she liked him. Did it matter if she didn't know where he grew up, what he really did? It hadn't mattered last night. Why should it matter now?

She believed that he was single. She didn't see him as someone who would lie about that. She was sure he was not a FedEx Driver. The huge shoulders and trim hips reminded her of her brother's friends who had been assigned to the Special Ops Command in Coronado.

She wasn't an expert on delivery driver tats either, but she knew plenty of Special Ops guys with skulls and other extreme symbols inking up their bodies. The skull plastered between his shoulder blades was a dead giveaway. Luke's barbed wire rings and bands of Celtic crosses were exactly what all the elite warrior types had.

Julie was trying to talk herself into believing she didn't mind that he was private. But she just couldn't understand why he wanted to be private today, when last night and this morning he'd been another man. And *that's* the man she wanted to have sitting next to her right now.

What the heck happened?

She recalled watching him at the beach before they spoke last night. She'd known she was safe to intrude into his private space there, insert herself into his world.

Did I actually do that?

They'd had sex, what, five or six times? She couldn't remember ever doing that before. But there had been something about the man who'd been sitting there, looking out over the whitecaps, drinking beer and clearly feeling melancholy, which had tugged on her heartstrings. Maybe she'd had no right to assume he wanted company. But then he seemed to need, in fact had even told her he'd needed, what she gave him.

She didn't think that was a lie, either.

They rode in silence past familiar streets, front porches and small picket fences and red tile roofs. She could feel him pulling away from her by the minute, though neither of them spoke. She got out her internal disclosure statement and double-checked her signature. Yup, she'd told herself this one could hurt if he never called her again. This type of guy was why she needed a disclosure statement in the first place. These were the ones where one moment you experienced the miracle of a life that could be, and the next you'd find yourself standing alone in the rain, locked out and without a friend.

She turned and decided to just do what she shouldn't do. Ask him. What could it hurt? She knew he'd already made a plan, one that either included her or didn't. And she didn't know any other way to reach him. She knew it wasn't smart, but she had to try or she'd regret it.

"So, what have I done, Luke?"

He had a vacant look, like he'd been deep in thought and had forgotten she was even in the car. She searched his eyes, but he didn't look at her. All he did was lean in her direction while he kept his eyes on the road.

"It's not you."

"What does that mean, Luke?"

"Means you didn't do anything wrong."

That stung. Sucked big time. It was difficult to hold the tears back. But no way was she going to let him see her cry. She wanted the dignity of a good cry in private.

Except it was such an almost-comical statement he'd made. In spite of what she thought was prudent, her lips turned up at the corners and she was about to laugh out loud.

She drew in a deep breath. "I did a lot of things last night, Luke, things I don't normally do," she said when he pulled over to the curb just outside her apartment complex. He started to get out, and she put her hand on his forearm to stop him. "Did some zombie swoop down and take over your body? I'd like to know where the guy I fucked all night long went, Luke. If you run into him again, would you ask him to give me a call sometime?"

She let herself out of the car and heard swearing coming from his side of the front seat, and then out of the corner of her eye saw his towering frame stand up just outside the driver door.

"Look, Julie. Don't blame yourself for any of this. It's all on me."

She turned and tilted her head until his eyes crept up to hers, and she finally was able to look directly into those icy blue wonders. She did see some pain and torment there, some of what she'd discerned from his body language before they spoke for the first time last night.

"Well, Luke, that's the most honest thing you've said to me in the last hour."

He tore his gaze away and stared at the ground. The car was an insurmountable barrier between them, still running.

"I'm a pretty understanding person, but this *is* all on you. No big deal if I said something that triggered some—"

"Like I said," he shouted over the sound of the car engine and over her voice. "It's not something *you* did. It's something I did. And I'm sorry, but I'm not going to explain it."

She watched him angrily throw himself back in the car and tear off down the street, squealing the tires as he rounded the corner. Out of her life forever.

CHAPTER 5

LUKE STOPPED BY the Rusty Scupper for a couple of beers even though it was barely noon. He sat at the bar, staring up at the pictures of guys they'd lost. The young Marine's picture should have been up there, but this wall was reserved for SEALs and the boat crews.

Being a medic, he understood the symptoms of PTSD. He'd had to pull guys from the arena due to the havoc it would wreak on everyone in a stressful combat situation. And having a guy not 100% was dangerous for all the guys around him.

He was going to speak to Kyle, his LPO, first. The last deployment had been hell on all of them. It was his first with this new team, Team 3, since he'd transferred from the East Coast just prior to their workup. His sister lived in San Diego. At first it had seemed like the change of scenery had done the trick. At first. He'd enjoyed working alongside Cooper, the tall medic who'd served with Kyle on four prior tours. In fact, all the guys in Kyle's platoon were solid.

The Navy knew why he'd requested a transfer. But Kyle didn't, unless he'd read his jacket, and he doubted his LPO had found the time, since they shipped out so soon after he arrived. With the escalating signs of trouble, his memory losses, mood swings, getting lost and finding himself in places he didn't remember traveling to, he knew Kyle would be all over him before it became a problem for all of them. He wanted to stay in. Requesting a discharge felt more like ringing the DOR bell—Drop On Request—instead of completing the BUD/S training. So if he was staying, he'd better take the initiative. He'd seen guys try to cover up their issues. It was never pretty.

Kyle sauntered in with Cooper at his side. The handsome leader flashed him a big, toothpaste smile. Cooper bent his enormous 6'4" frame in a silent bow.

"So, Paulsen, what can I do you for?" Kyle asked.

Luke briefly glanced over at Cooper and then looked back at his LPO. Nobody moved. Kyle was smart and wanted another pair of ears on this conversation, meaning he'd already begun to smell something.

"I'm wondering if I should take myself out of the rotation for a cycle."

"Oh, yes? Wanna tell me what's goin' on?" Kyle

said as he perched on the edge of his seat.

"I'm having trouble sleeping. I'm having the same dreams over and over again."

"What kind of dreams?"

"This lady with red lips—"

"Shit, you got that dream too?" Cooper hooted. "I've been married two years, and I still get that dream."

Luke tried to chuckle along with them. He decided to try a more direct approach so they'd take him more seriously.

"Before my transfer I was dating this girl." He looked up at Coop and Kyle and saw nothing register in their expressions. "Things got pretty hot and heavy, you know. I got her pregnant, so I was going to marry her. I mean, I loved her and all, but when I found out I got her pregnant, I had to marry her."

"Um hum," Kyle nodded.

"We'd gone down to Florida to visit her folks. Had a nice family weekend down there, and we told them about the engagement, figuring we'd have a little time to talk about the baby."

"Okay, so far I get you. So what does this have to do with you not sleeping now? Something go wrong?"

Luke nodded his head. "I started having trouble sleeping last deployment. A real fuckin' hellhole. We were training Afghan soldiers, and I just had this thought, this fear I couldn't get out of my head, that this was the one that was going to get me. But I came back, and felt, you know…"

"Survivor's guilt," Kyle said.

"Yeah, some of that."

Luke stared down at the bubbles in his beer glass. Cooper was chewing ice from his mineral water. Kyle had barely touched his beer.

"I fell asleep on the way home and crashed the car. She died there, Kyle. Died in my arms."

It was the same every time he told the story. His eyes would ache something fierce, but the tears wouldn't come until he closed his eyes. And it was usually when he was trying to sleep.

"I'm real sorry to hear it, Luke. I didn't have any clue that was your story. So what's going on now?"

"I thought the transfer would help. My sister lives in San Diego, sir. I seemed to be doing pretty good," Luke continued.

"I had no complaints. You did your job, from what I could tell." Kyle sighed. "So, this woman you're dreaming about, the one with the red lips?"

"It's not her. But the red is significant."

"Go on."

"I don't know who the woman was. She wasn't my, my—the girl I was going to marry."

"Say her name."

"Camilla."

"Okay, good."

"I—well, until last night as a matter of fact—I'd never seen her face. I just used to dream about the red lips. I was dozing off, dreaming that dream, when young Carson got hit. You remember?"

"Yes, two days before we came home."

"Yes. Well, the lack of sleep was catching up to me. He let me take a little catnap, and that's when he was hit."

"And you took out the bad guy."

"That I did. Without thinking, I did it. I can live with that part."

"Good."

"He died in my arms, just like she—Camilla—did. Just like her. I felt the blood, saw him pass over. I was there. Nothing I could do to stop it. I just witnessed it. And I was numb at the time, but now I have the nightmares, Kyle. I'm not sleeping more than an hour here and there."

"And what does it add up to?"

"At the most, maybe four hours' sleep."

"And that's not enough. You try using some meds?"

"No."

"I'd get you some, Luke. You've got to get your sleep."

"But now it's more than sleep. It's mood swings. I can be so incredibly happy one minute, and the next, I'm like in the pits of Hell itself."

"When are you up for extension?" Kyle asked.

"Eighteen months. Was going to re-up when I went over the next time, but now I'm wondering if I should sit out a cycle."

"You get to a doctor, first. You know we've just started those groups. Don't want you with the inactives. You stay with the active duty SEALs."

"I understand." He took the last sip of his beer. "Do you think I should wait out a rotation?"

"It's not for me to say. You're telling me all this…which is the right thing to do, by the way…so thank you for being proactive. We like that. But I've not seen anything to indicate you're not able to perform your duties. So we get you checked out. We do some PT evaluation. Your eyesight and hearing okay?"

"I'm fine in that department."

"You getting fucked regular, like?"

Luke wasn't quite sure he'd heard Kyle correctly.

"Sir?"

"Any things going on in your sex life you're not happy with? I gotta ask."

"No. Nothing's wrong, sir. Except—"

"What?"

"I feel a little too needy about it." He'd never admitted it to himself. Was this what was scaring him?

"Shit, Luke," Cooper interjected. "That's just normal. We all got it."

"I don't want to hurt anyone," Luke replied.

"Then you get someone strong."

LUKE PROMISED KYLE he'd check himself in for a complete workup, including a psych evaluation. He got medication to help him sleep, and he began feeling better after a solid month of ten-hour nights. He stayed away from dating. He stayed away from complicated.

But he thought about Julie every day. She was the first thing he pictured in the morning, how she'd looked that sunny morning in the motel room. And she was the last thing he saw at night before the medication kicked in.

"I don't do uncomplicated. I like it rich and complicated. Entangled. And I want to be sorely missed when I'm gone."

Well, the little lady had gotten her way. Trouble was, there was no fuckin' way she would ever know about it. It wasn't fair.

But it was the way it was.

CHAPTER 6

JULIE HADN'T TALKED to her brother in weeks, not since he'd announced his engagement.

"We're about to start having rehearsals. You ready for prime time, sis?" Colin asked.

"Doesn't Stephanie have some gorgeous friends who want to be her bridesmaids? I don't want her to think she's stuck with me."

"Nonsense. She's got five of those already. Besides, I think…outside of her…you'll be the prettiest gal there.

Julie remembered trying on the beautiful peach gown Stephanie had chosen for her bridesmaids, and how elegant and regal it made her feel. She wrote a reminder note to herself to schedule her hair, the final fitting, and to go hunting for the right bra, one that would give her the cleavage without looking like she was poured into a too-small dress.

Julie and Colin's parents were planning and hosting the wedding, since Stephanie had lost her mother in a commercial plane crash when she was in high school. Her father had been in the military and had been killed overseas some years before.

"So, when's the rehearsal?"

Colin gave her several dates, including the bridal shower and bachelorette party. She wasn't very close to Stephanie and didn't feel she should intrude on a private party with her girlfriends, but since Julie's mom was going, she'd make sure they left after a respectable showing, and she'd see to it her mom got home safely.

School would be out the week before the parties and rehearsals, giving her time to take care of all of the final arrangements and to give her parents a hand with entertaining the out-of-town guests and decorating the house and garden for the ceremony.

She had also arranged to rent a cottage from one of her friends so she could have peace and quiet when she needed a break.

She had to admit, she was looking forward to it. She'd been in a funk for the past thirty days, ever since the wonderful night and then the huge disappointment with Luke.

This was a welcome distraction while she planned her summer. It would be nice to spend a week up north, where she grew up. Get her summer vacation in gear. Shed the cobwebs of loneliness. It had been more challenging this year, thanks to a couple of whacko parents, but the kids were great and more exceptional than usual, and she was there for the kids, anyhow.

After her phone conversation with her brother, Julie glanced over at the brochures for vacation packages she was considering. She used to hate summer vacation, since she'd had no idea what to do with the time off. No man on the horizon. She began taking her summer trips in the middle of the hiatus so she wouldn't feel so lonely. And here it was again, another trip to Fiji, Hawaii or the Greek islands…by herself.

But it was better than staying home all by herself.

THE LAST DAY of school, her car already packed and gassed up so she could leave straight from school, she turned in her year-end paperwork that morning and stopped by the principal's office for an update on a disgruntled parent issue.

Dr. Connors frowned when she knocked on his door. "Come take a seat." He stood, pointing to the wooden armchair in front of his desk. "And close the door, please."

Julie's throat constricted. She did as she was told.

"I'm not making much headway with the Millers—Mr. Miller more than the Mrs."

"They need to get that child into counseling."

"Yes, I understand. They are willing to give her extra tutoring, but they do not want her staying back a year. You recommended she pass?"

"As a matter of fact, no, I didn't," Julie answered. "My reasoning is noted in the girl's report card, which I turned in with the rest just now."

"I'm going to have to ask you to alter them. The classroom incident aside, I don't need angry parents complaining to the school board. It would mean consequences for all of us."

Julie was feeling uncomfortable that her union representative wasn't present to hear this and to give her advice. She wasn't sure whether the principal was on her side or on the side of the parents. Julie thought she was the only one on the side of the student. Her parched tongue stuck to the roof of her mouth. Taking a deep breath, she finally asked the question she'd been dreading for the past five minutes. "Dr. Connor. Am I going to be fired?"

"No. Of course not. Not today, anyway."

It was just like him to wiggle out of saying something he didn't want to, which should have made her feel more comfortable since apparently there wasn't a planned trajectory to remove her from her job. But that didn't make her feel very secure, either.

"So they're still talking about suing the school."

"And me personally, and you personally."

"Me?"

"You are the one who they allege said things to their daughter in front of the whole class."

"Which is completely untrue, and I have student witnesses who are happy to dispute it. I would never say those vicious things. Those words aren't even in my vocabulary, Dr. Connor."

"Their attorney claims you are holding a grade or expulsion notice over their heads," he said solemnly.

"Their attorney? So now they have an attorney?" Julie could not believe how a lie the student had told her parents had managed to escalate to such a degree. And she partly blamed her principal for not acting more quickly. He'd elected to wait until the family had sent their third letter to his office.

"I'm sorry but we'll be dealing with this all summer. I'll be in touch."

"You want me to get the paperwork on the year-end evaluation?"

"No, I'll find it. I'll call you if I need anything else."

"Dr. Connor, I'm going up north today for my brother's wedding. I won't be around for another week at least. Probably ten days."

"Fine. No worries." He rose and extended his hand, which Julie shook, hoping he couldn't feel her nervousness. "Have a good wedding!" His cheery smile, plastered quickly onto his face, made her stomach churn.

Shaken, she found it a struggle to stay focused and drive safely during the trip to her parent's home in Sonoma County.

She solved the problem by listening to the seductive voice of her favorite narrator reading the latest novel from a romance series she loved. It was the perfect way to spend the hours on the road. It put her in the middle of an intense relationship with a strong guy who loved hot sex and wanted to protect her. She became the heroine. It was a pleasant fiction, feeling loved so intensely. She knew her fantasy life was good for her. And it certainly went a long way toward diminishing the uneasiness about her job and helping her set aside her heartache over Luke.

She wished her real life was more like this audiobook love story. And it had seemed so possible during the magical night with Luke. There was something about him, and she couldn't figure out what, exactly, that was so damned close to the hero in this audio romance. A hero who struggled with something from a past which had damaged him.

Julie wondered about the damage. She wondered what it was that haunted Luke. They'd barely spoken that urgent night…a night that still left her breathless every time she dreamed or thought about it.

And yet, something had been so right about being with Luke.

And at the same time, there was something so wrong about him.

The long driveway winding to her family home through clusters of oak and madrone trees was a welcoming sight. As she climbed the hill, she could see the valley floor below. Up north, the geysers were spewing steam, and the horizon was turning pink, indicating there would be a nice salmon glow at sunset.

Her mom came out to greet her before she could get to the front door.

"Julie, so glad you're safe. The guest room is all ready for you."

"No, Mom. Remember, I told you? I'm staying at a friend's house while they're in Europe. Besides, you've got tons of relatives coming from the east coast who arrive this week, right?"

"Next week. I just thought you could stay here. One night? Just one night?"

She always had a hard time saying no to her mother.

"Fine. But just one night. I need a little time to relax and clear my head. Yesterday was the last day of classes, you know."

"Not to worry. Your dad will be so happy to see you." Her mother picked up her duffel bag and hitched it over her shoulder. "Colin and Stephanie will be here to go over some details after your dad gets home."

"Great." Which meant another late night, Julie thought. Not exactly what she wanted, but she'd just have to get caught up on her rest tomorrow night.

THE REHEARSAL DINNER was a catered affair. The warm, early June evening was perfect for eating on the patio under the stars. Julie's parents' home was built in the middle of vineyards, overlooking a small lake. They had sent small boats holding votive candles sailing out from its grassy banks just before the sunset. Crickets had begun to chirp. An occasional frog mouthed off, telling her it would be a full-chorus night.

Stephanie looked radiant, as she always did. Colin was working to keep a couple of his five groomsmen away from her, and Julie enjoyed seeing him so possessive but happy. She hoped someday this would be her fate...having friends and family share in a glorious celebration of love here in her gorgeous childhood home.

One of the groomsmen was running late, so they sat around the patio sipping wine until they heard the doorbell ring.

Julie decided she'd play hostess and ran to answer, leaving her parents to mingle with the guests and deal with the caterer.

She threw the door open, caroling "It's about time you got here, Mr. Sixth Groomsman, we've been waiting for you so long, everybody's had a bit too much wine, and..."

Luke Paulsen stood on their doorstep.

He was dressed in baggy jeans and a light blue shirt. Though he was dressed casually, there was no mistaking the muscles beneath the cotton fabric, muscles that bulked out his magnificent chest, making the shirt spread deliciously over his breastbone. A trail of light brown hair lingered there, daring her to be inappropriate. It had been at least a month since she'd run her fingers up that chest, up the side of his massive neck, and pulled his lips to hers with consuming need, but she remembered so vividly it was if she'd just left his bed.

Her need was no less right now, standing in front of this irresistible man without touching him.

His hair was slicked back a bit from a recent shower, emanating the faint scent of soap and just a little aftershave. But his blue eyes bored into her, making her knees wobble. She felt so light-headed she could almost float up into the night sky.

He was obviously surprised, too, but a wild, kind of feral look crossed his face, an involuntary lifting of one corner of his lips. His chest expanded as he inhaled hard enough to suck her right into his arms, which she refused to do.

She'd steeled herself for the possibility of running

into him in San Diego, but she never thought she'd find him standing at her front door. For an instant she thought perhaps he had found her, was coming to the house to apologize for his behavior in San Diego, but then it dawned on her.

Luke was the sixth groomsman.

CHAPTER 7

"JULIE," HE SAID hoarsely. "What are you doing here?"

She exhaled, trying to shake off the dark circles beginning to gather, narrowing her vision, because she'd been holding her breath. "I live—lived here. This is my parents' home."

She could see he was troubled. "Then Colin is your brother?"

"Yes."

"Stephanie is my sister."

Knowing this marriage meant Luke would soon become part of *her* family sent panic from the base of her skull down to her toes. This man, who had at first brought her unspeakable passion, who had awakened something deep within her and then rejected her, was here to participate in the union of their two families.

It was wrong on every imaginable level. And so totally unfair.

"Luke!" Colin called out as he walked towards them. "Hey, bro, I see you've met my lovely sister."

How could this be happening?

"Yes," Luke said, avoiding eye contact. "We just met."

"What did I tell you? Huh? She's single, and I think she'd be just your type."

I'm not hearing this. This isn't real. "Julie, Luke, here, is a Navy SEAL."

Check that one off my list. Figures.

Her anger at how completely fucked up this all was gave her strength. "Oh, is that so?" She lowered her eyelids and spoke while tilting her head back, viewing his face through the tiniest slits her eyes could make. "Looks more like a UPS driver to me."

"Ha. You're funny, sis," Colin said. He leaned into Luke and whispered just loudly enough so she could hear him. "I think she likes you," following it up with a waggle of his eyebrows. Colin threw his arm around Luke's shoulders, which looked ridiculous since Luke was nearly three inches taller and probably outweighed him by forty pounds. He dragged Luke to the kitchen.

Julie slammed the front door so hard it sounded like a sonic boom. Voices in the other room immediately stopped. Her mother poked her head around the corner, her eyebrows knitted.

"Sorry. The wind caught it."

Her mother smiled and disappeared again.

Luke stood by his sister and was shaking hands with several of the other groomsmen and being introduced to family members. He shook hands with Julie's parents, which was one of the strangest scenes Julie had witnessed in a long time.

Julie decided she'd just ignore him. Whenever he moved into her line of sight, she'd turn her back. She'd stare to the side to avoid having to see him out of the corner of her eye. She'd look down or check her fingernails—she'd look anywhere and everywhere but in his direction. There was no way she was going to tolerate his scrutiny before she'd had a good and thorough talk with herself and perhaps a nice, long, private cry.

Very quickly, Julie ran out of places she could look without appearing to be a social deviant. She began to feel like one. Her mother had come over to her several times, asking if she was feeling well. That meant her efforts to look casual and unaffected were definitely not working.

The minister arrived, and the rehearsal began in earnest. She was put into position behind Stephanie's friends. And—of course!—Luke was placed in the corresponding position on Colin's side.

Great. She wondered what else could go wrong. And she didn't have to wait long to find out.

The minister wanted the bridesmaids and groomsmen to walk in together, all the pairs from the wedding party, arm in arm. She tried her very best not to touch him, which was naturally impossible. She tried not to have their legs brush against each other, which was also impossible. She tried not to think about the electric sizzle of his arm as he hugged hers to his side. And while she got more and more tense, he relaxed.

And he threaded the fingers of his right hand through the ones on her left, holding them tight against his chest. He rubbed the length of her forefinger as she tried not to move hers, but the warmth of his fingertips on the back of her hand, along the sides, and between her fingers in an intimate linking was making her ears buzz. She even had to tolerate a knowing smile from her brother and his wiggling eyebrows. She gladly parted company with Luke and took her position at the end of the line of bridesmaids.

Thank goodness they didn't have to do that again. The rehearsal was declared a success and everyone retired to the kitchen to get their food.

She scrutinized Stephanie carefully, maybe subconsciously looking for some evidence she wasn't really Luke's sister, which she already knew was ridiculous. Julie could see the family resemblance. Stephanie's blue eyes were the same shade as Luke's. Her lips were full. She was pretty, and appeared to be having a good time.

Glancing around the room, she couldn't find Luke and began to relax, thinking perhaps he had decided to leave early. He couldn't have misunderstood her coldness. Perhaps he'd gotten the message, finally.

But no such luck. Her back stiffened when she heard him call out to her from behind. Though it wasn't very smart, she turned around. No helpful distractions were within earshot, unless she yelled.

"I've thought hundreds of times about what I'd say to you if we met someplace. All the things I rehearsed have just gone out of my mind. Completely vanished." He pressed his fingers against his forehead.

She didn't want to drink in the cool blue liquid of his gaze, but she couldn't help it, finishing it off with a quick glance to his lips that grabbed his attention. His nostrils flared and his breathing deepened. Within seconds, their breathing was in tandem…the magical chemistry enveloping them both.

She saw movement at her waist and saw one hand begin to rise.

She immediately took a step back.

"Don't," she said.

"I'm sorry, Julie. I truly am."

"Good." She whirled away and marched back into the kitchen to join other partygoers.

JULIE DIDN'T HAVE any trouble avoiding his gaze the

rest of the evening. Luke seemed to disappear. And then she was told he had left.

Thank God.

She poured herself a big glass of red wine and sank into the family room couch. She listened to the happy banter of the bride and her girlfriends. She watched her brother joke with a couple of his groomsmen. Her parents danced to something on the radio. The caterers were busy clearing the kitchen.

And Julie wasn't here at all. She was back in San Diego on the beach, replaying everything that had happened with Luke.

How could something, which felt so right, have been so wrong?

CHAPTER 8

LUKE WENT STRAIGHT to the motel and crashed. Up until tonight, he'd been sleeping well without the medication. Tonight, he wasn't so sure he could.

He knew it would be a mistake to watch TV. Something would snag him, and then he'd be off on that loop in his brain, like a hamster in its wheel. Of all the messed-up situations. He was now going to be family with the woman he'd had a truly momentous one-night stand with. It had been a beautiful evening and morning after, until his past had overwhelmed him. He knew he was damaged goods. It would have been better for her if they'd never met again.

But it was impossible now. The marriage of his sister and her brother made meeting Julie unavoidable. It was selfish on his part, but he was angry with his sister and her brother. Angry about their love. Angry about their normal future.

Not that he blamed them, actually. He'd made different choices with his life, and because of his choices he was forever altered in a totally fucked-up and negative way.

He could never have what Stephanie and Colin had. He knew how much work it would be for a woman to create some kind of normal life with him, and it was dangerous. In trying to save him, it could well cost another woman her life.

Julie was such a sweet thing. Which was why it felt so bad, knowing he had hurt her. She'd lovingly kissed his scars and tats, given herself to him with a full and open heart, unafraid.

I don't do uncomplicated.

No, she wouldn't understand the complicated jumble that was his brain, otherwise she wouldn't say such a thing. If she only knew.

I want to be sorely missed when I'm gone.

That was the thing, though, wasn't it? Falling in love meant losing someone when they didn't come back. That was no way to treat another human being. Much better to keep them from waiting at all, from ever knowing him. It would be kinder.

Except it was too late now. He knew her, all right. He knew her little mewling sounds, the way her body yearned for him, her pure heart. Though he'd known it was wrong, he hadn't been able to help giving her hope in a happily ever after. He'd wanted, for just one night, to live the fantasy of being someone's hero—to be *her* hero. The guy who could rock that sweet woman's world and give more than he would take. It was almost like a little piece of bright crystal had broken off her and had lodged in him somewhere. Some little piece of the good that was her spirit.

Though emotionally injured, he wanted to be the warrior who was worthy of the medals he wore, still worthy of the Trident he'd earned. Be the man who could feel emotions without having to cover them up under a hundred pounds of equipment. Who didn't have to dive from a plane at midnight just to feel fully alive, to be present without the risk of death to define his boundaries.

He fell into a deep sleep.

The woman in red came to him, finding her way under the covers, stretching out against him, her face hovering just above his. He was aware she was a dream, because he didn't feel her so much as sense her, see her. She gave him the look that said she wanted to be taken. But when he lifted his mouth to hers in his dream, her lips were not there. Her iridescent body called to him, just as her lips had, but he could not touch her. He could hear her, but couldn't hear the sound of his own voice. He heard the steady pulsing of her heartbeat and her breath pushing in and out of her lungs as if she was inside him. Their hearts beat in unison.

Luke, the lady whispered. *I'm waiting for you, Luke.* Her voice faded while he watched the ambulance take her beautiful, warm body to some eternal resting spot.

Where she wouldn't laugh or cry or hear the sound of her own child being born. He'd done that. He'd taken it all away from her. He'd taken it from himself, too.

Luke. I'm waiting.

He was just about to follow her, figuring he'd better hurry, when he woke up.

His body was heaving like he'd been running, and he was short of breath. He'd fallen asleep in his clothes, which were so soaked they dampened the sheets as well. His clammy T-shirt stuck the front of his blue shirt tight against his chest.

He sat up to listen. He'd heard breathing. Or was it the ocean? He'd seen her slip under the sheets, but he was above the sheets in his tiny motel room.

He lay back into the white cotton pillows, staring through the blackness toward the ceiling he couldn't see, and tears rolled from the outside corners of his eyes and onto the pillowcase. The torment and pain of knowing he was not whole scared him. Rolling to the side, he brought his knees to his chest. He buried his face in the cotton pillowcase, bringing one arm over his ears to block any sounds of her breathing or her heartbeat. If she called his name, he didn't want to hear it.

He began to cry in the dark and all alone, hoping sleep would come soon and give him peace.

CHAPTER 9

JULIE GOT A call on her cell from a number she didn't recognize. It was a San Diego area code, so she figured it was one of Stephanie's friends.

It was Luke.

"I hope you don't mind."

Part of her wanted to tell him to go to hell, but she heard something in his voice that alerted her concern. "I don't mind. Are you all right, Luke?"

He paused for a few seconds. She heard traffic in the background on his end of the line. He was outside somewhere or near an open window.

"No." He cleared his throat, and into the silence he asked, "Are you still there?"

"Yes, Luke. I'm here."

"I wanted to apologize for my behavior—"

"Where are you?" she asked.

"Over at Aroma Roasters."

She looked at her bedside clock. It was nearly seven

thirty. "You want some company?"

"Not sure it's a very good idea, Julie."

"Then why did you call me?"

"To apologize. I thought since we were going to be family from now on, we should bury the hatchet."

"Which hatchet? The one between my shoulder blades or the one between yours?"

"Funny."

She heard his breathing; it was a little raspy, like he was shaking between breaths. The smooth, confident sailor she'd been with that magic night had turned into a teenage boy, she thought.

"Why don't you give me a few minutes, and I'll come over and we can have breakfast."

"I don't think it's necessary. I said what I had to say."

"So you don't want to have breakfast with me?"

"Julie, talking to you is…hard. This is me, apologizing."

"Yes, and you haven't answered my question yet, Luke."

After a brief pause he said, "Yes, I would like to have breakfast with you."

"I'll see you in thirty minutes."

Julie scrambled to the shower. She washed her hair and shaved everything she could. She put on a black panties and bra set. Slipped her legs into her straight-legged jeans that were perhaps just a little too small. Put on a white cotton long-sleeved T-shirt. She checked to be sure she could see the black bra through the cotton fabric.

Perfect.

She bunched her hair into a crystal-studded clip, applied a little pressed powder and fresh, red-cherry lip gloss. She added a little color to her cheeks and applied mascara and some pearl white eyelid powder. Last she walked through the spritzer of cologne.

And then she took a good look in the mirror.

"What are you doing, Julie?"

The face stared back at her, looking perky and bubbly. Her lipstick was too red. Her blush a little too deep pink. The shadow of her black bra too obvious. She'd put on too much perfume.

She removed the hair clip, wiped off the blush with a damp washcloth, dabbed off some of the perfume and changed her shirt to a black one. She kept her jeans. She brushed her hair down smooth, tucked it behind her ears, and left it plain.

Aroma Roasters smelled wonderful and fresh. The place was packed with people sipping espressos at small tiled tables or bellying up on stools at the hammered copper counter overlooking the street. The scream of the machines punctuated the air. Taking a deep breath, she searched the room from right to left and spotted him in a shadowed corner. His chin rested against his fist, propped up by his elbow resting on the tabletop.

He was watching her, but didn't get up until she began to walk in his direction. She knew if she'd missed him somehow, he would have stayed seated and just let her go. Something in her heart ached over the man's coldness.

"What can I get you?" he asked.

"Just a cappuccino."

"I'll be right back," he said stiffly. She watched several women eye him appreciatively and give her a close inspection. He waited in line, got two cappuccinos, and then returned to the table.

She folded one forearm over the other as she watched him take a sip of the hot coffee, leaving a little foamed milk on his upper lip he licked away with the rough tongue that had done things to her body. She found it difficult to be angry with him, but decided not to open the conversation, instead to just watch and see where it led on its own.

He frowned and linked his fingers together on the tabletop. "Julie, I want to explain a couple of things to you. It was suggested I call you to apologize, and maybe give you a little explanation of what's been going on with me."

"Fair enough," she tried to look and sound neutral.

She reminded herself she had the handy-dandy disclosure statement tucked away somewhere in her mind, so she could prove to herself she'd been properly warned in case something happened which turned out to be painful.

He licked his lips, and then bit down on a small corner, turning his head to study the street outside. When he directed his gaze back to her, the blue eyes bathed her body in tingles, warming her all over. Unlike before, when she'd been sitting this close to him in the restaurant the morning when everything fell apart, this time she could see his eyes were filled with things he didn't want to say.

"Julie, almost two years ago, I was engaged." He twisted an imaginary ring around his fourth finger.

She heard "was engaged" and relaxed. It was, after all, in the past.

"I'd gotten her pregnant. I was going to do the right thing and marry her." His eye blinked several times. "We went down to visit her parents in Florida to tell them the news."

She braced herself for something she was pretty sure she wasn't going to like. *Is there a love child, Luke?*

He traced the rim of the white mug with his forefinger. The dusting of dark hair on the backs of his hands looked so sexy. She tracked it with her eyes until it disappeared under the cuff of his blue shirt. Again he looked away before turning back to focus on her face, eyes gently dropping to her lips this time, and then honestly returning hers.

"I loved her, Julie. I hadn't planned to get married, but I did love her, and I wanted to be the man she expected me to be."

"Okay. So far so good." Julie had the urge to take one of his hands in hers, but resisted the temptation.

He took in a deep breath and then let it out. "I'd had a difficult time overseas, and was considering perhaps not re-upping this next cycle. So I thought maybe this was a sign I should consider getting out of the Teams to do something ancillary, perhaps go private, stateside."

Julie nodded, and waited.

"So we went down to see her folks, to tell them we'd decided to get married. We didn't tell them about the baby yet. Perhaps we should have." He sat back and looped his thumbs into his jeans belt loops. "I hadn't been sleeping very well. I guess I was tired. I fell asleep and—" he swallowed, his chin down, hanging his head. After he dropped his eyes, he whispered, "I crashed the car, and she was killed."

Julie found it difficult to look him in the eyes, but she did anyway. "It could have happened to anyone."

"But it happened to *me*," he whispered, "and to her."

Julie leaned forward and touched his hand. "And it wasn't your fault. Don't you see that?"

"I had no business being behind the wheel with my lack of sleep. I wasn't careful, and I misjudged my reaction time. I should have known it."

"You made an honest mistake, Luke. Ask me how many times I've fallen asleep on trips from San Diego to visit my parents here. I can think of half a dozen times when I was too tired, shouldn't have been driving and was just lucky nothing happened."

He nodded, looking thoughtful.

"Why do I think there's a 'but' in there somewhere?" she ventured.

"With Stephanie in San Diego, I decided to transfer to one of the West Coast teams. I thought it would be a fresh start."

Her heart ached for him, for the torment he bore so bravely.

"And it worked, in a way. I worked up with Team 3, went overseas with the group. Two days before we were to come home, I was catching some quick Z's—just long enough for the young Marine who was covering for me to get hit with a round. He died in my arms."

"Thank goodness you were there to hold him," she said. She could tell her comment startled Luke.

"No, he died because of me. Just like—just like

Camilla."

Julie then placed her palm over his fist. "You didn't kill either one of them, Luke. They made decisions too, which contributed to what happened. It's nobody's fault."

He stared down at her fingers as they covered his. He released them to her care when he allowed their hands to merge.

"I remember this," he whispered.

Oh, God. She did too. The feel of him under her hands. The feel of his hands on her. The importance of touch to a starving soul. He had taken on the burdens of the whole world and held himself responsible for them.

Tears silently ran down his cheeks while he lifted her fingers to his lips and kissed the tips. "I didn't mean to hurt you, Julie. I—well, you remind me of her."

He didn't let go of her hand. "I thought I should just leave. Would be better for you if I just left. So I did."

She extended her arm further and brushed the side of his cheek with the back of her other hand. "Except it hurt. It hurt real bad, Luke. You see, I didn't want you to go."

He brought his other hand on top of their entwined fingers.

She thought about it for a second, doing a quick gut check. Was she up to this? Although she knew it wasn't wise, she decided she was. "And I still don't."

CHAPTER 10

THEY WALKED IN the early morning sunlight to where he'd parked his car. She recognized the feel of the tan leather, and the smell of it mixed with his own personal scent as he helped her in. Time stood still as she watched him walk in front of the car and then open the driver-side door to take his place behind the wheel.

He hadn't asked her to come with him to his room at the large hotel downtown, but she knew it was where he was taking her.

He held her hand possessively while they walked over the carpeted hallway to the upstairs room, where he inserted his key card and escorted her inside.

She knew there were no easy answers for Luke's struggles, and she'd need resources she wasn't sure she had in order to be able to support him while he found the right direction. Julie also knew she couldn't walk the path for him, that it was a journey he would have to take, feel comfortable taking, alone. There was no way she could take away the pain or share his burden, no matter how hard she might grow to want to in time.

But she could make sure he knew he was loved. Was that what she felt right now? Probably not. They barely knew each other even though, because of their intense passion for each other, they'd shared a level of intimacy she'd never experienced before. But it was too soon to call it love. And it would be unhealthy for her to do so, regardless of whether it was good for him.

Her students this year had been an especially bright and creative bunch. They were unruly on many days, and this seemed to be happening more frequently. Or maybe she was learning to be more patient with them, letting them explore more and spend less time focused on strict obedience of the rules.

She could almost see in Luke some of the same things she occasionally saw in those scared little faces when they were frustrated, trying to learn a new concept or pushing to find out where their boundaries lay. Her job in the classroom was to ignite and stimulate their curiosity and not turn them off to a life of learning, exploration. First she had to earn their trust, and then they'd follow. She'd learned early on she couldn't force a lesson plan on them, just as she couldn't force compliance. They had to want to be good students.

The hotel room was dark, even though it was morning and there was not a cloud in the sky. The drapes were closed, and he did not turn on the lights.

She swallowed hard. A trickle of fear traveled down her spine as she suddenly thought this might be unwise. The promise of great sex was in the air. She could easily fall right back into where they'd been before, in her own words, "entangled" between the sheets. But it would mean ignoring the huge red flags surrounding him. He'd already told her of a tortured past. Now she began to worry if perhaps he wasn't being totally truthful with her.

Were his tears intended to snag her heart, make her do something unsafe and unwise?

Images of her former boyfriend, Dan, flashed in front of her eyes. He was a young Navy recruit she'd met at a back-to-school night. He'd said he came with his niece who was in another grade, a different class than Julie's. Said he was filling in for his sister who was out of town.

Why did men have to lie? She'd found out, after several all-consuming nights with him, that he was indeed married plus having a string of kids born outside his marriage all over the globe.

Was it happening again?

Luke sat on the bed and pulled her towards him.

"I'm not sure I can do this, Luke."

His roaming hands stopped immediately and he stood, brushing her aside.

He began pacing back and forth at the end of the bed. She didn't think he was faking some intense emotional turmoil.

"I'm sorry. This was my fault. Again."

She felt sorry for the man whose chest was heaving, whose breathing was labored, and who kept restlessly running his fingers through his hair.

"By accident I've learned a few things about you and your family," she began. "But I'm still not getting any answers from you, Luke. What is this all about, then? You want sex, but you don't want to talk? You want to take from me, and you don't want to give?"

She watched for signs he was getting angry. If she saw any signs of it, she'd be gone in a heartbeat.

"Talk to me, Luke. Tell me something, so I don't have to ask. It's a good place to start." She walked over to the drapes. "May I open these a little?"

"Sorry. Of course. I hadn't noticed." He quickly moved past her and began pulling the sides back, his arms grazing against her backside unintentionally. All the heat began pooling between her thighs again.

Damn.

Her ache for him was dulling her common sense.

What he did next made all the difference. Sitting on the edge of the bed, facing the light streaming in from the window, he patted his thigh. "Come here, Julie. Please. No reason to be afraid of me. I would never do anything, ever, to hurt you."

She did as he asked. He wrapped his arms around her waist, pulling her face to his chest, tucking her just under his chin. His hands didn't roam. He held her quietly.

"Camilla was a teacher, just like you. In fact, she also taught elementary school."

Julie arched back to examine his face.

"You remind me of her. I think it makes it even harder, for me at least."

She didn't want to ask, but she had to. "Am I a substitute for someone you miss?"

He didn't pull her towards him to try to convince her. "God, no, Julie. It just surprised me. All the guilt about causing the accident came flooding back to the surface, and I went right into shut-down mode." He pressed his forehead against hers and took hold of her hands in one of his. "I'm in counseling now, and I've learned a few things. It's one of the reasons I wanted to apologize."

She smoothed his fingers, aware that their entanglement was deepening.

And she didn't care.

"I was told not to expect you'd forgive me. Or to hang my getting better on whether or not you wanted to have anything to do with me anymore."

She placed her palms on his cheeks. "I'm not going anywhere, Luke. I'm right here."

She'd forgotten how much she'd missed his kiss. When their lips met, it was so natural to open to him, let him taste her, feel his mouth claiming her and let their tongues mingle. When he groaned, she felt his need, his loneliness rise to the surface. She gave him back everything she could, kissing his eyes, his temples, fondling the hair at the nape of his neck.

"God, Luke. I never realized how much I'd missed you until right now."

"Baby. Stay with me. Don't go, sweetheart."

"Yes." There was nowhere else she could go. Her whole world was right here in this room with her.

He slid his fingers under her cotton shirt, squeezing her breast as she recalled her naughty black satin bra. He bit the side of her neck and she hissed, arching back, pressing herself against his torso. She kissed every button she unbuttoned down his chest, flicking his skin with the tip of her tongue, drinking of the salty, musky scent of him. She heard the vibration of his guttural response when her lips touched his chest, her tongue encircled his nipples, and her teeth nipped at him gently.

She was breathless, starved for him. He rewarded her sighs by lifting her in his arms and laying her on the bed. He watched as she wiggled her way out of her jeans. He matched her by removing his and then uncovering his massive torso. She watched his corded muscles move just under the surface of his tanned and scarred skin.

Fully bare to him, she let him gaze at her in the morning light. Her peach was dripping with anticipation. After sheathing himself, his beautiful frame came to kneel over her. Then he gently pressed down his body, holding himself flat, like one long plank, touching her first with his cock at her belly button and then covering her warmly, as she lifted her knees and wrapped her legs around his waist.

She fully accepted his girth, riding him, moving her hips to his penetration, at first slow and deliberate, and then settling into a rhythm that ignited her. She felt how easily he slipped in and out of her wet channel. Arching backward, the back of her head rooted down into the pillow, she dropped her legs, pressed her heels to the bed and met him, shoving her pelvis onto his shaft while he plunged in relentlessly deep. The pre-orgasm drowning sensation, the feeling that she would never get enough of him, like she needed more air, overtook her and her internal muscles began to pulse and snap tight against him.

"Yes, baby. Sweetheart, fly away with me, baby."

"Oh, God, Luke. I love this."

"Yes, it's good for me too, baby," he whispered, burrowing his face into the side of her neck and beginning to suck.

Her bones were made of rubber. She merged all around him, rubbing his ass with her palms and then pulling him deeper. Crying out for him as her shattering rocketed throughout her body. She began to whimper, her self-control now fully gone. She was pliable, putty in his arms, needing his hardness, needing to feel his muscular shoulders, taste the sweat at the top of his breastbone. He was arching, groaning and she wanted to feel his groan in her mouth so she rose and begged, pressing her lips to his and sucking his tongue deep.

The jerking of his cock while her sensitive walls clasped him encouraged him to spurt his seed—gave them delicious seconds of respite. The refreshing satisfaction of two bodies in perfect synch, both needing and serving up each other's passion equally.

As he collapsed against her chest, she traced her fingertips over his back and butt cheeks, rewarded with an occasional jerk her touch stimulated in him. She loved the feel of this warrior's body on top of her, in her, all around her. His strong arms held her as no other had ever done. The world was a magical, safe place again, as long as Luke was there with her.

CHAPTER 11

LUKE WAS DELICIOUSLY tired from their lovemaking. Afterwards, as they were catching their breath, she didn't stop the soft caresses at his back, and he found himself slipping into a pool of apricot light. He felt safe. Loved. He was grateful he'd had enough sense not to scare her away. He was also grateful he'd gotten a chance to make things a little more right with her emotionally. Or at least he hoped it's what had happened. In his current state, he wasn't quite sure.

He told himself it wasn't just because they were going to be family, it was because he'd known it was the right thing to do, even if she never wanted to have anything more to do with him after. He'd hated himself for how he'd treated her and hoped she didn't still feel he had taken more than he had given. It was worth the risk, and at the first sign of resistance he planned to stop.

But she went with him to the place where there

wasn't any pain, where the future wasn't a dreaded, dark place. Where everywhere around him the people he cared about hadn't left him. She stayed, holding his hand for those few delicious moments.

He sank into a deep sleep in her arms.

HE WOKE UP refreshed, but alone in the bed. The sun had dipped lower, telling him it wasn't early evening yet, but he'd spent the day sleeping, with the curtains open. It was a very hopeful sign.

"Julie?" he called out, not seeing her clothes on the floor. No sounds came from the closet or bathroom. "Julie, are you still here?"

There was no answer.

He fell backwards into the bed, worried he'd done something to set her off. Her scent was still in the sheets, but the place where her body had lain was cold. He missed her terribly.

He got up, searching the room, looking for evidence she had been there on the off-chance this had all been a dream, like so many of the other dreams he'd been having lately. On the dresser, near the TV, he found a note.

Thank you for breakfast. Just had some things I needed to do for the wedding and thought I'd give you some space. Try to get some rest.

He fingered the note, the swirling, perfect script of her cursive handwriting. It was nice of her to leave it for him, but it was also nice of her to give him some room. She'd not asked or said anything about getting together again, although it was certain they'd see each other before the wedding. But he liked that she didn't cling to him. He knew he wasn't a very good prospect to cling to anyhow.

He called his LPO, Kyle Lansdowne, overdue to check in.

"You getting rest?" Kyle asked.

"Yes, even took a nap this morning."

"Long night?"

"Actually not. We had the rehearsal and dinner last night at Stephanie's in-laws. Nice people."

"Glad to hear it."

"Actually feels kind of fuckin' normal up here. I'm relaxing, Kyle."

"Yeah, until you meet someone. Luke, you be real careful with your behavior, hear me? Maybe caution on the side of keepin' it zipped?"

"I understand," he said, not wanting to find out what Kyle would think of his breakfast date.

"And use this time to get some rest. Next workup, I want you in it, but I also want you whole."

"Roger that."

"Say hi to Stephanie for me," Kyle said. Luke could

hear their toddler, Brandon, in the background.

"You babysitting again, Kyle?"

"Fuckin' A. Someone's got to pay the bills."

Christy was a successful realtor and made far more money than her SEAL husband. But she also had a tendency to spend more than most of the rest of the wives combined.

LUKE SHOWERED AND decided to stop in at a Navy recruiter, as was his custom when he traveled. Most of the men and women who worked there were more than happy to have an active duty SEAL for their young prospects to talk to, ask questions of. The office was sparsely populated, although all the branches of service had offices in the same building. A pool table was in one of the big meeting rooms. A video was streaming in the corner, showing training tapes just above a table filled with recruiting information.

Luke watched a Navy SEAL video showing a boat crew barreling down a river somewhere, firing guns and soaking the surrounding riverbanks with twenty-foot plumes of water. The virtues of joining the Teams were being extolled between scenes of gunfire and water blasting. One segment read: Enjoy Wildlife. In the background, the SWCC boat crew was silent until a large sea bass leapt in front of the boat. The gunner in front shot it, causing it to fall into their boat. That clip always made Luke laugh.

He spent a few minutes talking with the recruiters there and with a couple of the boys who were inquiring about life in the military. He was always happy to talk to them, although the hero worship he saw in their eyes did make him a little uncomfortable. He never thought of himself as a very big deal. Especially not now.

Luke also knew every man's journey was his own. Every man's pain was his own to deal with. But asking for help was the hardest part…and something they all had to do.

He agreed to do some physical training with a few of the young recruits later in the week, if something could be arranged in time.

He called Nick Dunn, whom he had befriended during their last tour together with SEAL Team 3. Nick was building a house on a little ten-acre patch in the middle of a valley floor surrounded by vineyards. There'd be another wedding some time later in the year, when the house was finished. Nick and Devon wanted to be married in the gardens his sister, Sophie, had started several years before she died of cancer.

"Holy shit, I didn't believe it when Kyle told me you might be up this way."

"I'm here, all right. Can I come see what you're doing?"

"You are most certainly welcome. I'll even let you

use my hammer," Nick said. "You got old clothes you can get dirty, or are you fixin' for a hot date?"

"I'm good with the getting dirty. And the girl might be okay with me dirty. But I got no plans right now." Luke felt a pang of regret that he didn't have plans, but knew it was best for the two of them to have some space. In fact, he was grateful Julie wasn't all over his phone, texting and calling. It made it a lot easier to relax until he could figure out what was best for both of them.

Luke drove out Bennett Valley Road, enjoying the vineyards flipping by like cards being shuffled. The leaves were lush and green, some of the dark fruit hanging visible in their shade. He'd always wanted to spend time in the wine country. Something about it made him feel at home.

He turned left onto a gravel driveway. Nearly a half mile later, he could see a beautiful, contemporary home taking form. The structure rose from the ground like a giant, wooden crystal. The lines of the house extended in several directions, with large second story windows overlooking the vineyards and tops of golden hills surrounding the valley floor. The roof was made of a dark green metal like he'd seen in snow country. The outside was still papered in white construction membrane.

Nick greeted him, shirtless and tanned. Luke

thought he looked good. He'd have to say happy. He knew what a rough tour Nick had as well and knew he was sitting out the next rotation, just as Luke had considered doing.

"Great to see you, man," Nick said once they'd completed their man-hug and backslapping.

"You, too. Look at this place," Luke said, and whistled, studying the unusual two-story structure.

A dark-haired beauty in jeans walked outside, removing her pink gloves, dirt smudged on her cheeks and wearing a white T-shirt so big it fell off one shoulder. With a commanding voice, she extended her hand to him. "Hi, I'm Devon. Welcome."

Luke noticed how quickly Devon wrapped her arms around Nick's waist and let him pull her close. He was pleased to see his former teammate so happy and settled. It was one of the things he wanted to discuss with his buddy if time permitted.

"So, show me around," Luke said.

"Well, this was my sister's nursery." Nick's jaw flickered, like he was gritting his teeth. It had only been a few months since his sister's death. "Sucked as a nursery, but she sure as hell got the location right."

Luke examined the golden, oak tree-studded hills, the gentle breeze blowing over the tops of the grape vines over the fence, making a whirring sound he found very peaceful. Rock walls bordered a rose garden and a vegetable garden. Sunlight flooded from the sky as it retreated for its nightly rest behind the golden hills.

Luke walked into a huge great room two stories tall. The light was warm, coming from more than thirty windows. He walked on a polished concrete floor which looked like granite. Everywhere he looked there was an eclectic blend of furniture, including pieces from India and Africa, as well as carpeting from the Middle East. The place was ablaze in color.

"This is incredible!" Luke said, stunned at the imaginative display. "I've never been in a house that felt so much like a place of worship." He noticed how his voice echoed against the windows, the flooring and large pieces of furniture.

"Yeah, it truly is a special place," Nick answered. "Sophie would have loved it."

"I think she still does," Devon said with a whisper to the ceiling. "I think she still comes here and watches us transform this house into the showplace she always wanted."

Devon and Nick shared a moment between them, followed by a chaste kiss. Nick nodded while he rubbed his thumb over Devon's lower lip. He turned to Luke. "I'm very happy here. Not sure I want to go back."

Luke understood this. Devon slipped away to the kitchen.

"Been thinking the same thing, Nick. I've got some demons, and they're keeping me up at night. I have trouble focusing."

"Yup." Nick pointed to a black leather couch covered in several quilts, where Luke took a seat.

"So, you're getting some help?"

Luke nodded. "It's the sleep, mainly. It's better, but I still have trouble with it. I know that's no good."

"I sleep like a baby now. Of course, I have to let them know my plans in the next sixty days. And right now," he looked over at Devon, "I'm not sure what they'll be. Devon makes good money as a realtor. I'm sure I could get work up here, maybe do something medical."

"I've thought the same thing. Don't you worry you'd miss it?"

"Yes, I do. It was the only thing I wanted to do for so long. Not sure I'd be good at much else, you know?" Luke felt Nick's eyes bore into him, as if Luke had the answer to his buddy's question.

"I keep asking myself if I should get out before things get really bad, or if I can get patched up to go back out there in the arena. Our work isn't done, you know."

"Roger that," Nick said nodding. "They need us now more than ever."

"Then I guess I better quit complaining and get

myself healed, right?" Luke smiled and was grateful Nick took the joke.

"You got someone good you can hold onto?"

Luke hesitated. "Not sure," he whispered to the ground.

"Okay, I got beers. You're staying for dinner, hear?" Devon handed Luke a longneck microbrew, then handed one to Nick, sealing it with a kiss before heading off to the kitchen before anyone could object.

"The boss has spoken. I've seen her angry, and man, you do *not* want to get her within a hundred yards of a baseball bat when she's angry," Nick said, chuckling.

"I heard a coupla times about your world-famous bat incident."

"Shit," Nick said as he shook his head. "I'm just glad the police got there in time."

Devon had stopped Nick from murdering the man who had murdered his sister, by the simple expedient of threatening to bash his head in with a baseball bat. It had been the sole topic of discussion for months among Team members.

"I note you're avoiding my question," Nick stated.

"I have a lady I've met. Shoot, Nick, I've only known her a little longer than thirty days. But she's the younger sister to the guy Stephanie is marrying. We're actually going to be family, know what I mean?"

"Like kissing cousins."

"I'm afraid it's gone a little further."

Nick sat back on the couch and took another long drag on his beer. "And?"

"I'm not sure I have anything to give her, in my current mental state, Nick. I don't want to cause her any pain."

"Since when is falling in love painless?"

They both laughed.

Nick started slowly. "Well, I'm going to tell you what my sister told Devon. She said to give me a chance to show her my decent side. Just give me a chance."

Both men looked down at their feet.

"You let her decide whether it's right for her, but you take the chance if she's giving it to you. Take the chance, Luke. Don't force it, just let it happen. If she wants to give you a shot, then you just let her do it." He flashed Luke the green-eyed smile he was famous for. "Besides, man. You do know the woman always chooses, don't you?"

Luke was puzzled.

Nick continued, "Oh yeah, we think we're in control. But it's the woman who decides on us, not the other way around. Didn't your mama ever tell you that?"

CHAPTER 12

JULIE ACTUALLY DIDN'T have a million errands to run, but she wanted to stay away from Luke just to see if he'd take the initiative and contact her. She thought he would, but she wasn't going to pin her hopes on it, just in case.

She'd gotten her heart broken before with a soldier she thought was available to give her everything he had, but had been mistaken. And looking back on it, she could see she should have known his actions didn't quite live up to his words. She had been so in love with being in love, she hadn't looked too carefully at what was beneath the surface.

She wasn't going to make the same mistake this time. Though she longed to pick up her phone and text or call him, she was going to resist the temptation. She'd go to the wedding, even if he never called her back, and try to put her blood spatter apron on and deal with it, deal with being in close proximity. She wasn't going to let him think it affected her in the slightest.

But the slow, rolling burn in her belly, the way she craved his kisses and caresses, his voice rumbling in his chest while he pressed himself against her, those were things she already missed so badly she felt almost hollow. And she knew it wasn't good enough. She'd be excising him with a dull knife, but she could do it. She'd done it before, and she could do it again. She just wished she could will herself not to fall for him. But she already had.

Julie wondered why she had such strong feelings for him. Was there a need to protect him, to take care of him, or was it something else, something which wasn't healthy? She'd heard about co-dependency. Was she doing that? Was she imagining things? Was he merely a fantasy guy?

So that's the steel resolve she'd work on this week. She'd occupy herself with everything else she needed to do for the wedding. Help her parents care for house-guests and the relatives from Germany and Norway who would arrive tomorrow. Time enough for Luke later on.

She laughed at what she'd told him that night a month ago. "I like entangled." Yes, that was the truth.

But, in this case, was that what he needed? It was more than getting him to want to be with her, he'd already told her he did. It was whether or not it was an honest, equal relationship. She didn't want a hookup. She didn't want to play house or erotic lovers. Being someone's fuck puppet wasn't her idea of fun. She'd never been that way. She was out for the real thing. Dared she hope this could be it? Was this guy too damaged, or was her need to save him clouding her vision?

She shook her head and spent the afternoon going over lists of To-Do items at her mother's house.

"You've been kind of quiet today, Julie. Everything all right?" Her mother had radar which could spot an earthquake a year in advance.

"You know how it is, Mom. End of school. Everything is rushed to get the grades posted, get the room packed down." She didn't want to mention the problem parents. Every year there were problem parents, but not to this level. It had to remain a secret or her mom would start digging until she wiggled it out of her.

"Right. I remember those days." Her mom had been a teacher as well.

Her mother prepared another green tea for each of them and then sat down again. "Colin's friend is nice," she said, looking over her mug at her daughter.

She knew exactly who her mother meant. But she decided to play dumb.

"Which one?"

"You know, the one with the big chest," her mother smiled and looked down at her tea demurely. "The one you couldn't stop looking at all night last night."

They stared into each other's eyes. Her mother didn't flinch, but her sweet smile was warming and nonjudgmental. The unspoken suggestion that a man like that would be able to protect and take care of her hit Julie like a furnace blast. In addition to having great intuition, her mother was rarely as subtle as she thought she was.

"I'm guessing you and Dad have also talked about this," Julie said as she sipped her tea.

"Oh, dear, your dad loves war heroes. He said that, in addition to being very handsome, the young man is extremely intelligent."

Julie decided to prepare them for a less-than-perfect outcome, to be realistic. "Mom, he's not ready to settle down, and frankly, neither am I."

"But how convenient you both live in San Diego where you could see each other occasionally," her mother persisted.

"Well—" She was going to lie to her mother and then thought better about it. "Of course, we might run into one another."

That was putting it mildly. They'd run into each other, all right, and the sparks were still flying. She closed her eyes as she sipped her tea. She knew her mother watched her with the unerring eye of an experienced police detective.

Julie didn't care.

ON THE WAY home, Julie got the call she'd been wishing for all day.

"Hi there, Luke. You get some rest?"

"I did, as a matter of fact."

"Good."

Julie squeezed the steering wheel and turned up the car speaker volume. She could hear his heavy breathing and some music in the background. She guessed he was calling from a restaurant or bar.

"I just called to say thank you for this morning. It was very nice."

"You're welcome." She was careful not to put anything in there she'd regret later, in case this was the call that could go quickly the other direction from what she was hoping.

"I slept hard, even with the drapes open."

"Wow. I can't do that," Julie answered truthfully.

"I was wondering if you'd be open to having coffee with me?"

"Coffee?"

"Um hum." He said.

"Like breakfast this morning?"

His chesty grumble was sexy as hell. “Something like that,” he whispered so softly that her spine tingled.

“I’m on my way to my temporary home-away-from-home. I can make you some coffee there, if you like.”

“I’d like.”

She gave him the address of the cottage. “Behind the main house, just drive past the open iron gate. You can park up front since the owners are out of the country and I have barely enough room for *my* car.”

WHEN SHE DROVE up the gravel driveway, Luke’s Mustang was already outside the main house garage. He was leaning against the car, legs crossed at the ankles, his blue jeans generously endowed in the front, emphasizing his package. His thighs were easily the size of her waist, and the physique under the tucked-in black T-shirt stretched tight across his chest made her panties wet.

And now she could see him following her car in the rearview mirror, just like she was honey and he was the bee. She stopped the car and turned off the ignition. The confident trajectory while he came toward her made her pant with anticipation.

The niggling worries racing around her head were instantly silenced when he hauled her up out of the car, threw his arms around her waist, brought her tight against his abdomen and covered her mouth with his. He was as dangerously delicious as he had been that very first night, and perhaps more so now that she knew what those muscles, those hands and those hips could dish out.

"I wasn't sure this was going to be okay with you," he whispered.

She leaned back in semi-shock, as if staring at a big, green third eye between his bushy eyebrows. "I'm making you coffee. What did you think?" She tried not to smile but couldn't help it. He lifted her up by the waist as she threw her arms around his neck, wrapped her thighs around his hips and let him carry her to the front door.

"I've been thinking about all the things I've wanted to do with you the last thirty days. Just not sure where to start."

She felt his hot lips on her neck as she threw her head back and savored his hunger. Yes, she needed this. Even if it the timing was wrong, she needed this tonight, just like she'd needed it on the beach that night, and needed it this morning. It wasn't the sex as much as his strength. He wasn't afraid to claim what he wanted, show her what he liked, unlike some of the metrosexual males she'd dated and endured fastidious movies or dinners with. This guy was all muscle, all about getting to the bottom, the basics of things, who fucked like it was the last day on earth and liked taking and then asking for forgiveness afterwards. She'd known guys like Luke were out there, she just had never met one until that night.

And here he was again, asking for more.

Their kisses were urgent and deep. She sucked at his tongue, needing everything he had to be inside her, filling her to capacity. He tasted salty and musky, but there was something fresh and exciting about him, like the taste of his mouth on hers would cause her to crave him more, the more she kissed him.

He was serious sexual candy of the yummy, dangerous kind. When he groaned into her ear and whispered her name, 'Julie, Julie, Julie,' she came completely undone. Bones to rubber, flesh upon tingling flesh, his sexy rumble while he penetrated her mouth, invading her like a conquering army.

She slithered down his torso to unlock the door and walked backwards, watching the delicious creature facing her come stalking toward her in the moonlight. She was through with being careful, appropriate and considerate. She wanted to be loved by someone who was used to loving hard. Loving possessed. Claiming every cell in her body.

He allowed her to stay just out of arm's reach while she removed layers of her clothes, until she stood next to the double bed in nothing but her underwear. He didn't touch her, but gazed, looking at the spot between her legs as if it belonged to him, licking his lips and examining her breasts and her lips while he slid his pants down and tore off his T-shirt. His chest was heaving. The dark stubble on his face framed lips that mated in a thin line while he licked them again, and smiled.

"Coffee?" she asked, feeling a bit naughty.

"Later. Much later," he growled.

The next instant he was on his knees, pulling the panties to the side urgently, whispering his approval as his mouth found her sex and swiped his, hot sandpaper tongue over her sensitive lips, pressing onto her nub. He sucked as her body responded to his kiss, his pull at her puckered core, plump and ripe from the lovemaking of earlier this morning. Her need and ache were such that she grabbed his shoulders and then ran her nails down his back. He deftly placed his palm under her knee and lifted one leg up over his shoulder and lunged into her deeper, which sent her backward, falling into the bed.

She laughed at his play. He climbed on top of her, holding himself with his massive arms in a straight, full-body pushup without touching her anywhere. But there was no mistaking the feel of his heat radiating down, covering her quivering nakedness.

"You like things a little rough, Julie?" he asked,

holding himself back.

"I don't know." She didn't, either. Her former dates and boyfriends were like wobbly-kneed boys on a basketball team, afraid of their own shadow. "What did you have in mind?"

"Can I tie you up?" He was watching her to be sure there was enough of a green light to go forward.

"Would you stop if I said no?"

All of a sudden he flinched in pain, whirled off her body and sat on the edge of the bed with his back to her.

What did I say?

Into his hands he said, "I'm not ready for this." He got up and collected his clothes, eyes averted.

"Luke. Wait a minute."

"No, Julie. This won't work. I'm not ready for this. I can*not* be trusted."

She ran around to face him as he bent over to put his feet into his pants. Instinct told her it was best not to touch him or get too close. She could feel the boiling of something dark and oily within him, something caged he was trying not to release.

The look he gave her shafted her heart with a javelin. His eyes squinted like they were standing in a sunny room—too sunny. But his jaw was tense. His soft, full lips were creased into a thin line and his breathing hitched. He held the tops of his jeans tight-fisted while he yanked them up and hauled the black T-shirt over his head.

Julie knew she shouldn't stop him. She knew that it wasn't sex, or even compassion he needed tonight.

It was distance.

CHAPTER 13

LUKE WASN'T AS careful as he should have been when he exited the gravel driveway and headed out onto Warm Springs Road. He nearly collided with an SUV full of soccer players and a very scared mom behind the wheel. Her panic splashed across him as his headlights lit them up, spurred him to overcorrect, nearly landing him in the ditch on the other side. But the soccer kids and their driver were safe.

Smoke billowed from under the hood of his Mustang, and he thought he'd totaled it until he recognized the smell of burning rubber from his tires. The soccer mom was well on her way out of the area, honking a couple of times. He was sorry he'd nearly scared the poor woman to death.

I've almost lost it.

He was grateful he'd only had one beer at Nick's house. Didn't stay for the ice cream because—because—

Because I wanted to fuck Julie senseless. He'd been so fixated on her that it had been the only thing on his mind when he left Nick's place.

He was suddenly out of options. And he knew he couldn't be alone.

He dialed Nick.

"Oh, good, you decided to join us for ice cream after all," Nick said.

At first Luke just tried to restore his breathing.

"Luke. You all right?"

"No."

"Talk to me. Better yet, get your butt over here."

"Okay."

"But I gotta ask you, first. You packin'?"

"No."

"I'm searching you before you step into my house, hear?"

"I deserve that."

TRUE TO HIS word, Nick did a quick frisk to check for weapons before he unlocked his front door and let Luke inside. There had been an unfortunate incident last year where someone came home and shot up a Team guy's family, and ever since then they'd been required to take protective action. Luke didn't see a vest underneath Nick's shirt, but he wasn't sure.

"Your keys." Nick held out his hand.

"I'm not giving you my fuckin' keys."

"Then you go outside and kill yourself for all I care. Now quit messin' with me and give me your God. Damned. Keys."

Luke surrendered his keychain.

"So what happened?"

"I don't know, man. I'm just a mess."

"Alcohol or coffee?" Nick asked on his way to the kitchen. "You choose. But you're not leaving here tonight, or if you do, you walk, understood?"

"Not coffee. I need to settle down."

Nick pulled out four long-necked beers from the refrigerator, brought them over to the couch placing two on the glass table in front of Luke and two in front of his spot next to Luke.

"So what happened, Luke? You went to see the girl...*and*?"

"And I got spooked."

"Fuck sake, Luke. Now you're pissing me off," Nick said before taking a deep swig.

"I was afraid I wouldn't be able to stop. I wanted her, hard."

Nick was pensive. "I feel you."

"It was too hard."

"So you pulled away because you weren't sure you'd be able to stop yourself from hurting her? Is that what you're sayin?"

Luke shrugged. The beer tasted good. He could almost feel the tissues in his stomach absorbing the alcohol. He was suddenly filled with unspeakable sadness. He looked away.

"It's the *thing*, Luke, not you. You're going to have to work on it. I can see it in your face, the way you hold yourself, man. You got those peaks and valleys, the highs and then those awful lows. You have to form a *practice* to take care of it. And you're not gonna want to do it, man. But it's just like PT. Hell, it's just like the BUD/S training. You don't just fuckin' stand there in your shorts and expect they'll award you the Trident."

Luke had never thought about it that way. Nick was making some sense.

"You're gonna have to train yourself back to some place—I can't call it normal, because there's no fuckin' normal out there. Just some place where you'll feel you can trust yourself again. And only then is when you can trust someone *else*."

Luke did feel glimpses of what his life used to be like and what it could be like again. Without all the dreams. Without the mood swings. And he didn't want to be coping with life using a jar full of pills, either.

"You gotta want to get well more than anything else in the world," Nick said. "And you gotta stop trying to control it, and just let it be. Quit dissing yourself for not being better. You're wounded."

Luke didn't like hearing that at all.

Nick picked up on it. "Yeah, you don't care for that label. Well, it's not like you lost a leg or an arm or something. Part of your soul leaked out, and you're gonna have to learn how to compensate."

Luke must have given him a puzzled look.

"You'll need help with that. Counseling. No shame in getting help. Just like in our training, no one gets through on his own. This is no different. Honest. I mean on my own, I was one sorry sonofabitch. I was headed nowhere, man."

HE AND NICK talked until two in the morning. They ran out of beer after the second six-pack was consumed, but Nick absolutely refused to allow them to go to the store for more. The point wasn't to get drunk either, so they didn't open wine or get into Nick's special stash of bourbon.

"Just means it's time to go to bed," Nick said.

He showed Luke to the downstairs bedroom, which had a fireplace and private bath. He got the fire started and then threw a towel at him. "Wash up before you sleep on my wife's expensive sheets, okay?"

They embraced briefly. Nick eyed him suspiciously. "You going to be all right? I'm not going to have to do anything heroic tonight, am I? I'm tired as hell."

"Thanks, man. Appreciate this."

"And you sleep in tomorrow. Sleep is good for you. Got your pills?"

"Nah, I'm not going to need them. I'll take a shower and just crash."

"And no fuckin' leaving until the morning, *after* breakfast, right?"

"Right."

Luke stripped off his clothes for the second time tonight. He couldn't help but remember watching Julie's naked body beneath him as she anticipated a beautiful lovemaking session. He loved watching her *need* him. That's what he saw there. And he wanted in the worst way to fill that need, scratch that itch. Just that it wasn't right. It would have been like heaven, but that still didn't make it right.

He let the warm water sluice over his body. He lathered up with some lemon shower gel and then enveloped himself in the fluffy towel sheet that reminded him of how Julie would smell. Wrapping it around his waist, he walked barefoot into the bedroom.

A sea of pillows covered half the bed. He carefully stacked them onto two overstuffed chairs nearby. Dropping the towel, he slipped between cool sheets and watched the even gas flame of the fire. He caught himself looking for answers in the golden flickering plumes, reminded himself it wasn't the right place to find them.

You have to treat this like a practice, Nick had said. Well, that's one way of looking at it. He had never thought getting well was something someone would have to practice. He thought it was something you just had to wait and let your body do.

He tucked his head back onto the firm pillows, watching the fire patterns on the ceiling dance back and forth. As his eyes closed, he heard the crack of an automatic, but was too tired to open them. Besides, his sleep was taking him to the noise, not away from it. He was back there. Blood on his hands. Camilla in his arms, the red liquid warm against his thighs. He realized he'd not remembered that she'd looked up at him.

She watched him, her eyes, surprisingly, not full of pain. He could see she knew she loved him more than he loved her. He was doing the right thing, but his feelings for her weren't as strong as his sense of duty and honor. His goal was to never allow her to feel unloved, even if he had to spend his life pretending. He would be a father to a child he hadn't planned on raising, because it would make her happy.

Because it was his duty.

For the first time in his dream, he searched her eyes. As the red blood trickled down the right side of her mouth over her startlingly flawless white cheek, her red blood-stained lips called to him and he heard her voice.

Goodbye, Luke.

JULIE DIDN'T WANT to be alone in her bed, but she didn't want to expend the energy to drive anywhere on the off-chance she would see someone she knew. She thought about calling one of her teacher friends in San Diego, but checked the clock first. It was only nine o'clock. Numbness set in as she took a hot bath and then slipped on a comforting flannel nightie. She called her co-worker, Annalise, who picked up on the first ring.

"Well that makes two of us who don't have dates, then," Julie forced herself to say.

"So what else is new? How's it going up there, Julie?"

"Oh, okay, I guess."

"Any cute new guys hanging around? Your brother has some hunky friends down here."

"I've been busy with the arrangements. Mom has me pretty tied up the next two days, going back and forth to San Francisco and Oakland airports to pick people up, get them to their hotels. I could probably become a chauffeur or do wine tours if I lost my teaching job."

It grated on her that even though she had a master's degree, she could only get a sixty percent contract to teach. That way, the school district didn't have to pay benefits. Although if it hadn't been for that, she wouldn't have had a job at all since enrollment was declining.

"Speaking of which," Annalise's voice now sounded conspiratorial. Julie's mind drifted back to the afternoon session a few days ago in Dr. Connors's office. She didn't pay attention to Annalise until the words, "and she said he wanted you fired."

"Who said that?" Julie asked.

"The girl was talking about it in school the last day, how you weren't coming back. You haven't had a conversation with Connors I don't know about, have you?"

"No. I even asked him. But you know, the guy won't give me a straight answer."

"Well, Julie, maybe he doesn't know."

"One thing's for sure, he isn't going to risk his job. Just wish he'd jumped in, been more proactive with the family."

"He probably thought it would all blow over," Annalise said.

It is going to all blow away. Everything is going away. Sharp, warm tears filled her eyes. That's when it hit her. She'd been clinging to her strong side, holding everything in, and what she really wanted to do was have a seriously sloppy, slobbery cry.

Suddenly it didn't matter if Annalise had information about her job. Her job could take a flying leap. The prospect of teaching in San Diego, a place where she'd loved living, was suddenly unappealing. Especially because she'd be looking for him everywhere. It would not give her any rest.

Better to go away, perhaps back up to Oregon, or try to come home and get a job up here. Then Colin and Stephanie could come visit her here, where Luke wouldn't be. Except there'd be pictures of him she wouldn't be able to avoid. Stories about what he was doing. Who he was sharing his life with.

Someone other than her in the picture.

Annalise finally noticed Julie wasn't listening. "Hey, kiddo. What's going on? You called me, but I'm getting the feeling you don't want to say a word. You just like listening to me go on and on about boring things down here? I thought you'd have a great adventure up there. I was hoping for it anyway."

"Thanks, Annalise."

No. Nothing *much* is going on *except my heart is broken.*

Again.

She wiped tears from her cheeks with the backs of her hands. "I'm going to go now. I'll give you a call later in the week. You doing anything exciting?"

"I'm thinking when you get back we'll go to Vegas

for a weekend. Sound good to you?"

"Sounds perfect. Girl's weekend out. Just what I think I need." She continued brushing the tears from her face. "Thanks for picking up. Take care."

CHAPTER 14

WHITE LINEN TABLECLOTHS graced rounded patio tables surrounded by folding chairs decorated with peach and green ribbons Julie had tied all by herself. There were one hundred of them. She'd tied the balloons all along the approach to her parents' house, along the mile-long driveway through massive oaks and tall bay trees.

Colin and Stephanie had made a wooden arch out of pieces of fallen tree branches from the woods surrounding the estate. It was rough-hewn, but they'd covered it with garlands of flowers and more wide satin green and peach ribbon. A dance floor had been laid down over her parents' lawn yesterday, and Julie had settled fifty votive candles in little metal boats to float on her parents' pool so they'd twinkle in the dark.

Her mother's garden was in full bloom, even more abundant than in years past. She'd planted golden yellow black-eyed Susans and white Shasta daisies around her blooming purple and pink hydrangeas which stood easily six feet tall. An array of snapdragons and sweet Williams dotted the front levels of the raised rock garden walls. In between, large South African lilies sent out a heady fragrance.

The gardeners had worked furiously over the past week and everything, including the multiple colored pots overflowing with annuals, looked like it had been trimmed with a pair of scissors. There wasn't a blade out of place, and yet the gardens had an exuberant, joyful look. Bench seats built into the rock walls were shaded with burgundy and green umbrellas, stuck into plastic piping embedded in the base of the seats. At night, the solar lights would come on and give it the magical glow they'd worked so hard to achieve.

She was still putting on finishing touches when her mother came out onto the patio.

"Julie, you'd better get inside and get dressed. People will be arriving in a half hour."

The sounds of the caterers clanging around in her mother's kitchen drifted through the open doorway. She surveyed the chairs and umbrellas she'd decorated and called it good. Behind her mother came two young men carrying the flowers for each of the tables and the buffet, sending her scooting out onto the patio.

"Oh, my God, I totally forgot the flowers!" her mother exclaimed as she dropped her shoulders and looked at Julie with her head cocked.

"It's cutting it rather close, I'd say. The boys better be careful they don't encounter guests on the driveway on the way down," Julie said as she watched the flower handlers set their box down and place little sprays at each table.

The driveway was a single lane. They'd hired a couple of high school boys with walkie-talkies to manage the traffic and to drive guests up and down in a trailered golf cart for the faint of heart or legs. The property owner at the bottom had agreed to loan his bare land to serve as a parking lot. When Julie was in high school, some partygoers had driven off the steep hill and wound up entangled in oak trees, lucky their descent had been halted by the sturdy trunks.

"Good point. I'll go let them know." Her mother darted back into the house.

The sky had remained cloudless on this beautiful June afternoon. A gentle breeze fluttered the ribbons, made the tall flowers of her mother's garden bob as if nodding at her in agreement. She'd always thought her wedding would look like this. Today she could look at it all, and actually feel happy for her brother and his fiancée. The sting of Luke's rejection had dulled, and she sternly reminded herself this day wasn't about her and her feelings, it was about her brother's. She would not let anything interfere with that.

She ran upstairs and began showering, washing and styling her hair and rubbing Tuscan Orange body cream everywhere. She took out the pink box and peeled back the peach tissue, revealing a light pink brocade corset. It hugged her waist, making it easily two inches smaller, made her already flat tummy even flatter, and rode down her hips and rear. She attached her peach stockings with the adjustable garter clips. The corset boosted her breasts up and gave her a luscious cleavage to accentuate her small waist.

Julie drew the lovely silk and voile bridesmaid's gown over her head, smoothing it down her breasts and waist, making her body shudder under the shush of the cool fabric. She zipped it up the side and walked in a cloud of peach to the bathroom to do her makeup.

She applied creams, powder, added some dusting powder with sparkles in it for her shoulders and used a pearlescent face powder. She lined her eyes in dark brown pencil, adding bronze eye shadow at the corners. With a generous serving of mascara, eyebrow gel and a last minute fluff-up of her long curls held tousled by spray gel, she looked at herself in the mirror. Nodded. It was as good as it was going to get.

She reached for the light pink lipstick just as she heard cars outside and saw her brother and the groomsmen get out of the SUVs. She wasn't going to look for him, but her brain counted them.

Six.

She lifted the tube of pink lipstick to her lips and stopped. Setting it down gently, she reached for the bright red lipstick and at first dabbed it sparingly. It was an afternoon wedding, after all. But she evaluated her looks and decided she needed to go full-on red. Full-on, sexual-siren-drop-down-and-beg-red. The *come over here and fuck me* kind of red. It was a statement to herself. She was ripe and ready to party, with or without the handsome SEAL. In spite of the handsome SEAL. She'd be aloof, pouty, difficult, and nobody's fool. She'd flit about this afternoon and evening, and not even look in his direction once.

She sprayed the room with the expensive bouquet Audrey Hepburn had created, walking through it and feeling the tiny atomized droplets hit her body. At last she put her peach satin ballet shoes on, twirled to see the layers of crinkle chiffon and voile rise up as if on a breeze created by angels' wings.

Exiting her old room, she heard people talking downstairs and identified her brother and several of his friends. She grabbed her skirts nearly mid-thigh to hold them up while she traveled to her parent's room, where the bride was being primped for her big day. She found her mother and the makeup artist busy working on Stephanie. Her small, heart-shaped face was framed in off-white lace worn like a tiara on top of her head.

Her bodice and sleeves were made of delicate cording held together by lace webbing populated with a generous supply of crystals. She wore crystals in her hair which sparkled under her veil. She was the most beautiful bride Julie had ever seen.

"Sister!" Stephanie said, holding out her arms. The makeup artist barely had enough time to get her large brush out of the way before Stephanie moved past her to give Julie a hug. Afterward, the two held hands and beamed at each other's beautiful gowns.

"Stephanie, you are absolutely gorgeous. I've never seen someone so happy, so radiant. Colin is just going to die when he sees you. He'll have a stroke, honest!"

"Oh, silly. I think there is going to be one SEAL who is going to step on his own tongue this afternoon. Honestly, Julie, you'll be the prettiest one out there."

"Nonsense."

The makeup artist demanded Stephanie's exclusivity again, and then looked at Julie's face and applied some blush and powder. Even her mother was attended to. A gentle knock on the door was the only warning before a bevy of peach and pink lovelies came squealing in, jumping and hugging the bride and getting caught in her veil. Julie enjoyed the happy banter and laughter of the bride and her attendants. She was so happy for all of them.

Julie and Colin's dad was going to walk Stephanie

down the aisle. Her father was smartly dressed in a three-piece black suit with a silvery brocade vest. He'd kept his trim figure and proud bearing, looking more like an older SEAL than an architect. He came over to wrap his arm around her waist and whisper to her ear, "Sweet Julie, next I'll be walking you down the aisle."

She threw her arms around his neck, kissed him on the cheek, and then squeezed him in a tight hug. "Not today, Daddy. Today belongs to Colin and Stephanie. I'm just so happy to be able to be here to enjoy it."

He gave her a squint and tilted his head to the side. "There isn't a single man downstairs," he pointed to the floor, "I'd object to you landing as a husband."

"In time, Dad. But don't get your hopes up. I'm happy being single." He held her face between his palms and kissed her gently on the lips. "My good girl. Always Daddy's special one. Always will be."

He gave a hug and kiss to his wife and then addressed the bride as if he'd just noticed her. "Oh, my heavens! You look just like an angel, my dear," he said. The bridesmaids giggled softly. "My son is one very lucky man," he said, winking at his wife.

It was arranged so the grooms stood in order at the foot of the stairs and the bridesmaids followed each other single file down to them. Stephanie stayed alone in the bedroom with her future mother-in-law. Julie made her way down the stairs carefully and watched over the top of the crystal-enhanced hairdos of the other bridesmaids while they paired up with their grooms.

She deliberately didn't look for Luke, and then when she realized she was close, instead of looking into his eyes as all the other couples had done, she looked down. Luke hooked his arm out to the side and she tucked hers through it, gently pressing her upper arm against the back of his and resting her fingers on his forearm next to his elbow. This had all been choreographed and scripted, and she followed along as instructed. She moved with him as he escorted her across the concrete floor of the living room and out the ten-light double doors towards the patio. She carefully stepped over the threshold. Part of her dress snagged briefly on a rough spot in the wooden doorjamb.

In an instant Luke was there in front of her, kneeling, looking for where the fabric had hung up. The delicate material looked soft and luscious in his large, callused hands, like he was handling armfuls of whipped cream. He pressed the fabric he'd freed back into her skirts and she felt a gentle touch of his fingers on her voile-encased thigh. That's when he looked up at her and his blue eyes seared her, and in spite of herself, she focused on his lips, thinking it would be safer than his eyes, until she realized he had done the same.

Their look mated. Both of them did a deep, controlled inhale, and both of them noticed the other doing it. Neither one looked away as the rest of the room faded to the background of muted voices and faded, blurry colors.

She had gotten used to his constant dark stubble, but today he was clean-shaven, his cheeks smooth and shiny, like they'd been oiled, but she knew it was his aftershave lotion. The lemony one he used, and yes, she could smell it. The light fragrance would still be on his fingers. His full lips were deep pink. Without his stubble, she noticed he had a dimple on his right side which was usually hidden, even during their ardent lovemaking. She'd thought she knew every luscious detail of his face, so this discovery was thrilling.

And that's what she was thinking about when he turned and brought her through the doorway, the last couple to make their way across the patio, across the dance floor to the corner of the stone wall near the large cascading fountain. At the sight of Colin's face, his eyes sashaying between the two of them, his lips raised in a private grin, she and Luke drifted apart and took their respective positions at the end of the procession on either side of the ceremony center.

A lute player began playing an old English hymn, and the minister instructed everyone to rise and turn to see Stephanie standing at the edge of the patio with Julie's dad proudly at her side. There was a collective gasp, and for a second Julie thought the audience would break into spontaneous applause.

Though Julie was focused on the bride and frequently bringing her warm, loving gaze back to Colin, she felt Luke watching her. She could feel the heat of his smoldering gaze, the attraction that was still so strong, especially since it had been given a little encouragement earlier with the snag of her dress and the gentle brush of his fingers against her. She hadn't flinched or stepped back at his subtle touch. Her heart still pounded at the closeness to him, at the feel of his eyes perusing her body carefully while everyone else's was focused on the bride. She was doing her own private lap dance for him though she barely moved.

When Stephanie approached her future husband, Julie allowed Colin's head to obscure Luke's face. She noticed the SEAL stayed put and then moved slightly to the side so she got a clear look at his questioning blue eyes. She rocked back on the heels of her slippers and he was obscured again, and she turned her eyes downward as if she hadn't noticed what she'd done.

In an act of boldness rising from somewhere deep within her, she licked her ruby red lips, raised her chin and stared straight into the blue heaven of his eyes. Her heart fluttered and protested the pain of needing him so much, but took solace in the equal need she saw in his.

CHAPTER 15

DAMN IT! LUKE'S inability to focus wasn't helping today. He was tethered to the sight of Julie, like a big peach wad of cotton candy, ripe and exploding on his taste buds, the image of her delicate flower underneath all those petticoats and the way she would writhe beneath him.

Is she feeling it too?

Why couldn't they just sit and talk first? Why did it always end up being about sex with her? He wanted desperately to plunge into her, but the need to be understood…to be loved first…was filling him with an angst which normally would make him incapable. Not today. He was drilling deep with his eyes, as if he could convince her he had the best of intentions, but couldn't think until he was next to her, inside her, breathing her spice and tasting her juices.

At her fuckin' brother's wedding. He felt an unmistakable, and damned inconvenient, rock-hard erection.

Maybe the pain of his need was spurring him on. Was it the PTSD, making it so he wanted to lose control, take her, lift up her skirts and bask in the glory of her pink, quivering peach?

God in heaven, I'm a fuckin' dog. He made quick apologies to Mama Guzman's God, the one they all prayed to on Team 3.

Help me out, here.

And then he saw her wet her lips. She was all pink and innocent except for lips the color of blood. The crack of the automatic, the feeling of warm liquid on his thighs, Camilla's blood, the whisper from his beloved, the one he had held onto every night, in spite of how much pain it caused him, the familiar things of his memory and his life, slipping into the slots of his brain and one by one faded, until all he could see was Camilla's lips saying, *Goodbye.*

Black circles began to tighten around his vision, and he thought he might pass out. He could see Camilla fading, almost floating, in a red satin gown floating all around her, the vision moving away from him, color going grey, and then was lost in a puff of smoke as his focus returned to the present.

"I now pronounce you husband and wife. Ladies and gentlemen, I present to you Mr. and Mrs. Christensen."

Colin and Stephanie first kissed modestly then

turned and faced their well-wishers. The audience stood and clapped for them. Their happy profiles obscured Luke's view of Julie for a moment, but he was rewarded when the newly-married couple stepped forward and down the aisle and Luke saw her blush—blotchy red marks on her chest above the indescribably beautiful heaving breasts needing release. Her body was almost shaking as she struggled for breath. God, he wanted to fill her need. He knew he was the one to do it as no other could.

The other couples met in the center and followed the bride and groom out through the audience. At first Luke presented an arm for her to hook through, but at the last moment clasped her hand firmly, and they walked, not as was rehearsed, but fingers entwined, slipping over each other's fingers, squeezing, exploring, tips touching the juncture of each other's fingers until he thought he would explode.

He led her off to the side of the house, not inside with the rest of the bridal party. He didn't look at her, but instead held up a finger to his friend, Julie's brother, and asked for a private moment with her. The moment was granted, and he searched for a place where they could just be alone.

There was a small rose garden on the west side of the house, behind a white gate covered with a pink blooming climber. He clicked open the gate and heard the creak of metal hinges, closed it behind her, brushing the beautiful fabric aside from the weathered wood on either side of the gate and from tiny thorns of the climbing rose.

He felt her eyes watching him while he fixed her skirts, smoothed them and brushed them like he was preparing a large doll for display. And then he stepped to her, placed his palms on either side of her face, pressed her cheeks together, puckering her beautiful wet, crimson lips and sank himself into them. The soft pillows of flesh parted for him, complete with her delicious, high-pitched whine.

"Julie, Julie, Julie. I can't stop thinking about you. I can't stand being away from you."

He stepped back and searched her eyes, which were watering. Her arms carefully moved up along his back, rubbing over the black fabric of his tux.

In a moment he did not understand, she whispered, "Help me." Her eyebrows had quirked into little tents. The warm brown eyes looked back and forth between both of his, looking for something he hoped to God she'd find there.

"Baby, I need *you* to help *me*," he said honestly, rubbing his lips against hers, nibbling on her mouth, tasting lingering toothpaste and stroking her lower lip with his tongue. "I have nothing to give you but pain," he said sadly, searching for an answer in her eyes.

She smiled and returned his nibbles, her long dark lashes fluttering as she examined his lips by kissing them. "No, you don't give me pain. You give me pleasure, you give me hope. You give me something I've never experienced before fully until today. You give me your love, and I accept it freely. All of it you can give, Luke. All of it, along with the pain and whatever else you have going on. I want all of you."

The words she spoke began to sink in. She must have seen his doubt.

"*All* of you, Luke," she said again, as she cupped his head between her hands. "I want entangled, complicated, and I want to be *missed* when I go, just as I've missed you these past few days."

"Julie, are you sure?"

She drew back and looked at him, ready to speak what he thought was going to be a scolding remark. "You telling me I don't know my own feelings, Luke?"

"Of course not. But I'm—"

"Perfect just the way you are. Let me help you put back the pieces and grow the ones that are still missing. I can help you do this, Luke. If you'll let me in."

Let her in? Hell, yeah.

Just like the night at the beach, she had reached in and grabbed his heart. His soul was touched, his body was on board. His brain was still screaming *what ifs*...but it didn't matter. He wasn't going to go anywhere but deeper.

He started searching, turning his head from side to side.

She reached up on tiptoes and whispered into his ear, which made him tingle, "Follow me."

Julie took his hand and they went through the white gate again, into the back yard. Off to the left stood a brick pathway curving behind a row of large shrubs. As they rounded the corner, Luke could see a vintage airstream trailer with its blue awning extended over the front door. She pulled the lever, opening the door, and stepped up into the cool, dark trailer. He followed.

It had a musty, unused smell, but the windows were open and the curtains fluttered in the breeze. They could hear people laughing and talking, some dance music playing. He knew they didn't have much time before the wedding party needed to pose for pictures, but he hoped to God they'd understand.

She walked down a short corridor, past an efficiency kitchen to a bed in the back with a light green satin bedspread and colorful pillows. She turned around, looking up to him as she sat in the peach whipped cream of her dress. Her body needed to be unwrapped, each layer peeled back slowly and savored. Her blush made him gasp.

He pulled off his jacket and laid it gently on the

front couch, then undid his bow tie, dropping it to the floor. He removed his vest and dropped it. Bisecting the distance between them, taking his time to look at every luscious petal of her picture, he unbuttoned his shirt, pulling it out of his black pants. Her hungry look spurred him on. He sank to his knees, smoothed his palms from her ankles to her knees under the fluff of her skirt as she closed her eyes and licked those damned red lips. He moved his hands slowly up, like a swimmer doing a breaststroke, against her soft thighs, encountering the garters of her corset.

It's going to be a challenge. But he'd make do. He dipped his head underneath her skirts and inhaled her womanly desire—

Two loud raps on the door broke the spell.

"Luke, Julie. We're all waiting on you two," Colin's voice came boldly through the door. Luke whipped his head out from under her skirts, still hungry for the taste of her and faced Julie's shocked face.

"Oh, my God. Ohmygod," Julie said as she jumped up, her hands flying around her skirts. She ran to help Luke find pieces of his wedding attire, helping him slip on his vest while he buttoned his shirt.

"Colin, we'll be right out. We were just having a private conversation. Sorry."

"Yeah, I'll bet. But Jules, I came over here because Dad was steamed when he saw you two come here. I'm afraid the whole wedding party kind of—"

"Not to worry, Colin. We're coming," Luke said as Julie darted him a look, blushing. He couldn't help but wiggle his eyebrows. She appeared not to have gotten the joke. He picked up his jacket. At least he hadn't taken his shoes off.

As Luke was fiddling with his bow tie, Julie opened the door to her brother.

"Sorry, guys. But we're hot and crabby. Everything's waiting on you two."

Luke, grabbing Julie by the waist, whirling her around before bending to give her a deep kiss, his tongue as urgent as hers. Colin wouldn't be able to mistake his intentions.

"Wow. Slow down there, pardner," Colin chuckled. "If you make my bride wait any longer, I'll not gonna get lucky tonight like you guys are obviously gonna do."

Julie giggled and tried to pull away. Luke loved the feeling of catching her and bringing her back to his chest.

"Luke, let's get your bow tie straightened out."

He submitted to her fussing over the little thing he wore willingly, especially since her scent and the delicate feel of her fingers on and around his neck was so pleasurable. She checked him over. She smiled. "What?"

"I like how you fuss over me. I can't wait either, Julie," he blurted.

"Guys!" Colin was getting impatient.

"Coming, coming!" Julie said breathlessly as she ducked out of the doorway. Luke slammed the door behind him and, taking Julie's hand, allowed himself to be dragged back to the public part of the yard and the waiting wedding party. He couldn't bring himself to look at Julie's mother or father, but several of the bridesmaids bore expressions of shock, one young lady covering her mouth to conceal what he suspected might be a grin.

Well, what did they expect? He was going to get under her skirts sooner or later. This would just heighten the anticipation.

And then he'd go for Veteran's Day, Memorial Day and the Fourth of July all at once. It would be an evening she'd never forget.

CHAPTER 16

LUKE HAD BEEN goofy all during the photography session. He'd been inappropriate, exasperating the poor, skinny photographer, but his assistant, who looked like she'd been around the block a few times with bikers, loved their play. Luke would break after their pose and grab Julie.

"Take this one," he'd say, picking her up, his face obscured by the creamy peach, floaty material. He asked to have the bridesmaids and grooms photographed separately, as couples in a group, and he would not allow a stiff, formal picture. In every one he was hugging her, his face close to hers all the time, and he'd kissed her so many times in front of God and the whole world without anything held back, eventually she just stopped worrying and went with it.

Even the elder Mr. Christensen seemed to enjoy it, although her mother, ever the practical one, wanted old-fashioned wedding photos first, and then would indulge his folly if he insisted. She'd told him so several times, but Luke pretended not to hear. He was the most deliciously handsome bad boy, and Julie loved how he didn't care.

Finally the group drifted off to different corners of the house, the patio and the pool area, leaving Luke and Julie alone. He snagged a bottle of champagne and whispered, "To the Airstream, love?"

Julie's cheeks flushed for at least the tenth time in the short hour they'd been with the photographer. He walked around behind her, one arm pulling her by the waist into him, her rear cleavage feeling his hardness. "Or should we go somewhere they don't know about?"

Giggles erupted in spite of scolding herself to behave.

"Mmmm. I like those little sounds. I love the way you laugh. I love the way you do everything."

She turned around, placed her arms around his neck and let him pull their bodies together. Hard against him, she felt safe. And she also knew he wouldn't always be like this. He would have his difficult, possibly even insane moments, but for right now, she'd enjoy the way he was and the way he showed her how much he cared for her.

He was sipping on her lips, making her dizzy, while people walked past them. She didn't care and closed her eyes so she could just experience the hardness of his body, the soft, lemony scent of his cheeks and the tender way he worked over her mouth, stroking and pleasuring her tongue.

"I don't want to leave the party, Luke. And I don't think this can be done discreetly, but I'm still all for it."

"Mmmm. Music to my ears, baby."

He led them back around the hedges, down the brick pathway and back to the Airstream. She made sure all the shades were drawn, and she clicked the door locked.

"No deadbolt, so if someone has a key we're screwed," she said, and then giggled. "Or, actually *not* screwed!"

"I love your potty mouth, Miss Christensen."

He untied his bow tie again, setting it on the countertop, placed his jacket carefully on the couch. Tore off his vest and walked up to her in his pants and white shirt, having kicked off his shoes.

"You do it," he growled, inhaling deeply and presenting his chest to her.

She began unbuttoning his shirt, kissing the warm, smooth skin underneath the cotton. She pulled his shirt from his pants, letting one hand squeeze his package lovingly.

"I want you to know it's more for me than just missing your body, Luke. And I—"

"Me too, princess." He interrupted her by migrating his kiss to her neck while her hands slid over the ripples in his chest, squeezing a nipple between her thumb and first two fingers. "It's way more than sex for me. I'm not ashamed to say I need you, Julie Christensen. I need you in my life."

She examined his face. He allowed the distance between them.

"Luke, I know there will be some rough patches. Like I said to you earlier, just bring what you can."

"I'm hoping we can make this work, sweetheart."

"Me too. But—" she covered his mouth with her fingers. "You don't have to make any promises. I'll take any part of you you're capable of giving. And I think we can work on the rest, if you're into it."

"More than into it. It will be my mission in life. But the instant I feel out of control, I'm going to leave."

"No, Luke. No. You stay and finish it. I can handle anything you dish out. I figured that out while we were separated. This is crazy fast for me. We have so much to go over and talk about, and now with the sexual angle—not knocking it, of course—but I want to explore *all* of you."

"Doctor, I am all yours. I will never hurt you, Julie."

"That's just it, Luke." She took his hand, and they sat on the couch. "You won't be able *not* to, because I care for you, and we will both do things to disappoint the other. I have one request, though." She looked at him levelly. His eyes were steady on hers. He didn't flinch or frown, which was a good thing. "No quitting."

At that, he cocked his head.

"Like your training, Luke. If we do this together, no quitting, saying it's too hard, walking away. I won't live that way. Being separated from you is bad enough during the day, but if I'm around when you're deployed I will wait for you, because you *will* come home to me, right?"

He nodded. "Absolutely I will come home to you. And dream about you every day and night."

"And if your dark places come up, you show them, Luke. You work with me to understand. We work on both our dark or scared places, so we understand each other. We don't quit. You don't run away or ring our DOR bell."

He was serious for a second, and then smiled. "But, Miss Julie, I love ringing your bell."

She smiled back, feeling the heat on her chest and face. "Yes, and you do it very nicely. But I want to make sure you understand, it's just like the night on the beach. I don't do uncomplicated. I like entangled. I won't do casual. I want it all, Luke. You don't hold back. You show me everything, and we work on it all together. But I won't live with those days of being apart because you leave me. You don't walk away. You don't quit on me. Never. Understood?"

He inhaled like he'd been slapped. Looking first down to his lap he thought for a few moments. "If I get to a place—"

She stopped him again with her fingers on his lips. "You let me decide if it's too much. You let *me* decide. You don't take the decision away from me. Because, Luke? I'm not quitting. Ever."

It would have been easier to just fall into the love-making and bask in fantasy love with him, but what she wanted was a real relationship with the real hero who had sacrificed himself for her and the rest of the country. She wanted to grow, to be his right hand, the person at his side, not the person who watched from the sidelines.

"I don't deserve you," he whispered.

"I could say the same. So let's learn to heal each other. But understand it's the *real* you I want, not someone you're pretending to be, Luke. I want you to be my hero just by showing up."

He nodded. Their foreheads touched. "You have me entangled, Miss Julie. But, unlike your statement to me on the beach, there is no fuckin' way I'm going to miss you, because I'm going to hold on tight to you. I'm never letting you go. And you already know I'm not a quitter."

"Yes. I'm going into this with my eyes wide open, Luke. I'll take all of you. All the parts. You just have to show up."

"Agreed."

She could tell his restraint was hurting him a bit, but he was making sure she understood he wasn't going to just jump her bones even though it was clearly on his mind. He wanted her to lead him. And it was just about the sexiest thing he had ever done.

"Come," she stood, pulled his arm and he walked behind her, his shirt wide open, showing off the delicious abs and pecs peeking. His trim hips and long gait followed. His eyes stayed tethered. His fingers entwined with hers while he allowed himself to be led. She sat on the end of the bed with her crinkly chiffon flounces out to the sides. Exactly where they'd been interrupted.

He knelt again. "Thought about this all during the photography," he whispered, removing first one slipper and then the other. "Thought about this," he hissed as he ran his palms up from her ankles, over her knees and pressed her thighs open. He looked down on the layers of dress, his arms buried underneath, and his fingers found her panties. His clear blue eyes searched her face while he breached the elastic and his fingers rubbed her up and down, circling her clit. She was parched. The delicious feeling of him searching, taking his time, being gentle but persistent with his invasion, made her wet. When he slid two fingers inside her sex melted against him.

He moaned at her readiness for him. He lifted the petticoats with his other hand and buried his face in the juncture between her legs, breathing hot against her satin panties, rasping his teeth along her lips through the fabric and sucking the little nub which stood up in blatant invitation. She heard him groan again as his hot tongue hooked under the edge and found her warm sex ripe and waiting for him. His tongue on her opening made her cream with delight. The first lap and suck of her nether lips sent her into a shudder of pleasure.

She lay back on the bed, raising her knees and propping them on the mattress by his ears. She raised her pelvis to his mouth as the fabric crinkled under them. He peeled the layers of organza back, laying them on her chest while he exposed her to him fully. Then he removed her panties.

He stared down at her while removing his shirt and trousers. Fully naked, he placed his hands under her bottom, lifted her sex to his mouth and licked and sucked the delicate folds of her opening. His tongue plunged deep, making her rock with pleasure, forcing her pubic bone against his nose. She could feel her own juices spilling for him as her sex puckered, swelled and released to his mouth.

His two fingers massaged inside her and around

her clit as he climbed up on top.

"I hope you don't mind, but I want to fuck you in this dress. It's the fantasy I've been having ever since I saw you coming down the stairs. I wanted to fuck you with this soft peach fluff floating all around us."

"Yes. I was thinking the same thing," she laughed. "Could hardly wait."

"I don't want to hurt the dress,"

"Shhh." She found herself saying, "It's like me, not nearly as delicate as it looks."

He got to work pulling her stockings off, sliding them carefully down her legs and placing them on the floor by the bed. He climbed up on the bed, sliding her up with an arm under her shoulders.

"Help me with this fantasy," he whispered in her ear.

She couldn't help but smile when he propped himself up at the head of the bed, his cock large and stiffly saluting the ceiling, while he drew her, pulling her forearms so she was climbing him. He helped her smooth the skirts out to the sides, while her bare knees found his hips and slid to hug him there underneath the skirts. She rose up on her knees, then rocked down and back, feeling his penis ride the little gully of her sex, getting snagged at her opening.

And then he was in, just the tip. He clutched her hips and ground her down along his shaft. She felt her liquids release, her body accepting his girth, holding and milking him as he lifted and pressed her body alternately, riding his cock. He was huge, filling her deep. They began with long, deep strokes, but soon she was rolling her hips against him, pressing into him while he raised his hips to plunge deeper. She rocked back and forth, loving the delicious feel of the dull ache she'd carried for days being fed, satisfied, inflamed.

After several minutes, their fucking became urgent, her need for full penetration increasing, and when she began to feel the buzz and tingle of her new orgasm, he came on even stronger.

He was pushing her pleasure, knowing she was on the edge, not letting her stop, fueling her fire. She found herself arching backward, moaning to the ceiling while he rammed into her, his hips mating hers, giving support to his cock embedded deep.

He unzipped the side of her dress, peeling it down around her shoulders till it pooled at her waist.

He sucked in air as he finally got a good look at the light pink brocade undergarment. "Oh baby. That's nice, but how the hell do I—"

"You don't. I'm leaving it on."

"But I want to see you, all of you."

She was still rocking, feeling her inner muscles spasm delightfully. "You will," she groaned between thrusts.

"God, how I love hearing you when I'm fucking you."

"God, I love how you fuck me." She squeezed her elbows together forcing her breasts out in front, her knees hugging his hips. His hands had been roaming under her skirts, up the back of her butt cheeks, but in a flash they were over her own hands as his fingers forced hers to squeeze her own breasts under the stiff bones of the corset. He rose up, arching forward, kissing her neck, raising his knees to lift his pelvis and drive his cock deeper. The dress got more and more bunched up in front of her, partially obscuring his face, forcing him to peel it back just so he could suck her nipples.

Finally he lowered his knees. "This has got to go. I liked it at first, but this just has to go *now*," he said with determination. He lifted the frilly dress off her and she was left with just her corset. She continued to ride him. His hands still gripped her waist, moving her up and down his shaft, rocking her to the sides, rocking her deep.

"Baby, this is real nice, but—" He was staring at her breasts, still partially hidden from him.

"It stays, for now—" she began. "Patience," she said as she leaned forward and kissed him.

He rocked deeper still underneath her, mumbling urgently, "Patience has never been one of my strengths."

"No," she sighed. "Urgency and action," she said as she moved on top of him in circular motions. "Lots of fucking, definitely your strong suit."

"God, baby—" He began to spill inside her. She pulled hard and quickly unsnapped the corset down the front, watching as he took such a deep breath he nearly sucked her inside him.

He had her off him in a flash, pushing her down on the bed, throwing the corset to the side, hiking up her knees. He thrust himself in, rooting deep. He was still spilling, but getting harder and bigger as he came. Forcing aside the lips of her sex, filling her. He stroked long, ending each time a little further in, and then with one last push, pressed his cock firmly against her cervix, and held himself there while she felt the delicious spilling of his seed and he stayed still so she could feel its full force.

Her body answered his with a long, deep, rolling orgasm in tandem, leaving her completely wrung out. He stayed pressed inside her. She loved the way their bodies joined and rode the wave of their pleasure all the way to the top of the hill and down the other side, where they slid into mutual entwined serenity.

HE WOKE UP groggy from their lovemaking, not sure how much time they had been sleeping in the little vintage travel trailer, but loving the feel of her body beneath his. Her lips were still red, even though he'd kissed most of her lipstick off. He loved gazing at her while she slept. She was all the things he wanted in a woman, and she'd said she was in it for the long haul.

He thought about what Kyle had told him, and Nick had underscored. She not only was the someone he would lean on, he would learn in time to trust his need instead of trying to cover it up. His own beliefs had told him he wasn't good enough, that he needed to stay away, that he wasn't worthy. But she stood up for the part of him who wanted to connect on this intense level. The little thread which knew it was okay to ask for help, to need someone. That being a man was about facing your fears, and not always conquering them. He knew she would love all the rough edges and bumps out of him.

And for the first time in his life, he'd found someone strong enough to handle what he knew he might dish out. Her telling him not to quit had made a big impression. He knew about not quitting. He knew about not ringing the bell.

"I'm still here," he whispered to the line of helmets he'd seen at BUD/S. To the line of men who hadn't had a chance to find what he'd found in a woman. He was overwhelmed with gratitude.

'I like complicated, entangled. I want to be sorely

missed when I'm gone.'

Baby, there's no fuckin' way I'm letting you anywhere out of my sight or my heart again. Not ever.

CHAPTER 17

THE PARTY WOUND down, and finally the mobile DJ played to an empty dance floor, using up his already paid-for time. Caterers appeared and began cleaning up plates and gathering paper items in large black garbage bags.

Colin and Stephanie bid the dwindling crowd a farewell. Just before they left, Luke's sister tried to toss Julie her bouquet, but one of the bridesmaids stepped in front of her and snagged it for herself, holding it up in a triumphant salute as though she'd won a gold medal.

Luke ran to Julie's side immediately, as if to quell the bad luck. "You don't need one of those. You already got the guy."

Her fresh face leaned into his lips to accept the kiss he planted on her cheek. "Tell me more about this guy," she said, as she turned, weaving her arms up around his neck and losing her fingers in his hair.

"Does he like to go camping?"

"Only in Airstreams," he said with a growl. "And I like my ladies to wear peach chiffon, which matches..."

He realized his voice was carrying when her fingers closed over his mouth and she shushed him with a kiss. Somewhere behind him he heard titters. He reacted by giving Julie a moan. When they separated at last, he whispered while nibbling on her lips, "Julie, you are too delicious for my health. I just want to spend the next week staying naked in bed with you."

"Camping."

"Whatever you like, sweetheart. But room service sounds better than making you slave over a campfire."

Her right eyebrow lifted. "You'd rather have me slave in the bed underneath you?"

"Yes, baby. Absolutely. Underneath me or anywhere for that matter, Julie. As long as you're naked. As long as we're both naked."

She giggled and snuggled into his neck. The smell and feel of her in her chiffon was such a turn-on he was going to have to work to keep himself paced. He glanced around the winding-down party. The DJ looked sad as he played a slow song, swaying from side to side in tune with the music, earphones bulging and tethering him, eyes closed, in his own private world of music.

"One last dance?" he whispered.

"Love to, Sweetie."

He led her to the dance floor, which would be removed shortly. Taking Julie in his arms was so familiar. The way she arched against his chest and allowed her thighs to straddle his as they made slow progress across the floor, pressing their abdomens together was a thing of beauty. The sound of her flounces reminded him of the gift of her sex he had opened earlier, like a favorite birthday present wrapped in tissue. The delicate flower of her pussy made his mouth water. He kissed her neck, and she slid her arms up on his shoulders, locking her fingers behind his head. She scraped her pubic bone against his right thigh, and he nearly lost it. He angled himself so she could feel how hard he was for her and was rewarded with one of her little moans, and her eyes twinkled back at him just before she closed them.

He wanted to say something but suddenly felt hesitant. Everything had gone so fast, he didn't want to spook her. He was unafraid to show her how much he loved being with her, especially since she'd promised to visit him in Coronado. They'd see where things went from there. It might be like the cart before the horse, but he wanted to ask her to marry him right now, at this impulsive moment, but he held himself back.

Being the wife of a SEAL was a special assignment, and there was no training for it except the school of hard knocks. There was a community of wives who looked out for each other. And not all the stories from overseas made it home to them. The smart wives knew this. He knew it was a lot to ask of someone. He didn't want to fall for a lady who couldn't possibly understand what she was getting herself into.

But that was a completely crazy thought, because he'd already fallen for her. He decided he'd just put it out of his mind and not discuss anything future-related, to keep the pressure off them both. Nothing wrong with having a little bit of—well, a *lot* of—fun in the next few weeks before his deployment.

He held her under the starlight. Feeling eyes on him, he saw Julie's parents eyeing him from their kitchen window, smiling. He couldn't maintain the eye contact though, because odds weren't in his favor. He wasn't Prince Charming or Sir Galahad riding in on his white horse. He was just a guy other guys sent in to blow stuff up, grab people and hopefully get out before getting shot or caught.

And his intentions, although he liked to think of them as honorable, were merely to do everything in his power to be as irresistible as possible to her so when he left, *he'd* be the one she'd miss. And then maybe she'd wait for him. Maybe she'd wait until he got fully well. It was a lot of ifs.

The music stopped while he was kissing her ear

through her hair and holding her tighter as she melted into him. He liked that they were dancing, because their thighs made soft caresses, and the dress, that yummy dress, made all those whispering noises. He just knew every time he heard the sound of layers of chiffon, he'd get hard. It was going to be something he'd have for the rest of his life.

Unwinding from her warm body, he pulled her across the party floor towards the house. On the way, he asked her a question he was hoping she'd answer in the affirmative.

"I still have the room at the Hilton."

Her breath hitched a bit as her spine straightened. *Okay, the Hilton is a non-starter.*

"So what is it you want, Julie?" He held her elbow to keep her from crossing the threshold into her parent's kitchen.

"Someplace else," she said to her shoes.

"I know a spot Nick told me about."

"Nick?"

"My buddy who lives here. He's starting a winery. Retiring from the teams."

"Okay. Something not like the Pink Slipper in Coronado, right?"

"Right." He squeezed her and whispered, "Sorry about that."

"I think at the time I was just glad it wasn't a public

beach or the back of a pickup."

"Funny. But it was all I could think of."

"Roger that, sailor. I was in the same boat, trust me."

Julie rushed up to her room to get a few things to bring along. He wished he could follow her there. He wished no one else was in the house, that he could be with her under the twinkle lights, pay the DJ to play all night long so they could dance and go out to the Airstream or barricade themselves in her old bedroom. Something normal and warm and happy. He liked the light-hearted feeling she created around them. He had visions he could get used to this feeling, and it had been too damned long since it had been part of his psyche.

He slung her bag over his shoulder and led her through the gauntlet of the remaining few partygoers. He thought they'd made a clean exit when her mom waylaid them at the front door.

"Sweetheart. Your dad and I want to have breakfast tomorrow morning with you two. Can you join us?"

Luke's heart skipped a beat or two, and he decided to let Julie handle it. "Mom, we might be taking off. I'm not sure what our schedule will look like tomorrow."

Her mother was not taking "No" very well. "Silly, before you leave, then. We can do it early, if you want. Then your dad and I can go to church afterwards." Her mother went in for the kill shot, had been holding Julie's hand and then reached for Luke's and squeezed it. "Please. One little favor to humor the mother of the groom?"

She had a way of looking down coyly like Julie that pulled on his heartstrings. The woman was lethal.

Then her mother delivered the kill shot. "After all, we're family now."

There was no way out of coming to breakfast tomorrow morning, of having to spend time face-to-face with the parents of the woman he was going to fuck all night long. He'd get to look into their eyes and try to make at least a little sense, while he munched down his eggs, and chewed bacon, and sipped black coffee. All while having the biggest hard-on imaginable. He could see the scene already in living color.

What are you doing, Luke? You are a freakin' dog.

Oh yeah, there was the earlier thought about the life together with her. The part about how he loved her. That part. And yes, they were family. And yes, he'd be the gentleman, but tomorrow morning, not tonight. Tonight he hoped she'd be anything but a lady in his arms.

"I think we can arrange it, Julie," he said to her disappointed face. "We can make the time, don't you think, hon?"

Julie frowned. It didn't appear to be what she'd had

in mind at all, but she went along with him. "Okay, Mom. We'll come by, but not early. How about nine?"

"Fine." Her mother beamed. "See you then." Her sparkly eyes were the last thing Luke saw, since they'd lingered on his face longer than on her daughter's. The lady knew full well what he was about.

He wasn't quite sure she approved.

But what difference could it make anyhow?

HE CHECKED OUT of the Hilton after making sure the hotel Nick recommended was available. It was going to set him back a quarter of a month's pay, but he went ahead and took the room for two nights.

When he drove up to the Waterwheel Inn, the silvery lights illuminating the olive trees at the entrance echoed the carpet of twinkling stars scattered across the dark sky. The texture of golden stucco walls was highlighted in shadows created by ground-level lighting hidden in the landscaping. When they entered the reception area they could hear water flowing beyond glass doors which opened onto a courtyard fountain. Maps painted directly on the walls and frames of old early California artifacts adorned the reception area like an upscale museum.

They checked in. He was struggling to remember if he had enough on his credit card for all this but forced the thought out of his mind. He wanted this to be special for her. Right now, it was all that counted. He wanted to blot out their time together at the Pink Slipper—not the urgency, but the cheesy locale. He vowed she'd never have to stay in a seedy place again for the rest of her life. At least, not if she was with him.

They ambled along the wet walkways to the sound of water sluicing over paddles of an enormous waterwheel. It churned slowly, emptying its contents into a shallow koi pond meandering throughout the property. This place was every bit as nice as Nick had said.

Up narrow, flagstone-lined steps, and there was their room. Luke opened the heavy hand-hewn oak door, and his chest tightened when she slipped past him, the whispers of her textured chiffon tickling his heart. She turned and looked, gazing at the tall exposed beam ceilings, the fireplace and overstuffed reading chairs at the hearth, the heavy tapestry curtains and bedspread on the massive king bed in the center of the room. Like a marionette her head dipped to the side as her dress rustled, and then she faced him.

Whatever he had been before, she'd washed clean. He hoped he would be worthy of her love, and not just in a physical sense. The shadows of his PTSD would return, he was certain of it. More than a little sadness remained with him though. They'd have to work through those times carefully, and he prayed for strength to be gentle with her on those days.

But for tonight all that was way off in the future he hoped they'd have even though, deep down, he still wondered if he was good enough for her.

Tonight was his opportunity to be the man he wanted to be, loving the woman he knew he had been created to love. And he wasn't going to walk away.

Ever.

CHAPTER 18

JULIE WATCHED LUKE linger just inside the doorframe after the big hinges creaked and the lumbering door boomed shut behind him. With his back against the wood, his hips slung at an angle, he'd raised his chin, peering across the small foyer at her, his lips hitched up on one side, punctuated by a prominent, sexy dimple. He was so drool-worthy in so many ways, but especially because of the way he made her wait for him to walk over to her slowly, letting her anticipate the feel of his arms around her waist and the warm softness of his nourishing kiss.

She smoothly melted into him, brushing her palms up his white shirt and over the knots of nipples she could feel under the starched cotton fabric. His body heat was always set on high. Little beads of sweat popped out on his upper lip and at his temples, and he tasted her slowly, giving her the encouraging moans she longed to hear. Add in the feel of his powerful arms around her, and the combination of sweet manhood and fierce protector made her knees wobble. If only she could spend the rest of her life like this, wrapped in his arms, protected from everything that would dare to invade her space.

The intensity was almost pain, she loved this man so much. And here he was, ready to love her physically, sending her places she'd never been before. Each time they were together she went deeper into a fantasy from which she never wanted to return. God help her if she ever had to get over loving him. She was certain she never would recover.

His slow pace drove her into an erotic frenzy. She needed him inside her, now more than ever. The afternoon had been but a tease. She was ready for the full course dinner and couldn't wait to be fully consumed by the smell, the taste, and the feel of him touching her everywhere.

He dropped to his knees after slipping off his shoes. Without touching her, he unbuttoned three of the top buttons of his white shirt, pulling the tails out of his pants, and sat back on his heels with his palms on his thighs, just looking at her. His eyes traveled down her chest to her waist, then lower to the hem of her crinkly chiffon confection of a dress.

He inhaled deeply and smiled up at her.

She wasn't sure what he was trying to tell her, so

she started to raise her hemline with one hand, but he stopped her with his large paw.

"I'll do it. I want to do it all."

She leaned back. "Oh, God. You are killing me, Luke. Would you please get your hands, your mouth, *something* on me, or I'll die!" She felt the fullness of her breasts in her own palms as she looked into the fervent gaze of her lover, who was letting her squirm in her own juices.

"All good things come to those who wait," he whispered while he reached under her dress with his right hand. His knuckles rubbed the inside of her leg and then traveled upwards until his fingers touched the satin crotch of her panties. He barely touched her there, and it was driving her crazy.

"But why, when we could spend more time in each other's arms?" she whispered back.

"Meaning you don't like this?" he said with a lopsided grin, letting one finger slip under the elastic at the top of her left thigh. "Or this," he said while an errant finger rubbed the length of her labia. Her knees parted and she wobbled.

Slowly his forefinger found her opening. "Or this," he said, inserting it before diverting his attention to the peach chiffon covering the triangle of her sex. "And what about this?" he said, lifting her skirts and blowing his warm breath onto her pubic bone while he inserted another finger. His tongue followed the trail his fingers had blazed. She arched forward, bracing her hands on his brawny, bulging shoulders, and splayed her knees further apart to give him as much access as she could.

She held the fabric of her skirts up with one hand, watching his curly dark hair and the strong neck and powerful shoulders disappear into her underthings. His hot breath and tongue added fuel to the flames of her own desire. Her fingers sifted through his hair as she presented herself to him. He spoke his hunger with a deep growl that vibrated against her leg while his tongue explored the lips of her folds and took her juices.

"God, Luke," she sighed. The ache was getting worse, not better, the more he pleasured her. She wasn't sure she could remain standing.

His bright eyes came out from under her skirts, his lips wet with her arousal. "Just hold your horses, Julie. We've got lots of time, sweetheart." He smiled and all was right with the world.

Standing, he wrapped one arm around her waist and, as she leaned into him, he led her to the bed. Like a life-sized doll, she sat. He kneeled in front of her again and just looked at her. She removed his shirt while he watched her. She undid his belt buckle, and he rose and removed his black trousers, laying them on the overstuffed chair. His red, white and blue boxers made her laugh.

She stood, turning so he could remove her dress. He kissed his way down her spine while he slowly unzipped her, triggering a shiver of pleasure. Her wet panties got wetter.

After removing the rest of their underthings, they slipped into bed. She relished the length of him against her. She raised her arms above her head, inhaled and raised her knees while he made his way down to nibble between her legs again. Although she loved the feel of his hot mouth on her, she wanted him inside and tugged under his arms, encouraging him to climb the length of her body to mount her.

"I want—no, *need*—you inside me, Luke."

"Of course. Love being inside you, Julie," he whispered to her ear.

"Do you have something?"

Luke stopped. Julie could see he hadn't even thought about it, and he cursed himself silently. He told her he didn't have anything left and had not thought to stop and get more. He started to pull up. "No, sweetheart. I'm sorry—"

She stopped him. "I don't care. I need you right now."

"Julie, this isn't wise."

She smiled back up to him. "Just this once, Luke. We'll be careful next time. Make love to me bare just this one more time. To celebrate. Please."

She could see he was having second thoughts, but his body was fully engaged. It wasn't like he was forcing himself on her. He was trying to show he was strong for the both of them, but when she reached around and squeezed his balls she felt him cave into his desire.

"Fuck it," he whispered.

His hot cock forced her open as he filled her to the hilt in one long thrust which left her breathless and seeing stars. She was urgent to feel him root deep, she wanted him fast and hard.

Her fingers and toes tingled from touching the strong muscles of his back while he worked against her pelvis, sending her falling through the depths of her own desire. She arched and accepted him as completely as she could physically accommodate him. And he wanted more.

He abruptly stopped, scooted down, and tasted her sex. Her clitoris vibrated under the little bite of his teeth as he sucked and played her little nub like an instrument. Her breath hitched, she let out a cry as he growled and swallowed her juices. His fingers worked on her opening, one big thumb working over the gatekeeper of her core until it released to him and he drank her passion.

As if it had renewed his strength he was on her

body again, pumping her in long, liquid movements, pausing with their bodies entwined and pressed against each other, only to pull away and then enter her again fully.

The manly breath on her neck and chest, his whispers of passion and need, the way he wanted her hard and demanded she give herself to him without holding back, were consuming her. He was not careful, and it was perfect, because she wanted to be taken—not made love to, but taken.

"Take me with you, baby," he said as he began a series of thrusts and groans, forcing himself deep. Her internal muscles clamped down on him, drawing him deeper still until something snapped and she was ravenous for him. She pushed him off and quickly straddled him, pushing down his thick cock to feel the full force and length of him against her needy channel. Her bones were rubber as she ground her pelvis against his slim waist. His hands lifted her by the butt and set her back down on him. He sucked in through his teeth, inhaling, and then she felt him explode. She rode his pulsations and her own.

Their bodies relaxed simultaneously while they watched each other's faces, listening for their sounds of breathing like wind through the trees. She was lost in the icy blue of his eyes and the enormity of the possibilities she saw there. Their mating had been intense and all-consuming, yet so much more than the physical coupling. The beauty of how this man loved her, used her completely, and how she was able to give herself to him had her emotions spiraling out of control, and she teetered on the verge of weeping.

And then she saw he had moisture in his eyes as well.

She lay against him, pressing herself into the nook under his chin, while his huge arms held her secure. Julie felt compelled to say something, but had no clue what it could be. She focused again on the rise and fall of his chest, on the sound of his strong heart thumping, sending hers on a rhythmic dance to match. Whatever was going to be said would have to wait until her head stopped swimming with the smell, the feel, and the sounds of this warrior's powerful body.

Whatever her destiny, it mattered little what would happen in the future as long as he held her like he was doing this afternoon. If he loved who she was half as much as his body loved hers physically, she didn't care the cost to her heart. She gave it to him willingly.

CHAPTER 19

Luke hoped Julie's mother didn't notice the difficulty he had looking her squarely in the eyes, the way he hung his head, pursing his lips together in humble reflection. He really didn't want to be there. Could she tell? Her dark eyes examined him without showing judgment or approval. She had a stealthy way of watching for whatever he didn't want to show to make an appearance, very much like interpreters did when they'd bring in a high-level target for questioning. They assessed the women to look for a weak spot in the family they could exploit so they could get their information. He'd seen the look when Kyle relayed to a translator what he was to tell the wife or daughter of a man they were going to take in. The strong women had that stare, holding back judgment and masking their feelings. But watching, always watching for non-verbal signs their life was about to change.

Julie's father was a different story. He was protective of his daughter, but seemed to have accepted their new relationship without strings. He was genuinely pleased to see her and be in her happy company. Luke liked that. And Julie was talkative, clearly her father's favorite.

Julie took the opportunity to rub her palm over his thigh, which Mrs. Christensen noticed immediately, to his embarrassment. She gave him the benefit of focusing on her daughter's movements under the table and not pressing either of them with a direct glare. Thank God.

He halfway thought Mrs. Christensen had some preternatural sense of smell and could detect the sex on them both, even though they'd showered right before leaving. He halfway expected her to ask him if they'd been safe, if they'd used protection…and of course they hadn't. Her lips smiled, but her eyes did not, as though she knew the answer to that question.

Then she probed his past and managed to dig out things perhaps Stephanie hadn't told her about living with his parents. She even found ways to find out how Colin was behaving, since he lived in San Diego. She asked about the SEAL Teams.

"When do you deploy next?"

"We never know for sure. There are things in play right now which might require we leave soon, Ma'am." That got Julie's attention, too.

"You're headed to the Middle East?"

"Not sure." He knew it was North Africa, but he decided to keep it close. He wasn't sure he'd even tell Julie just yet. And he hadn't told her he was leaving so soon either and felt a little bad about it.

"You guys meet in San Diego, then?" Mr. Christensen asked.

Julie said yes and Luke said no, remembering he'd admitted to meeting her for the first time at the rehearsal dinner.

"We knew of each other and sort of met," she gazed into his face, "through Colin and Stephanie."

Her father nodded, but her mother wasn't buying any of it.

The rest of the morning was strange. Luke really wanted not to be there, even though he knew Julie's parents had good intentions. He did not like the scrutiny. As if sensing it, Julie told them they had to go. She took Luke's hand and led him up to the guest room, which used to be Julie's bedroom.

It looked like Julie had never left. Old posters from her high school days still pinned to the bulletin boards. A poster-sized collage of her friends, some pictures going all the way back to grade school. Her smile was intoxicating as she watched him look around the room, learning about the life she'd lived and how she'd grown up. Unlike his own upbringing, Julie had spent nearly her whole life in one place and one house. Luke knew more about moving than he ever wanted to. And he recalled how his mother had loved it even less.

Today he found himself missing her. She would have been happy for Stephanie. She'd be curious but happy for Luke too, perhaps a little amused by how they'd gotten together. What would he have told her, anyhow? "Met a girl at the beach and, well—" He stopped because he didn't know what he'd say to her, or if she'd approve. His relationship with his father had never progressed into a loving one since he was gone for so much of Luke's childhood on deployments. He'd made a promise to himself he wouldn't put a child of his through then when it was his turn to settle down.

"You like my room?" She snuggled up and accepted his arms about her waist.

"I like, Julie, but I'd like it a lot better if we were naked somewhere so when I make you come it won't disturb your parents."

She grinned up at him. Yup, he thought. It was a pretty good line.

AFTER COLLECTING HER things from the cottage and securing the property, they visited Nick Dunn while Devon was at work. Luke was disappointed he wouldn't be able to introduce the two women. Nick began to explain they had just optioned the former neighbor's fifty acres of prime vineyard.

"Where'd you get hold of that kind of money, Nick?" Luke wanted to know. "Certainly not on a SEAL's salary."

"Amen to that, brother. Devon sold her condo, and we used the proceeds to build the new house, and then used some of the money for the option. Got ourselves a little 'LLC,' so you're welcome to pitch in if you want."

"Afraid I can't help you there, Nick. Shoot, I'll bet Libby's parents would love to invest here," Luke said, referring to Calvin "Coop" Cooper's wife's family.

"Already in. And we caught a break with the relatives of the former owner, who is now serving a ten-year sentence for his involvement in my sister's death. He needed money for legal fees, and his sons gave Devon the option without much of a fight. The woman is amazing."

"Yes, she is," Luke said as he lovingly glanced at Julie, who blushed.

Julie walked outside to view the gardens Nick and Devon had planted on the old nursery property, while Luke lingered in the doorway, watching her.

"She's beautiful. A keeper, Luke. You okay?" asked Nick.

"Fuck, no. We just reconnected yesterday at the wedding. I'm taking it slow," he lied.

"Sure you are, you horn dog. I can see how slow

you're going," Nick said as he swiveled his hips in Luke's direction. "When you get back, you keep up with the meetings and make sure you ask for medication if you get strung out or get to feeling weird. Okay?"

"Yeah, I'm doing okay so far."

"Don't mess with it, Luke. Stay connected to the community."

"Shut up, Nick. I got this part." But Luke understood how fragile the thread was. He'd felt fuckin' great the last twenty-four hours, but the shadows could descend on him again without warning. He told himself Julie was helping keep the demons at bay and that being with her was the best thing he could do for his mental health.

Miss Fresh Face looked radiant while she made her way through the gardens to the two SEALs waiting at the back door. Dressed in jeans and a big shirt, she looked like she belonged in the middle of the waving flowerbeds and bright sunlight. He'd reveled in the beauty of her mom's gardens and realized, sadly, she'd be disappointed to see his hole of an apartment, which didn't have gardens—not even a balcony or ocean view. He wondered if she'd ever fit in with his lifestyle, since it would be very different from what she'd grown up with.

"This is a piece of heaven," she said to Nick.

"I've said the same thing myself. My sister was very happy here until she got sick."

Luke watched Julie frown and peer at her toes.

Nick brought them inside and poured fresh coffee. "I'm sorry Devon couldn't be here. She works most Sundays with open houses and such," Nick began. "She'll be sore she missed Luke," he said as he wiggled his eyebrows. "If I didn't know better..."

Luke felt himself blush. Devon had a way of being so direct it embarrassed him sometimes. Julie was just like her.

"You know anything about running a winery?" Luke asked.

"Learning. A lot of it you can hire out, but it still means I have to do lots of research so we don't get ripped off," Nick answered. He shifted on the bright patchwork fabric high-backed chair Luke remembered as one of Sophie's favorites. "I hired a good vineyard manager, and luckily for us, Mr. Rodriguez knew what he was doing when he planted and began maintenance. The newest part is now coming into its first good season."

"Love how the sun plays on the vines. You have the same rock walls my parents have," Julie offered.

"We got lots of rock here in Bennett Valley, that's for sure. It was probably the most difficult part of getting it ready to plant. Did you know there are ranchers all over this valley floor with old rock walls going back more than a hundred years?"

"What are you going to call your wine, Nick?"

"Sophie's Dream Winery."

"She would have loved that, Nick." Luke knew Mark Beale, Nick's best friend and BUD/S partner, had fallen hard for Nick's sister during her final days. It was fitting for Sophie's vision of the property to be realized and enhanced a hundred percent, since it was now to be part of a Team project. She would have liked that too, he thought. Sophie had loved her SEAL brother and all his Teammates.

"You teach in San Diego, Luke says," Nick said to Julie.

"Yes. I have the best job in the world. I mean, the kids are great, and they're why I do it. I could do without some of the administrative hassles and the parents, though."

"What grade?"

"Second. Love kids at that age. Still excited about being in school."

Luke remembered how Camilla had loved her students too. He felt the jolt of pain tug on him while Julie chattered on about her classroom. Something about it was too familiar. He decided to push it aside for now and just enjoy the time they had left together.

ON THEIR WAY back to the Waterwheel, Luke offered to accompany Julie back by car to San Diego the next day.

"A road trip with you sounds like a fun idea," she said with a coy smile. Her hair was flying in all directions, waving out the open windows to the early summer day. "I do have to be at school on Tuesday for a teacher meeting though, so we can't dawdle, much as I'd love to."

"Another time, then."

"No. I think I'd like you to take me home. But we have to stop at a drugstore on the way."

He searched his memory and then blushed, hanging his head. "Condoms."

She nodded. There was something else clouding her enthusiasm.

"You okay about last night?" he asked.

"I've got some issues to work on when I get back. We have a parent situation I'll have to deal with first thing." He could tell her smile was forced. "Maybe my principal has made it go away, but it isn't likely."

"I'm sorry. Anything I can do?"

"Just love me, Luke. It's all I need."

He intended to. Fully.

CHAPTER 20

JULIE WOKE UP with a slightly stiff neck. They were nearly halfway to San Diego County, and Luke had pulled over for gas and to grab them some lunch. She'd been more tired than she thought she'd be, but then they hadn't gotten much sleep. In between their heavy lovemaking, the sound of the waterwheel outside their door had kept her awake until she found herself drifting off to sleep just as the sky turned pink with sunrise. Her rest hadn't lasted long.

The popular restaurant's parking lot was filled with motorhomes and long-haul trucks. She found herself getting tense as they got closer to home. The sparkle of the emotion-filled weekend began to fade, revealing some fears she was surprised to discover. Was this thing with Luke just a fantasy?

She could tell the bloom of their rekindled relationship had worn off for Luke as well. He looked tired, and they spoke little while they ordered. The footsie was gone. Knowing smiles were gone. They'd had plans to perhaps stay overnight somewhere and then get up early to get Julie back just in time for her meeting, but now Luke seemed hell-bent on driving straight through.

"I can spell you, if you like," she suggested. They had nearly four hours to go.

"Not necessary," he answered without looking at her. She could tell something was eating at him, and almost hoped it was his military past and not something she'd done. Then she chastised herself for such a ridiculous thought.

Maybe it was lack of sleep. She pushed the off button on her better judgment, something she would soon regret.

"So is there something I've done wrong, Luke?"

He gave her a confused look, knitting his eyebrows and squinting, especially on the side he favored, his right.

"Excuse me? Why would you think that?"

"Just you've been so quiet, and I thought—"

"Julie, I've been letting you sleep for Chrissake."

"Well, yes." She instantly regretted she'd said anything. Now she wanted to be compliant, and then realized it would just put him off even more. It would have been best to ignore the niggling question and just leave him alone. But of course she couldn't. Maybe it was knowing they would go their separate ways when they reached San Diego, and nothing had been said about seeing each other after the trip.

"You've been awake, what? Twenty minutes while I gassed up the car?" The emphasis on *I gassed up the car* made it sound like it had been an imposition, not like a man who was devoted to the woman he loved. As if it was her fault.

Was it just her company? But that was nuts.

"I'm sorry, Luke. I should have insisted I drive part of the way. You're tired. And you're crabby."

She could see his control waning. "You don't know anything about how I feel, Julie. Don't do that."

"What? Just what am I doing, Luke?" She said it a little too loud, and several of the customers turned to look. Luke didn't flinch or seem to notice, but she knew he had.

"Quit prying."

"We talked about this."

"No *this* isn't what we talked about, Julie." He delivered it sharply, like a saber cutting through silk. He hissed the words, spinning out his enunciation with irritation oozing through every pore.

Was she ready for this? She told herself she was. She also told herself she shouldn't back down, even if it risked a blowup. She had to show him she wasn't afraid of what he had going on emotionally. But she was getting more uncomfortable by the moment. Something in the back of her brain was shouting *'No'* but she didn't care. It was past time to fully engage.

"I don't think it is anything we talked about either, except I've said before that I didn't want you to check out on me, and from what I can see, it's exactly what you've done."

Anger flared in his eyes, and he swiped his forearm across the table so his silverware hit the floor, attracting attention.

"Don't start this, Luke," she held firm.

He pointed at her face and then gratefully thought better of it. She drilled a look to him and again would not back down. The first word out of his mouth was going to be 'You.' She could tell.

"You have no idea what you're talking about. I'm just fuckin' tired, and I've been trying to be careful to let you sleep. What, I have to entertain you 24/7 now? Not enough to let you get some rest while I'm sitting on my ass dodging motorhomes and stupid truck drivers?"

"You offered."

"Well, that wasn't such a good decision now, was it?"

She sat back and watched a brother and sister throw ice cubes at each other. Everything around her irritated her too. She felt as tired as she knew he did.

But the memory of their intense, nearly all-night, sexual encounter left her aching for more of that closeness…that soulful connection she might possibly have imagined after all…and missing him already.

Shaking her head, she decided to try reminding him how it had been between them last night. "Luke, have you forgotten why we didn't get any sleep last night? Is sleep really the issue here?"

At first he blinked, as if he couldn't parse the words. And then he took in a deep breath and let it out slowly, dropping his eyes to where her fingers rested on the tabletop. He plastered a smile on his lips, and when he looked at her, some of the sparkle returned to his eyes.

But he was measured. He was guarded. And it broke her heart.

Just tell me, Luke. Let me in. No need to play nice. Just be honest with me. I can handle it.

"I guess you wore me out a bit. I enjoyed it last night. But—"

She grabbed his hand and squeezed it. "Just stop. Look. I'm sorry. I'm a little on edge too. Let's just hit the reset button, Luke. I didn't mean anything by it."

The gentle pat he returned was just for effect. He wasn't feeling anything at all, though she could tell he was trying to.

"It's been a pretty intense few days. We both have

things we have to go back and do, things perhaps we aren't looking forward to," he said. "And I'm not much of a talker, either. I don't do small talk. I never know what to say. I'm pretty much an action guy."

"I've experienced that first hand," she said with a blush, which was not warmly received. "It's part of what I find attractive—"

He was up in an instant. "Going to the john," he said as he practically ran from the table.

What just happened? He'd gotten a couple of cell phone texts. Was there a problem back in San Diego?

Their food was delivered just before Luke returned to the table. A droplet of water was at his temple, and it looked like his hair was wet. His smile to her was almost sheepish.

He waited until she took the first bite before he began. And then she knew she wasn't going to like whatever he was going to say.

"Julie, there's no question I'm attracted to you. I guess what's going on with me is I'm having an extreme attack of conscience. I feel like I've led you someplace I didn't intend to go myself. Does that make sense?"

"No. Not really."

He checked the table to his left, watching the family with the warring children interact. His face was an expressionless slate, except for the jaw muscles that rippled as he ground his back teeth. He didn't look up at her, just leaned forward over his hands, tented his eyebrows, and continued.

"Look. This is hard for me. I'm not sure I'm ready for the kind of intense relationship you seem to want. And I feel real bad I've led you on."

He did a quick check to her eyes and then darted back down to his hands.

She could have said something, but what she really wanted to do was throw her ice water in his face. Fucked nearly every way possible, and now the guy had a pang of regret. Her fury escalated to a slow boil.

It was what her mother used to say to warn her about men and sex. "Boys just want to get in your pants," she used to say. "They get what they want, and then they're on to the next conquest." In fact, she could see her mother's face nodding and saying 'I told you so' which just infuriated her further. And the woman was wrong. Dead wrong.

But where did it leave them?

Nowhere. That's exactly where it left them. There was no "they." There was a memory of something briefly beautiful, something she could see dying right in front of her, being eviscerated and torn apart by some black spirit which had taken over the man she thought she loved.

Yes, Luke was damaged all right. Maybe it was the

lack of sleep, but today, this afternoon, sitting at this table in front of strangers with the ridiculous elevator music blaring in the background where the food suddenly tasted like cardboard, she wasn't so sure she could keep her promise to him.

"Come on. Let's hit the road," he said before she could.

The fresh air, though laced with dusty gasoline and exhaust fumes from the busy freeway, helped. The absence of disapproving looks lessened the tension a bit for her.

"I'd like to drive, if you don't mind, Luke," she said, without looking at him.

"No. Not an option."

So now she was also an "option."

"Let me give you a chance to catch a cat nap. I'll wake you up in an hour. I promise."

He was searching the buzzing traffic on the freeway, as if there was an answer there.

"Suit yourself," he said, and dropped the keys in her palm.

JULIE DIDN'T WAKE him up in an hour. She drove him all the way to San Diego, and in the evening light, touched his arm and saw him flinch. Disoriented at first, he glared at her when he realized he'd slept the remainder of the trip and she had neglected to wake him up.

"You need to tell me where to drop you off."

It was as if she'd said something so distasteful he could hardly stand to listen. He appeared to think about something and then shook his head. Then he flopped back, pounded his fist into his thigh and swore.

"Fuck. My car's at the airport. We've passed it already."

"No problem," Julie said, turning off the freeway to the overpass that took them north again on I-5. She was working hard to remain unflappable, but her armpits were sweaty. She'd had several talks with herself before waking Luke, and that had helped. There was no way she was going to let her crushing disappointment and hurt show. She'd tell it to her pillow when she cried herself to sleep after a long, hot shower.

"I'm at Terminal 1 parking," he pointed to the sign.

She drove through the gate and followed his directions until they were parked behind a huge, deep blue Hummer. Of course he would have a big monster car.

She popped the trunk and got out for what she hoped was a goodbye hug, perhaps some semblance of a kiss. Was she hoping he'd talk about seeing her again?

Yes. It was definitely what she hoped for.

But what she got was a peck on the cheek and a

shrug. "I had fun. I'll call you sometime."

He wasn't even careful how he sounded, how he delivered the age-old line she should have been prepared for, but wasn't.

Well, it was her own damned fault she thought as she handed the attendant her ticket and was allowed to exit the parking lot. She'd laid the ground rules, told him it was not acceptable for him to mentally "go away," and he couldn't help himself.

He'd told her he loved her, something she couldn't simply discard. But the part about letting her decide whether or not it was too much, giving her the choice, he'd still done that. Yeah, he allowed her to choose whether to answer her phone when he called, *if* he called. It just wasn't exactly what she'd hoped for.

Well, she thought, if there was a God of teachers, he'd save her from problems with the administration. She could go on her girls' week in Vegas with a couple of friends. They'd get drunk, watch the male dance reviews and maybe a nudie show and ogle the firemen or policemen—something *other* than a man in military uniform.

And she'd learn to forget by throwing herself into next year's lesson plans in the anticipation of bright, young faces, eager to learn.

And hope to God she could stop thinking about the icy blue eyes of the man who had wounded her.

Because she realized she did love him still.

CHAPTER 21

LUKE SAT GRIPPING the wheel of his Hummer and pressed his forehead into it.

You freakin' asshole!

Sweet Julie had given him just about everything he ever wanted in a woman and more. And he had to go all cold on her. The shadows of the past had sneaked in and draped themselves over his sensual weekend with her, graying out her beautiful, warm spirit. The crowd of old voices shouted in his ear things like, '*You don't deserve her,*' or '*You better watch out or you'll kill her, too.*'

He'd been released from the dream of Camilla and her red lips until a week ago. And then Julie and all her pure pinkness, just like Camilla had been for him, so willing, so easy to fall for, her body calling for his to take them over the edge of passion like never before. Why was it going to be taken away from him again?

He knew he'd have to book a meeting with his

counselor. He didn't want to be honest about the medication he *wasn't* taking, because he didn't like how it made him feel. Told himself he was stronger than everyone else. And yeah, the doc had told him he'd start to feel normal and he'd think he could go off the meds and play Superman. It was just that he didn't want to be dulled down, miss a single eyelash or freckle on her beautiful body. He'd wanted to have all of it without missing anything.

So what did he do? He destroyed it. He blew his chance.

Clearly he wasn't ready for this kind of intense relationship. He'd rushed up to Colin's wedding, was shocked to find Julie greeting guests at the door to her parent's home. He was in the company of a bunch of strangers who were so nice to him, not because of his military service, but because they were decent people. They didn't know what kind of a hot-and-cold guy he was, what kind of a time bomb was ticking inside him.

Normally he'd have tired of the girl. His entanglements with Julie were golden strings which cut into his flesh. Something about the pain was delicious in a fucked-up kind of way. His aching heart was somehow atonement for Camilla maybe, or something else.

Yeah, the doc had told him the confused state of mind would come and go. That if he started feeling numb or confused, if he lacked motivation to go work out or even fold his clothes, to watch out.

Something had soaked into his pants, leaving his thighs damp. What was weird was the steering wheel was dripping on him.

Holy fuck. My tears.

Time to rein in those feelings. He pushed the button to start the Hummer, but it didn't. He rummaged through his backpack to make sure the keys were there, and put them closer to his lap in the tray at the console. This time his Hummer roared to life.

His beast wanted to run flat out like a good racehorse. The freeway called to him. He was running home. He knew it just like the cowboys of old who pushed their horses to get them home before sunset. He needed the brotherhood to rub off all the rough edges, or pound them off as sometimes happened.

He dialed his LPO.

"You back, Luke?"

"Yup. Anything going on tonight?"

"Sanouk's got a poker game planned. Not sure I'm up to it, though. Brandon has been hell on wheels."

"He's your boy. Only makes sense."

"Christy's been working a ton. He's getting used to torturing his dad."

"So bring him along."

"Not a chance. You know what he said to Christy this morning?"

"Wait a minute. He's talking already?"

"Shit, Luke. Where you been? He's fuckin' three and a half."

"Like I'm supposed to know the development cycle of my LPO's kid. Kyle, no offense, but I'd rather pay attention to what Christy is wearing than check out whether or not your rug rat is talking."

"Watch it, Luke."

"Okay, it's a big deal to you. I get it."

"No, man. It's a big deal what he said."

"So hurry up and fuckin' tell me."

"He dropped his spoon on the floor. He said, 'Oh, fuck, I dropped it.'"

Now that was funny. Luke could just see the scene.

"What'd you expect? You just said he's been hanging around you more these days. You think he'd start talking college prep?"

"I caught hell from Christy."

"As you should. Not likely he picked up his language from her side, ya know?"

"Yeah. So I'm trying to limit his exposure to stuff like poker parties. But I'll come if Christy gets home and doesn't have other plans."

"Roger that, then." Luke was happy for Kyle, who had found a woman he would let boss him around the house, even though on the job Kyle was usually the one in charge. He chuckled when he dialed Fredo's number and didn't get an answer. He did get hold of his fellow teammate, Tyler Gray.

"So Colin went ahead and did the deed."

"He sure did."

"When did you get home?"

"Um. Just now."

"You see Nick?"

"Sure did. He's got a fine little place there. Going into the wine business."

"I hear he's leaving the Teams."

"Not sure. It happens, Tyler. You know that. Comes a point when it's not fun anymore." He was thinking about his own battles. Was this what was going on with him? Was it getting to be time to get out? He'd already transferred from the East Coast teams. But he liked Team 3 and his LPO. If he couldn't make it here, he wouldn't be happy anywhere.

Something else to talk to the doc about.

"So Tyler, you ready for some fun tonight?"

"I'm not feeling too good about the poker, but we could meet at the Scupper for a couple of brews."

"Works for me. I've been driving half the day."

"Thought you flew."

"Came back with someone."

"As in of the female kind?"

"Affirmative."

"And why the fuck aren't you tied up this evening?

You losing your touch, Luke?"

Nothing wrong with my touch. It's my head.

"Long story. Tell you later. Meet you at the Scupper in an hour?" he said while he turned toward Coronado.

"I'll be there."

He decided to check in with his Chief, Timmons, who turned out to be in a foul mood. He called him on his cell, since he hadn't thought the man would be working. He was wrong.

"Shit, Luke, you sound like hell."

"I didn't want to call you either."

"You okay? Back from…where-the-hell-were-you?" Timmons growled.

"Sonoma County. My sister got married to a guy from up there."

Luke heard rustling. "I'm looking out this window at some barracks, some palm trees growing despite the Navy's efforts to kill them through neglect. I've got to go home and have dinner with a woman who hasn't talked to me for over a month. I'm wondering, son, why you ever came back."

"Had to, sir. It's my job. You know that." Luke wondered whether Timmons's inquiry about his mental health had as much to do with his own issues. Sounded like his household was anything but happy.

The pause meant they were done talking.

"You okay, sir?" Part of him welcomed the distraction, and he took it as a good sign he cared about his chief.

"I'm about as okay as a third tit on a warthog. You know I'm leaving the Navy soon. I dunno, is it okay?"

"So, take a side trip to Sonoma County. It's beautiful up there. Maybe look for work up there."

"No can do, son," Timmons barked into the earpiece.

"And why not?"

"They don't have a doll factory up there, and my wife would never tolerate it." Timmons's wife had filled their bedroom with a museum-level doll collection that everyone knew he hated. Luke suspected he spent most nights in his recliner in front of the TV.

"So you go by yourself," Luke posed. "Just for a vacation. Go look up Nick. He's adjusting well to living away from the community for now."

"Keep your fuckin' eyes in your own yard."

"Yeah. Take good care of those dolls."

"Fuck you!" Timmons roared. The rustling in the background intensified followed by a crash and tinkle of shattered glass.

Which meant the frog statue was toast again. Luke would have to tell Kyle to order their sixth replacement of the Team gift and mascot. Another three hundred dollars down the drain. But he liked to think the frog might wind up in Timmons's bedroom keeping the dolls company. Then Timmons would know his boys on Team 3 were thinking about him.

Luke drove into his apartment complex. It was perched on a hill, and the ocean view would have been nice if it hadn't been for another apartment building which had appeared overnight and completely obscured the vista.

His apartment was sparse. Since he never spent any time there, it wasn't furnished with anything he couldn't pick up at Goodwill or the local discount furniture store. One of his buds had pointed out he was still eating his dinners on the floor, so he went out the next day and bought two chairs and a small, stained card table. Now they looked shabby. He remembered seeing Julie's old room, and could easily guess what her place in San Diego looked like. Her classroom was probably the same. Filled with light and color. Stimulating all the young minds in her care. Filled with happy chaos.

He chastised himself for thinking so much about her. He needed *lack* of stimulation, lack of chaos and color. He needed clean, sparse, maybe a little cold, to calm him down. Maybe a midnight swim. He needed the distraction of a couple of beers and the intense friendship of one of his brothers. He needed to "plug in." His exploration into the free-flowing, soft, warm side of Julie was a dangerous place where he'd lost control. He wasn't ready for that. He didn't trust himself. Not yet.

He thought about his sister, Stephanie, on her honeymoon, about what they were doing. He imagined his sister and her brother walking on some white sand beach together. Warm. In love. Happy. He saw romantic dinners and midnight swims naked in warm water. Warm water, not like the cold waters of Coronado when they were doing a wet and sandy.

Good for you, Stephanie. They hadn't been especially close while they were growing up. Luke had gone into the Navy while she was still in braces. She'd gone away to boarding school when their mom died. Luke lived with the family of a friend and finished his last year of public high school and then decided to go into the Navy without college. But Stephanie had the opportunity for an educated future, and she'd met Colin in San Diego at school. When Luke transferred to Coronado he struck up a friendship with Colin, who couldn't stop talking about his sister he was constantly trying to hook up with him. Funny how things turned out.

His eyes stung again at the thought of what might have happened if Colin had arranged the blind date he'd been threatening for a couple of years. Luke wished he could hit a reset button, like in the movie, so he could meet her again for the first time. He'd have gone slower this time. He'd have taken his time and told her about his struggles with PTSD *before* he'd fucked her. Before he'd let her form an emotional attachment which no doubt was causing her some pain. Maybe some anger. Well, he deserved it. He deserved all of it. God, he was such a dog.

The Scupper was bustling with a bachelor party. Some regular Navy guy and several of his friends were entertaining themselves, being louder than was comfortable for him. But then he probably had about five more years' military service in than they did. It was like looking in a mirror, way back to when he first made the Teams. He and a couple of other buddies had been downright obnoxious in Little Creek. Some older Team guys sat in on their little celebration, laughing right along with them, pleased with their enthusiasm, but warning them tougher days were ahead.

That's right, the only easy day was yesterday.

And yesterday was a pretty nice day, thought Luke. He felt like the healing he'd begun was here to stay. He'd felt like part of a family, like maybe he could maintain his share of the emotional stability. He trusted himself.

But what had occurred on the trip home made him question everything. Julie deserved more than a vacant shirt, or someone trying to just walk through life pretending he felt whole. And he didn't have the energy to "play nice" when he didn't *feel* nice.

He ordered his beer and took it out to the patio. The fire pit gas flame was lit, but the patio was empty. He sat down and enjoyed the heat from the fire, staring into the flames. Even though it was a warm San Diego night, the long ride, even though he'd slept for part of it, had given him a backache.

There were no answers there in the orange tongues of light. His eyes dried out from the heat and stung. Or maybe it was because he'd shed so many tears his tear ducts were trying to replenish themselves. But there was no question, his melancholy was starting to worry him. Big swing in emotion from yesterday.

Tyler sauntered in and took up his usual position, carrying a long-necked bottle.

"You look like shit, Luke."

"You weren't the first one I called either, asshole," Luke said to his best friend. Without looking at Tyler's face, he could tell the guy was taunting him with a grin and a sparkle in his eyes that told the world he was up to mischief.

"You gonna tell me about the sweet thing you brought back with you from up North?"

Luke rounded on him, ready to punch his lights out. He didn't like the way Tyler called her a "sweet young thing." It was disrespectful. He didn't have the right to talk that way about Julie.

Tyler was smart and knew how to work him: say nothing more. Let Luke stew in his own awkwardness. That irritated him too. "She lives down here. Colin's sister."

"Ah, the schoolteacher he's been trying to hook me up with," Tyler said.

"*You*?" Luke couldn't believe he wasn't Colin's only choice for a brother-in-law.

"You're fuckin' kidding me, Luke. You don't think I'd measure up, that it? Well I'll tell you something, asshole. If *I'd* brought her back, I wouldn't be here having some sad brews with you, old man." Tyler liked to refer to Luke as the old man, but he was only a month older.

Luke was at his limit, but he had to admit Tyler was right. He'd been an idiot today. And he was being an idiot right now too. Late to the party on both counts. Couldn't stop his mood this afternoon and couldn't stop it now.

But he still didn't like Colin trying to get both of them to take his sister out.

"I offered to drive her home. That's all, Tyler."

Tyler took a long drag off his beer. He signaled for another round for both of them. Two was usually their limit, unless one of them wasn't going to drive home, which was always possible. There was a Team guy named Darrell who lived not more than three blocks away from the Scupper. He could always crash there if need be. Then Luke realized Tyler was grinning at him.

"What?" he asked, irritation coming back.

"You fucked her."

Several of the customers at nearby tables, luckily all men, turned and looked at Tyler.

"It wasn't like that."

"You fucked her."

Luke stood up. He said, "God damn it. Of course I fucked her," loud enough even passersby on the sidewalk out front could hear him.

So much for the low-profile night he wasn't going to have.

CHAPTER 22

LUKE AND TYLER stopped by Sanouk's apartment for the poker game. The two buddies were not speaking, but Luke knew it was just the way it was going to be tonight. Tomorrow everything would be back to normal. Hanging around Tyler and a few others on the Team would either grind off or chisel off his sharp edges. He chalked it up to being a little testy from the long drive from Sonoma County and because he hadn't worked out in a few days or taken an ocean swim. He'd let himself get soft in the head. That's all it was.

Sanouk was now smoking cigars, which he'd justified as being better than inhaling cigarettes. When they walked into the apartment, he greeted them, tipping the green visor Gunny'd liked to wear for poker night. The thing had been chewed by a dog long dead before Sanouk had ever made it to the States. The Team had adopted the young Thai because he was Gunny's blood, and Gunny's blood was Team blood. The old Gunnery Sergeant was the one who had brought a lot of the crew home from parties, saving them from a DUI and Conduct Unbecoming charge. The regular Navy guys and MPs were only too happy to dish out their little slice of pain, fueled mostly by jealousy.

After Gunny passed, Sanouk and his mother had taken over Gunny's gym and had not changed one thing except to bring in a new glass case for the Popeye T-shirts and water bottles they sold. She also brought in a chair masseuse, a white-haired, ancient guy with incredibly strong hands. No one knew his name although he practically lived at the gym, and he gave the best chair massages anyone could recall. Turned out he was the relative living in California who helped Sanouk's mother, Amornpan, get her papers in order and lent her money to come over to see her grizzled husband before his death. Gunny had left Thailand while she was pregnant.

She did help Gunny die with dignity. She'd had something of a premonition about it. Though Gunny wasn't the husband she'd always wanted, she was the wife he'd always needed. She was held in a great deal of respect by Team guys and was always invited to Team events, like the mother of one of the Team members she almost was.

Amornpan was beautiful. Gunny said she'd gotten

more beautiful with age. And all the Team guys knew it was because of his love for this woman, in spite of all the years of separation. The Team wanted to get them remarried, but Gunny insisted there was nothing wrong with the first marriage and didn't see any need to change things. It was a fitting end to a man all the SEALs of Team 3 considered their surrogate father.

Now seeing Sanouk wearing the visor, Gunny's favorite hat for poker games, nearly brought Luke to tears. He steeled himself for the hazing he surely was going to get tonight.

"Hey, my man," Sanouk said to the two of them. Jones and Fredo moved over to make more room at the table. Luke begged off, saying he was out of money, which was partially true. The two nights at the Waterwheel Inn had cost him nearly a half month's take-home pay.

"Fuck sake, Luke. We're playing quarters, here. You don't fuckin' have a dollar on you?" Sanouk's eyes were dancing. A quick glance down at his winnings, and Luke realized why.

Quietly he got out his wallet, took a dollar bill out and laid it on the table in front of Sanouk. "Here. Just take it now. This way I lose it quick and painless."

Fredo shot daggers at Luke. "You fuckin' giving up before you fight? Who told you that was a good idea?"

"I just don't feel like losing my dollar slow," Luke

answered.

"See, that's the fuckin' point, Luke," Jones added. "You assume you'll lose it. How the fuck do you know?"

"Because all you guys are better players than I am, and look how he's cleaning your clocks," Luke insisted.

Fredo shook his head. "Fuckin' pussy. Go off to a wedding, man, and you come home and mope around—"

"I'm not fuckin' moping around—" Luke started, but soon it was a regular free-for-all. Everyone but Sanouk was standing up, arguing about the game, about Luke, about anything and everything. Though the language was blue with swearing and arms were waving about, the tabletop remained intact. It was an unspoken rule: you were the bad guy, regardless of the legitimacy of your claim, if you disturbed the game.

Tyler whispered something to Fredo, who nodded. Being the senior member of the group, not in terms of rank, but in terms of years of service, he spoke with authority.

"Okay guys. We go for a swim, and anyone who objects does some fuckin' wet and sandy."

Luke wondered what the difference was, since it would be freakin' cold out there right now. Fredo had drilled him a look and, amidst the grumbles and curses, the group put on their jackets and began to file out of

Sanouk's apartment.

Jones hated the midnight swims the most. He turned to Sanouk. "You should come." It was all the Thai youth needed. "Hell, yeah!" the kid said. He carefully put out his cigar and dashed to the bedroom, coming back shirtless but with a towel draped over his neck.

The poker game remained exactly where and how they'd left it. There was a good chance they'd continue the next day.

LUKE WAS ESPECIALLY cold tonight. The aches from the long car ride and his lack of sleep in the last twenty-four hours were catching up to him. He teamed up with Jones, the slowest swimmer on the Team. They all shed their pants and shoes in one communal pile. Some took off the T-shirts underneath whatever else they'd worn, which included Fredo who had been wearing a bright red Hawaiian print. Some, like Jones and Luke, left their shirts on for added warmth.

The nearly full moon reminded Luke of a BUD/S training on the other side of the island in an un-gated area of public beach separated with orange plastic netting for a makeshift divider. He'd looked at the moon during the training and imagined it was warming him. Now, as he headed to the water with the rest of the Team, he wondered what the fuck he'd been thinking.

The water was chilly, but not as bad as he'd expected. It did clear his head right away. Jones took off in a slow crawl following Fredo and Sanouk, who were in the lead by a considerable margin. Luke worked to catch up to Jones, and the two men began a swimming-in-tandem exercise like a couple of porpoises. The inlet was choppy and just as dirty as usual. He could taste remnants of diesel fuel and whatever else had sloughed off the Navy cruisers and small craft. In the daytime the water looked much better than it tasted at night.

Tyler, Rory and a new guy were in the middle of the pack. On cue they turned on their backs and eyed Jones and Luke bringing up the rear. Apparently satisfied, the trio rolled over to their bellies again and took off, leaving him and Jones behind.

At one of the light buoys, Fredo turned and then headed back. He didn't look up when he passed Jones and Luke going in the opposite direction, but did give them the finger.

They swam for nearly an hour. Luke knew the others didn't much want to be in the water and were probably cold as he was, but they were making damned sure Luke worked off some of the negative energy he hadn't been able to conceal. They were probably cussing him out, he thought. But the simple act of taking him on this swim and not leaving him alone in his misery was what you did for one of your own. Nobody got left behind.

Ever.

The sand of the little park glowed white in the moonlight when he and Jones collapsed next to each other, staring up at the stars until they could catch their breath. It felt good to be totally exhausted.

Luke knew he'd be able to get a good night's sleep now. Maybe even sleep in, if he could keep his room dark enough. Tyler punched Luke in the arm with a 'Later, dude,' but his arms were so frozen he barely felt the sting.

The others climbed into several vehicles and began to leave the parking lot. Fredo hung back.

"Luke, maybe you fuckin' come on over to my place for the evening, okay?" the short Mexican SEAL barked it more like an order than a question. "Mia's gone to PV with her girlfriends until the weekend. I could use the fuckin' company."

"Nah, I'm good," Luke said.

"I think, if it's all the same to you, tonight you should come over. Shit, my place is way more quiet than yours."

"You fuckin' don't have to keep an eye on me, Fredo. But I appreciate it."

"Shit, Luke. I'm gonna sleep, not watch your sorry ass. Just come over, okay?"

"But I sleep better in my own fuckin' bed, Fredo. Just leave me the fuck alone." There was no point in asking Fredo to come to *his* place since he didn't have a couch, and it was out of the question for two SEALs to share the same bed. So he would have to give up his bed for the floor.

"You call Kyle in the AM then, my man," Fredo commanded.

"Roger that."

Fredo had finished drying off with his Hawaiian shirt. Then he slipped it over his shoulders and wet undershirt. At least their pants were dry, but wouldn't be for long since their wet boxers would soon soak through. It did kind of guarantee Fredo that Luke wouldn't be making the rounds of the bars on Coronado Island, not with pants looking like he'd pissed them. Going home to change and then returning to the party scene just seemed like too much damned work.

"You call me if you get any fuckin' *thoughts*."

"Doubt I will. I'm fuckin' completely spent," Luke said.

"No, not technically," Fredo objected. "Spent is after you've fuckin' been with your woman for a few hours, bro." Fredo punched him in the arm. "You good?"

"Fuckin' fantastic. Not fuckin' cold either," Luke lied back to him, which was the answer Fredo had probably been looking for.

And like a good pair of shoes he'd misplaced and suddenly found, he was relieved he was able to sync in with Fredo and the other SEALs in the use of the word fuck, and mean it.

It was a very fuckin' good sign.

CHAPTER 23

JULIE MADE IT into her apartment, lugging the rolling duffel behind her. The bridesmaid dress was in a bag slung over one arm. The chiffon made the crinkled paper noise, which still sent a shiver up her spine in spite of the ache in her heart.

She managed to smile at a couple walking past hand in hand. She told herself she was okay with seeing lovers. This wouldn't bother her, she was "fine"—the word seemed to brush aside painful emotions, and although it made her tense, she felt more in control.

That is, until she closed her front door. Dropping the dress bag on the floor, she released the duffel handle and let it flip forward. She slumped to the floor next to it. When she saw the vacantness of her normally bright and cheerful apartment, she nearly burst into tears. She hadn't turned on the lights, but water from the large pool area below was reflected on her walls, and she could see lights at the little harbor beyond and the Bay glistening under a full moon.

She righted herself but stayed seated, watching moonbeams dance like faerie wings against the apartment walls. Tall palm fronds waved outside her balcony slider, their shadows clacking to an unknown rhythm against the sheetrocked walls.

That's when the tears came. And when they came, her chest heaved and her inhales were choppy, like she couldn't get enough air. The vacant hole in her heart was unbearable. She'd told herself it would be hard, but damn, she didn't expect it would be *this* hard. There was no way she would be "fine" today.

She'd told him she'd stay the course, and all she asked in return was for him to not walk out, not give up on them.

But that's exactly what he'd done. And no matter how much she ached, she knew the only thing for her to do was set aside the pain and throw herself back into her classes. She had things to prepare for the brief summer session she was scheduled to teach, and she'd offered to do it so she could help some of her struggling students.

In the dark and all alone, she vowed it was time to get busy and not pine for him. After all, there was no future with Luke, and thus it wasn't helpful to keep brooding about it. Eventually the feeling part would fade and she'd be able to see him again at family gatherings or hear about him and not feel the hole in her chest yawn open again. But she vowed, sitting on the floor watching the reflections of the night and water lights, someday the right guy would come along. He'd be the real deal, the real package, and he'd be available to her.

Because Luke was *not* and might never be.

JULIE'S SUMMER SCHOOL session was due to start in a week. She kept her appointment with the principal the next morning to go over a couple of items he'd wanted to discuss prior to classes starting. She needed to get her room in shape for the new class, simplify it by removing some of her history and math modules. It was going to be a combined group of slow readers from second through fourth grades. Slow readers had trouble focusing and concentrating sometimes, and too much stimulation could be counterproductive.

Dr. Connors was early and poked his head into the room as she was removing a large math chart.

"There you are, Julie. Mind if we have a little talk?"

Julie stepped down off the wooden chair, rolled up the chart and placed it in a large white storage tube with her other posters. "Sure," she said, dusting her palms together. "You want to sit here?" She offered him her desk chair.

"Um…" He was searching her walls, trying to be

casual, but Julie could see he was a bit tense. "Let's go into my office. Then we can speak freely."

Which was alarming. She was uneasy that he'd wanted privacy. But unlike some of his colleagues, Dr. Connors wasn't especially close to any of his teachers, so they'd all gotten used to his more formal ways without reading anything into it. Still, it was obvious he had something on his mind.

A cold wind whooshed down the concrete halls of the nearly abandoned school. The parking lot had only a handful of cars. It would get busier later in the week, when those teaching summer school returned to do their prep work. It would get the busiest just before school began in earnest in the fall.

She followed the principal, who had a runner's build and a loping gait. He didn't walk with her, so she followed behind and said not a word.

After sitting behind his desk, he motioned for her to take the chair she always sat in for his one-on-one discussions. Although she tried to engage him, his lack of eye contact was disturbing.

He leaned back, linking his fingers behind his head and glanced at the ceiling while he inhaled. At last he came forward, placing his forearms on the desk, and leveled a look at her, which froze her.

"The Millers are going to be a problem, Julie." He searched her face, lips pursed and a slight frown to his bushy eyebrows. "The District does not want a lawsuit, but it's beginning to look like things are headed there."

Julie was surprised at the term "lawsuit," but wasn't surprised to learn the Millers would be a bigger problem than Connors had hoped. They'd given the sweet, elderly kindergarten teacher a hard time, too. The first grade teacher had left early in the school year to have a baby. The long-term sub never had a chance. It was her first year of teaching. Dr. Connors, who had himself just arrived this year, knew about the previous years of complaints about the Millers, but for some reason didn't take them seriously enough, Julie thought.

Until now.

"I just don't see how they could have much of a case, Dr. Connors. I really don't."

"Well, just defending the district against accusations is expensive and isn't what we want to do. I have negotiated something I hope will help defuse the situation." Now Connors was beginning to look smug. Julie didn't think she was going to like anything he said next. And she didn't.

"I've told them she will pass to the third grade, provided she gets some special tutoring this summer."

"I think it's an excellent idea, Dr. Connors." Julie was actually relieved before she noticed he was eyeing her carefully.

"Mr. Miller wants her in your classroom this summer."

"But—" Connors wouldn't let her continue.

"And he says he'll pay for extra tutoring, if it is *you* who does the instruction, so it dovetails into the curriculum here."

Julie stood. "No. You have to understand how this could be. They've already complained about my teaching methods. I think another—"

"I've already agreed to it," Connors stated flatly.

"But not the tutoring. Surely not the tutoring."

"That, too, although you two can negotiate the times and salary." He got up and came over to stand next to her. "This is your opportunity to make things right, Julie. In order to keep your job, I'm asking you to do this for the District and for yourself. Consider your career."

"But my union rep—"

"Has already been contacted."

THIS WAS SO wrong on so many levels. She left a message for her rep, who wasn't answering. She called a co-worker and didn't get an answer, either. She lingered around the doorway of another teacher who was also preparing her room for summer school, but all three of the kids in the classroom with her were helping. Julie didn't want to expose them to anything about the Millers.

She returned to her room, quickly removed the remainder of the items she'd planned to take down, stored them and left.

Mr. Miller was leaning against her car in the parking lot as if he'd been waiting for her. She was so surprised by his boldness, it took her a minute to compose herself.

He remained perched there in a somewhat triumphant manner, legs crossed at the ankles, his eyebrows raised in defiance of anything she would say, and his lips in a flat, smug line. His arms were crossed too, and he looked at her with a slight tilt of his head.

He must have seen her flinch and noticed her expression change. Squinting into the sunlight, she hoped if she blinked he might disappear.

But he was no vision.

"Mr. Miller, what can I do for you?"

"Julie," his voice started out so syrupy sweet it made her teeth ache. "I want you to know I'm very happy you've accepted my offer."

"Your offer?" How could this man possibly believe he was offering her anything worthwhile?

"Yes. My offer to drop the lawsuit if you agree to tutor my daughter."

"Unfortunately, it would be outside the school's jurisdiction."

"I'm glad to hear you say so. I was hoping we

wouldn't have to conduct the tutoring on school grounds."

His comments weren't adding up. "Mr. Miller, I've agreed to be her teacher this summer. I haven't agreed to anything else."

"On the contrary. The District's representative assured my attorney you had agreed to some private tutoring."

"I told my principal I'd consider it. We have yet to work out the terms."

"Which is why I'm here." He feigned cooperation and reasonableness.

He stood up, hands relaxed by his sides. His smile showed he could be charming, in an evil sort of way. Julie was sincerely afraid of him. She checked her surroundings, using her peripheral vision without turning her head or giving away her intentions, but she was concerned there was only one other car in the parking lot. Mr. Miller's Lexus SUV was parked right behind hers, actually blocking her unless she drove across the landscaping.

Miller was dressed in blue jeans and light blue shirt. His well-worn cowboy boots made him move in a dangerous-looking saunter when he came towards her. He stopped just before she would have to back up to avoid touching. She backed up anyway, putting a clear two feet between them, which wasn't enough.

She was grateful for the papers she hugged to her chest, grateful there was a little traffic on the road in front of the school. She knew some of the boys would be coming by for basketball practice soon unless it was cancelled for the summer, so there would be parents in and out of the parking lot.

If she could just get to her car and lock the doors.

Miller looked at her like a piece of meat. She didn't want to meet his gaze, but he kept following her face around, demanding eye contact. She didn't give him the satisfaction. His shoulders were powerful, and she realized for the first time he was very tall, perhaps six foot three or so.

Most of the times she'd met him, she realized, he'd been seated and so had she. Also, his wife wasn't in the SUV, so the two of them were alone.

"Look, Julie," he said with raspy charm. His eyes were roaming all over her hair. He was trying to use a softer approach, and for a second she thought he might reach out to hug her or touch her cheek. The attraction vibe she got made her sick to her stomach. "There's no need to make this difficult. I'm sure if we cooperate with each other, we can come to some reasonable arrangement. All I want is for my daughter to have the very best education possible."

No, sir, something else is going on here.

"But Corey is getting the best education possible, if

you and your wife would only stop interfering." Julie thought her position was obvious.

He paused, blinked several times, as if he'd been verbally slapped and hadn't expected it. "Now there's where you're wrong, Julie. Our little Corey is quite a special child, and she requires special treatment." He moved closer, but Julie took a backward step in tandem, maintaining the two-foot distance between them.

"Mr. Miller, I'm not comfortable discussing this here, or right now. Perhaps we can make an appointment for another day this week before school starts? I'd like you to bring your wife as well, and I'll have my principal or another colleague sit in so we can, all four of us, put our heads together."

"What an excellent suggestion," he said, and his eyes lit up. "This is a very promising start. How about tomorrow? Say, noon?"

"Noon would be fine. I'll have to check with my principal."

"But you can find someone else if he's not available?"

"Yes." Julie was confident someone would be willing to help her out. She hoped her rep would be that someone.

"I'm very happy you'll be helping our little Corey with her studies, Julie," he said while he extended his hand. Julie did not take his hand, but instead walked around to the other side of her car, tweeted it open, got in and started the ignition. She quickly locked the doors with the touch of a button. She hoped he didn't notice. His little grin and three-finger wave didn't mask her abiding fear that he'd noticed everything and knew how afraid of him she was.

CHAPTER 24

JULIE WAS SO worried about the upcoming meeting with the Millers, she hadn't gotten much sleep. She also was uncomfortable because no one had called her back. Out of options, she dialed one of her non-teacher friends.

"Jules, I'm sorry, but I've got to be at work at nine and was planning on working through lunch."

"Not today. Gosh if you'd given me a couple days' notice, no problem," another one of her friends said.

She dialed her principal at school, and this time got a recording saying he'd be out of the office until Friday.

You chicken shit. Set me up and then leave.

Her rep finally called just when she was leaving for the classroom. "Julie, I've got another meeting at eleven. If I can get out of it early I'll zip across town and come join you. Can't say for sure I'll be on time, and I might get tied up."

"Thanks, Noreen."

"Listen, if you're so worried about it, I'd reschedule," Noreen said.

Julie checked her gut, looking out at the beautiful, cloudless morning. When it was beautiful, and it was like this most days, all things were possible. She wondered if it wasn't just her fatigue from the long drive, and her stress over the scar on her heart. The term lovesick came readily to mind.

Taking in a deep breath, she said, "You're right. I'm probably being more paranoid than I need to be. I'll just get it over with and then, if we can't come to terms and I think I need you, I'll tell them I need to think it over first."

"You know this is private stuff. Not something I have any jurisdiction to oversee anyway. But I do think Connors has come up with a creative solution, plus you'll make a little extra money. That doesn't hurt, right? And you'd be in the perfect position to make a recommendation to the district for next year."

It did have some validity as an argument. "Only one problem. Dr. Connors has told the Millers she will pass to the third grade. That stipulation wasn't based on any evaluation done by me. I don't think my opinions will even be considered."

"Well, that's my job. You know what they say. If you've got enemies, keep them close so you can keep an eye on their activities. This way perhaps the District will dodge the bullet."

"Thought you were supposed to be there for me, not the District."

"I am thinking about you first. The lawsuit is bad for you, and it's bad for the District. This has a chance to work, Julie. Let's give it a try. Better for everyone involved."

MR. MILLER WALKED into Julie's classroom alone, carrying a bouquet of flowers.

"Peace offering, Miss Julie," he said, extending the hefty bouquet.

She focused on the lovely flowers, but what stuck in her chest was the "Miss Julie" term Luke had used so many times when they'd made love. It had only been two days since she'd last seen him, but she'd begun to hope it wouldn't continue to be so painful.

She sighed and took the flowers from Miller's outstretched hand. "Thanks," she said, turning. She walked to the sink to get out a vase and put the bouquet in water. She removed the plastic, added the sugar packet, dropped the bouquet in, and stuck them on the shelf above the sink unceremoniously. She wasn't going to give him reason to believe bringing the flowers had melted her icy demeanor. And because Noreen wasn't there and he hadn't brought his wife, she was very worried.

She gestured to the chair across from her desk, which was piled with books and made a good barrier.

"So, Mr. Miller—"

"Please call me Carl."

She adjusted her tongue because she was going to say something she knew wasn't smart. The "C" in Carl would have stuck in her throat. "I've been instructed to address you as Mr. I hope you don't mind." She was proud she'd been able to give him a deceptively warm smile, even broader than she intended.

"No harm, no foul, Julie. I *can* call you Julie, though, right?"

"Of course."

So far so good. But a marching band with pointed hats was jumping up and down in her stomach.

"The root of Corey's problems is focus-related. Have you ever had her tested?"

"For what?" He blinked, and a serious crease appeared above his nose, as though the idea had never occurred to him.

"Learning disabilities. There could be some components of ADD, for instance—"

"Nothing wrong with my Corey. No tests."

Well, holy heck, what was she thinking? Of course he wouldn't want any testing on the girl, who swung from being so shy she wouldn't speak up to raging at her teacher the next moment for encouraging her participation. And she accused everyone of hating her and openly talked about it. These were things Julie would have found troubling in a much older child, but with a second grader, she was truly alarmed.

"Only thing wrong with her is she's struggling to keep up," he insisted.

"Well, yes, I certainly see that, Mr. Miller. Which is why I recommended she stay back a year, to ease her stress, the pressure she's experiencing. She's emotionally immature—"

"You know what I find most disturbing, Miss Julie? Your school gave her an incompetent first-year teacher and now wants her to pay the price by staying back a year? Where is the school's responsibility for the fact that she wasn't taught in a way which made it possible for her learn?"

It was an age-old complaint every teacher heard at some point. There wasn't anything wrong with the child, it was the teaching methods the parents found fault with. Parents who had a vested interest, which was as it should be, but who had difficulty trusting the school district and even its best teachers. And Julie considered herself one of the latter. She'd tried harder to work with Corey than anyone else in the classroom, but had found her nearly impossible and had constantly requested testing, which the principal never acted on.

She wondered if there was something going on in the home which could warrant an outside source being called, like Child Protective Services, CPS. If she could just find one scar, one bruise, the call would be extremely easy to make.

"Mr. Miller, I understand your reluctance—"

His pattern of throwing her off with his interruptions was noted.

"I'm not reluctant. I simply refuse." The evil smile which followed his comment chilled Julie to her core. She saw glimpses of something dangerous.

"If there is a tool we can use to help your daughter's progress, wouldn't you want to use it?"

He squinted back at her, indicating she was treading on delicate territory. "I want what's best for Corey. She is, of course, my child. My only child."

Julie looked down at her registration paperwork. "Mr. Miller, when you registered her for school, it says right here she has an older sister."

"Who has gone to live with her mother," he completed.

She decided it wasn't smart to mention that even though the girl didn't live with him, she was still his daughter. Or was she? And did it matter?

"Does Corey have much contact with her? I never near anything about her in class. But then, she's very shy, unless she gets angry."

"Yes, she's the same with me. Very sweet and docile, but she shares her father's passionate temper."

Red alarm bells were going off all over the place. Julie decided right then, there would be no private tutoring lessons, and any future meeting would take place in the presence of at least one, maybe two, other colleagues.

Damn you, Dr. Connors. She'd been hung out to dry. Sacrificed.

She leaned back in her chair, closing the folder on her desk and crossing her arms. The cell phone on her desk lit up and she saw the text from Noreen,

"Can't make it. Call me when it's over to discuss."

Damn. Sweat formed under her armpits and ran down her sides. Her right hand had a slight tremor. Glancing around the room, she saw he could easily corner her, keep her there, and no one would find her for hours. Suddenly her classroom felt like a prison.

Then she had an idea.

"Excuse me, Mr. Miller. I have to take this call." She held her phone to her ear, pressed the recording button and recorded a voice message.

"Noreen, so sorry! I forgot about the meeting." She hit her forehead with her palm. "Look, I'm just about finished here. I'm with Mr. Miller, you know, the father of the little girl in my class I spoke to you about?"

She paused a significant length of time to give the impression she was hearing another's reply, then began again.

"Yes, well, I can be over there in about...oh," she pretended to check the time on her cell, "...say, twenty minutes? Or would you and the officer like to meet me here?"

She chanced a glance up to Mr. Miller's face and was rewarded to see some degree of alarm showing there, quickly hidden.

"Fine, Noreen. I'm sure this won't take long, just a second." She tucked the phone under her chin and asked him, "I'm very sorry, Mr. Miller. Do you think we could reschedule? We've got a meeting with the Police Athletic League about a softball tournament coming up this summer, a fundraiser. I'd completely forgotten about it until just now."

"No. You run along. We can discuss this another day." He stood up as she pretended to finish the call. He paced back and forth in front of her in long, liquid movements, like a panther in a cage. She knew he was dangerous, perhaps borderline psychotic. He was powerfully built as well.

"Okay, Noreen. I'm all yours in just a few. Be right over. And please tell the officers I'm sorry." She ended the recording, hit send message and typed in her brother's email, which was the only one she could think of. Hitting done, she let the voice message go through the airwaves to a phone which was probably somewhere on a beach in the Caribbean.

She set the phone down when Miller approached the desk. Just as he leaned forward to say something, Julie heard the delivery zip tone, indicating the message had been sent. He righted himself and looked at her carefully. She didn't flinch but was relieved when he broke eye contact first.

"Tomorrow. I'll meet you here tomorrow. Noon. I'll bring lunch."

He turned around and left the room with stealth speed, and without waiting for her consent. She noted he was used to getting his way, which bothered her more than anything else. She was sure there was an unhealthy family dynamic going on there. There was no way on God's green earth she would attend the next meeting alone.

CHAPTER 25

KYLE HAD WANTED to see Luke in the morning. Luke was feeling pretty good and had placed a call to his psychiatrist at the medical center requesting an appointment earlier than the standing one he had next week.

He heard words being exchanged on the other side of the front door, and it was clear Christy and Kyle were having an argument. Kyle hadn't texted him to call the meeting off, so Luke knocked.

He heard a muffled, "It's Luke." Kyle opened the door and stared at his bare toes while he gestured for Luke to enter their cute but very upscale home a block from the beach.

Brandon immediately dropped toys in the middle of the living room and ran over to Luke to get a hug. Luke tousled the boy's sandy brown hair and allowed the chubby arms to hug his knees. He bent over and spoke softly to him, "How's it hanging, little man?"

"See, Kyle, that's what I'm talking about," Christy snapped.

Luke stood up immediately and looked to his LPO for guidance. Kyle reassured him with their hand signal, 'all clear,' sliding his palm through the air.

"We've got to get to Brandon's preschool to have a little parent conference. But it won't take long," Kyle said.

"You don't know that," Christy said with her hands on her hips. She was, as she usually was, dressed in a plain white silk suit which highlighted her blonde hair and tanned skin. Kyle was dressed in cargoes, flip-flops and a surfing T-shirt.

"Christy, come on. We're talking about *Brandon*."

"Hey, man," Luke began. "Why don't I stop by later on, after the dust settles?"

"Good," said Christy.

"No way. You're coming with us," Kyle responded right over the top of her. "He's gonna have to do this someday. Consider it research," he said to Christy.

She humphed to the kitchen, picked up her purse and keys. "You guys are on your own with Brandon afterwards if they won't take him. I have to work."

Luke was uncomfortable, but figured whatever it was Kyle had to say to him, it was better off said in the car and alone. Of course it would change in the years to come, but Brandon wasn't old enough to make out much of what they discussed, whatever was on his LPO's agenda.

They strapped Brandon into the car seat, and Kyle let the huge black Hummer roar to life.

He wanted to ask his LPO what was going on with Brandon, but figured it was a personal matter. He must have read his mind just then, because he offered an explanation.

"Remember what I told you yesterday about Brandon dropping his spoon?"

"Yeah."

"Well, he's f—" Kyle leaned in and whispered, "He's fuckin' doing it at school, too. And the teachers want to have a meet and greet."

Which was funny. It was Kyle's secret way of talking about the snatch-n-grabs they did overseas. A meet and greet with a SEAL usually meant you were the target of an investigation of some sort and wasn't ever considered a good thing by the target, but it was a great way to pick up intelligence.

"That all it is?"

"Think so. It's what they told Christy. And believe me, if she'd had a reason to bust my balls any more about it, she would have."

Luke sat back and was relieved it wasn't about anything worse than strong language.

"She's been grumpy lately. I'm guessing she's pregnant."

"Nice work, sailor. You knocked her up on the ship then?"

"Apparently so. But if I'd have known she'd turn into this, I'd have reconsidered it."

They both stared out the windshield for a few seconds. As if on cue, they looked at each other and in unison shouted, "Not!"

"Well, congrats, then," Luke finally said while they made the turn into the First Presbyterian Preschool parking lot. Christy was already standing by her Mercedes coupe.

"For what? I didn't tell you anything." Kyle looked in his rear view mirror and shouted to Brandon, "Lips tight, Brandon, okay?"

"Okay Daddy," came the enthusiastic response.

"You can't teach 'em too young." Kyle got out and leaned down to look back into the Hummer. "Come on and get your butt outa there. Time to learn a lesson in being a family. You'll have to do this someday."

Luke wasn't sure he wanted to accompany his LPO, but he figured he didn't have an option.

Brandon was spewing, "Get your butt outa here," and pointing in Luke's direction. Kyle immediately shushed him by putting his fingers to his mouth.

"Not now Brandon," he whispered tenderly.

Brandon put his chubby hands on either side of

Kyle's face. "Okay, Daddy," he whispered, and smiled, his eyes bright with the secret.

Christy was frostier than at the house. Luke suspected part of the reason he was along for the ride was so Kyle didn't have to experience a full-on assault from her, since she wouldn't do it in front of him. Which probably pissed her off more.

In the hallway they could hear children playing on the other side of Dutch doors open for drop-off and pickup. No other parents were present and, from the sounds of the voices, it appeared classes had started a while ago.

Kyle lifted Brandon in the direction of a young teacher who greeted him with open arms, but Kyle insisted he set the toddler down on the floor on the other side of the door.

"Brandon," he called to him.

"Yes, Daddy?"

Kyle made the motion of zipping his mouth up, and Brandon nodded and repeated the action. Then his LPO watched his son run to play with the other children.

Christy was standing a few feet away with a woman in a plum-colored dress who was holding a file folder.

"Kyle, this is Nancy Jordan, the preschool director."

Kyle shook her hand. She looked around Kyle to

Luke with a question on her face.

"Oh, sorry," Kyle said. "This is Luke. He's one of the men I work with. If you don't mind, Christy and I thought sitting in on a meeting would be good information for him, you know, when the day comes."

Luke could feel Christy's anger boil. She was way more emotional than he'd seen her in a long time. He understood all that. But her reasons were her own and impossible for him to figure out.

Nancy bowed and said hello, then led them to her office, which was just on the other side of Brandon's playroom. A two-way mirror had been installed on both the outside wall and the interior wall, so she could observe the children.

Christy and Kyle sat at her desk and Luke found a chair in the corner, settling in, trying to make himself small.

"Okay, well, thank you for coming in today. We generally don't do these sorts of meetings at the end of a school year. Everyone is so busy, but we felt this was important," the director said.

"Christy said Brandon was not behaving. In what way?" Kyle asked.

"I think I can show you best by playing a little video clip we took of him," she answered him.

Luke could tell this wasn't going to sit right with Kyle, since videotaping children was supposed to be semi-illegal in California, except for family members or unless permission was given first. Kyle and Christy looked at each other.

"That's illegal," Kyle said to the director. "You take this?"

"No it was taken as a teaching aid—"

"I don't care what's on the fuckin' video, if my son's picture is on it, I'm walking outta here with it today."

"No reason to take that tone with me, Mr. Lansdowne. I think you'll understand, if you'll just let me play it for you. Please."

Kyle blustered and sat back. "Go ahead," he mumbled.

"I'm going to erase it right after you see it. Not to worry, Mr. Lansdowne."

The TV monitor lit up and there was a view of the playground. Brandon was riding a scooter, propelling it with his feet, chasing one of his friends in another scooter who was holding up a piece of paper bag decorated like a flag. It was covered in scribbles and stickers. The boy in front was waving it proudly above his head.

"He's going too fast?" Kyle said to the monitor. "That what this is about?"

"No, Mr. Lansdowne. Just watch."

Another boy ran up behind the lead boy and

snatched the flag from his fingers, which prompted Brandon to stop suddenly, causing a backup on the roadway. Several other children collided due to the traffic jam. But Brandon had abandoned his scooter and run off camera. They all could hear yelling coming from around the corner, and two of the teachers, who had been supervising some organized play nearby, immediately sprang into action. Brandon came back on camera, chasing the little boy with the flag. He overcame the youngster and pushed him to the ground, then retrieved his flag and handed it to his friend.

Walking back to his scooter, he turned and, very clearly and deliberately, said, "You fuckin' axle."

Kyle closed his eyes and almost swore. He didn't watch while Brandon was led off the playground by one arm.

Luke thought it was kind of funny, but he knew it was serious for Brandon's parents, so he respectfully tried to think of something else so he wouldn't burst out laughing. He focused on the crack in the wood flooring, a dirty window, a fingerprint on the one-way mirror, anything.

He crossed his legs and sank further into the corner, resting his arms on his crossed lower leg and knee, placing his hand over his mouth and nose and shaking his head.

The director erased the video with the touch of a button. "There you go. All gone," she said with a curt smile. Then she turned off the equipment, her polished purple nails matching the color of her dress.

She angled her head and looked at Christy with affection. She was obviously a nice woman, and probably had never uttered a four-letter word in her life. Luke knew this was probably way over the top for her.

"So, Mr. and Mrs. Lansdowne, I'm afraid Presbyterian Preschool has decided Brandon cannot continue with the four-year-old program next year. However, there are a number of other schools in the San Diego area which might be able to take him, if you act quickly. Or, there are several day care centers on base—"

"No. He's not going to some fuckin' day care center," Kyle said before he could control himself.

"There you go," the director said, opening her palm in Kyle's direction. "He's hearing this language at home and frankly, Mrs. Lansdowne, I'm surprised you allow this to happen. I know your reputation as a very God-fearing woman who is fair and honest in her successful real estate dealings. Frankly, if I had a realtor—"

"I don't swear, but my husband does. He swears a lot." She shot Kyle a look Luke couldn't understand. Half fury, half sexual energy. He knew she'd seen her husband in little Brandon's actions. Kyle was smart to keep his mouth shut.

"It's an occupational hazard." She allowed one eyebrow to rise and licked her lips. Kyle closely monitored every tiny shift of expression. He was leaning back into his chair, viewing her with half-lidded eyes, almost looking like he was enjoying her intensity. And then with a start, Luke realized he *was*!

The director wasn't sure what she was witnessing. Squirming in her chair, she delivered a message to break the ice, "I suppose if you work on it over the summer, we could check on him nearer the fall, and see if his language has improved—"

Kyle was still staring into the eyes of his wife. "He doesn't understand what he's saying. They're just words to him," he said.

"Well, Mr. Lansdowne, we can't allow such language here."

Kyle slowly faced the director and nodded. "Then we won't waste any more of your time. Because I'm going to work with him on the appropriateness of his language, but if he slips up, I don't want anyone else telling him he's wrong. That has to come from me."

The director reacted like she'd been slapped. Slightly offended, she told them she'd allow Brandon to stay the last two weeks of the session and then offered to give them a list of other preschools, but no day care centers.

Kyle and Christy shared a look Luke would have to say was molten.

CHAPTER 26

NOREEN MET JULIE at school a half hour early. She was ten years older than Julie, single, and extremely attractive. Julie thought she would have been very successful in some kind of high-paying sales job. But Noreen liked her work and seemed to be good at it. Today she wore a simple pair of dark blue slacks and a cream-colored shell top with pearls. Her hair, which could be worn long, was pulled back in a ponytail. Her dark-rimmed glasses made her look very bookish, which Julie thought was done on purpose.

Julie would have to say she had dressed for a part in a play.

Noreen pumped out a bit of the hand cream Julie kept on the corner of her desk and began rubbing it into her palms. "This is real nice. Lemon?"

"Apricot."

"Where's it from?"

"Beautiful little inn up north in Kenwood. My

friend took me there after the wedding."

"The groomsman guy? The SEAL?"

"Yes."

Noreen leaned over the desk, pulling her glasses low onto her nose, and peered at Julie. "And you let this particular man out of your sight?"

"He's damaged. He needs time to heal."

Noreen placed her glasses back on her nose, crossed her arms, and gave Julie a stern look indicating she didn't approve of something. "I'm beginning to doubt your radar, kid," she said while she continued to work the cream into her hands.

"Come on, Noreen. Give me a little credit. And can we concentrate on what we're doing here today, please?"

"Okay, just for the record, Julie, what you guys decide to do about the tutoring is outside my purview, but here's the thing. If you continue to do things, and they are connected to your classroom teaching, then it kind of *becomes* part of the contract we have with the school. Does that make sense?"

"Think so."

"So just watch what you promise, sort of under-promise and over-deliver, if you will."

"I understand." She wanted clarification on the one thing she was the most concerned about. "What about having a witness? I mean, he wants to do tutoring off campus, and—"

"It *has* to be off campus. You cannot use the school for it."

"So I pick a public place, then?"

"Yes. Why do you see so many tutors in Starbuck's? Homeschoolers?"

"Makes sense."

"That way there are lots of eyes on the behavior. You start meeting him in his home, for instance, and then he can say anything."

"Gotcha."

Noreen came around the desk and sat on it, peering down at Julie. "You really think this guy is creepy? Couldn't he just be nuts about his daughter and her grades? I think that's a little more likely."

"Can you find out about her older sister?"

"No. Why would the union care about her older sister?" Noreen stood and looked out the window toward the parking lot.

"Because I'm starting to think she's a link to information that's important to this situation and connected to her little sister's problems."

"You're been reading too many detective or thriller novels, Jules. Besides, you're a teacher, not a private eye."

Something caught Noreen's attention outside. "Hello! Julie, that him?"

Julie craned her neck and saw Mr. Miller walking along a strip of landscaping carrying a white paper deli bag.

"Yes."

"Hubba-hubba. You sure about not liking the guy?"

"Wait until you talk to him."

"Gotcha. But boy, Julie, I definitely think you should have your antennae checked. He's gorgeous."

"And very married."

Noreen shrugged, fluffing her top and tightening her ponytail. She licked her lips and waited for him to walk into the room.

Miller paused at the doorway, as if stunned by something. His swagger was gone. He was smooth and lithe and, after the initial jerkiness, his movements were sleek and cat-like. His smile also looked all too feral for Julie's peace of mind. What was astonishing was the way Noreen fawned all over the man.

"Well, I didn't realize Julie had such a lovely younger sister. Are you a teacher, too?" Mr. Miller set the paper bag down and nearly ran over to Noreen's side, taking her hand and then lingering. Julie had never before seen such a technicolor scammer operating so smoothly.

Julie watched her scratch the back of her neck in a nervous gesture, slightly swaying from side to side, like a young girl at a school dance just asked to the floor for the first time. She could hardly believe her eyes. Mr. Miller's transformation since yesterday was unbelievable. Literally.

Julie stood. "Mr. Miller, this is Noreen Powers, my union rep."

"And she's smart, too!" His eyebrows rose. His eyes got large. He placed his other hand on top of their entwined fingers. "Wonderful to meet you. Noreen? Is it Noreen?"

"Yes."

"What a beautiful name." He stepped back and gave her a wink. "It suits you."

Things were going from bad to worse. Noreen had been Julie's first line of defense.

Miller retrieved his bag and brought it over to Julie's desk. "Well, I just took a guess and hoped someone else was going to be here to help us eat these things. I took the liberty of going to Hansen's and picking up some of their legendary Caesar salads."

He waited on the two women, giving them each their salads, napkins and a fork. He opened three bottles of lemon mineral water. Julie noted his attention to detail. Noreen's defenses were dropping by the minute. It was a smart move, Julie noted.

The guy was good. She could almost say diabolical.

By the time they had finished their salads and the scrumptious macadamia caramel torte he'd brought for each of them, Noreen had to rush off to another meeting. She made her apologies, even managing to roll her eyes at Julie before exiting the doorway. She'd lingered in Mr. Miller's handshake, never corrected him about calling her by her first name, and never noticed how he'd inched himself closer and closer to her while they slowly ate and shared small talk. He simply outlasted them with his charm intact.

Julie was starting to doubt her perception of Mr. Miller. She was going to hold back judgment for a bit, try not to come to any conclusion, and just stick to the facts at hand. He seemed genuinely warm and accommodating. Although she still didn't trust him, she felt herself soften. Maybe her perception had been colored by the painful breakup with Luke.

Luke!

She wondered what he was thinking this afternoon and what he was doing. It took her a few seconds to realize Miller had been talking to her.

"I'm sorry. What did you say?" She asked.

"I was asking if there was any reading material I could take home to study. I'd like to supplement what you're doing in the classroom with my own tutoring at home. If you approve, of course."

Me? Approve? What on earth was going on? Had an alien taken over the man she'd talked with in the parking lot?

"Of course, anything you do with Corey at home will help us here. She needs to be read to, and encouraged to read aloud." Then she had an idea. "I was never able to figure out what she likes. You'll want to read her things she is interested in. That's how kids naturally become readers. Even if she does have—" she paused at the beginnings of a frown on his face. "I'm not saying she does have any learning disabilities, but we can hold off on the testing until I've had the summer to help build her study skills."

She noticed he seemed to accept what she was saying. No use in requiring the testing, not if he was going to be this compliant.

"Everyone reads faster when they are given material they're interested in. Everyone," she said.

He nodded. "Rabbits. She likes rabbits and chickens."

"Good. Very good. See, I would have never guessed."

Miller was pensive. "Her sister used to raise them."

"Ah. Then she misses her *sister*. Perhaps that's part of what's going on, too. She's always so shy in my classroom. Perhaps this would bring her out of her shell. Any chance they could visit?"

Miller dropped his own guard a bit and spoke to his hands folded on the desktop. "Not a chance in hell."

To Julie's surprise, Mr. Miller didn't press her to schedule dates for the private tutoring, which was a great relief. She handed him a reading list for first grade, since Corey was nearly a full year behind. "My goal is to get her beyond second grade level and on into third grade materials by the end of the summer. It might be difficult, but if you work with us, it could be done."

"Thank you, Miss Julie. I appreciate your kindness. I'll buy all these books this afternoon."

"No. Let's not overwhelm her. Just one or two—perhaps take her to the bookstore and let her pick them out. If she's invested, she'll be more cooperative."

He leaned back on his chair and rocked it on two legs. "I like cooperative. Beats the hell out of the other way."

It was a strange comment, coming clear out of the blue, but Julie let it pass. She told herself she'd be able to spot the signs something was going awry long before it became a problem. She was also convinced Miller had a genuine desire to help Corey read and do better in school.

"We teach them not to be intimidated by the books they get. We in essence make friends with the books. We show them study techniques, even for elementary school-aged children."

"Make it fun," he said softly.

"Exactly." She noticed he had focused on her lips, which caused her to lean back and put more distance between them even though there was a large desk separating their bodies.

They concluded their meeting. Julie was hopeful the summer would be totally uneventful, that little Corey would get the help she needed, so she would feel more comfortable when school started. She hoped she could get rid of the niggling doubts she still harbored about Mr. Miller and his wife. She wished she'd remembered the woman more clearly. Her demeanor was very similar to the behavior Corey had exhibited in class. Very shut down, very quiet and retiring.

At the doorway he paused, turning on a charming smile she might have thought attractive if she was meeting him for the first time or didn't know anything about his daughter. "I'm feeling very good about this new direction, Miss Julie."

His words were careful and calculated. Because she could see him weigh and measure what he said, some of Julie's distrust returned.

"I'd like to apply the same principles to how we interact with one another," he added.

"I see no reason we shouldn't be non-adversarial. We are on the same side, Mr. Miller."

"Indeed, Miss Julie, indeed. You have a good day."

His smile seemed a little forced, but perhaps he had

to work hard to maintain control of his actions and emotions. She saw in him something very dark and dangerous. But if he could hold onto that control, Julie could help his daughter discover the world of learning and the love of books.

She decided it was the only thing she would focus on, and she'd let time heal everything else.

CHAPTER 27

LATER THAT NIGHT Julie got a call from her brother, Colin.

"I got this confusing voice message this morning. Came from you yesterday. Are you all right?"

"Yes, I'm fine."

"Well what the hell was it about? And why did I get it?"

"I was using you as my reason for ending a meeting with someone I didn't want to be alone with." She was surprised at her own honesty.

"Luke?"

She melted. *This is what you told yourself you wouldn't react to.* She knew it wasn't going to be possible to just forget about him and move on. He'd be a permanent fixture in her tight family unit.

"No. Not Luke. Someone else."

"Things not work out between you two? You seemed pretty close to me. Mom said—"

Julie had to stop him. "No, Colin. You got the wrong impression. He's fun, and yes, we had a good time. I'm sorry we created such a public spectacle." She chose her words carefully. "Colin, he has some things to work out, emotional stuff, you know?"

"Yeah. A lot of those guys do."

"I'm guessing he has more of a past than you know. Perhaps it just never came up, but he is a sweetheart, just not the type of guy I can spend very much time with. That's all."

"He's been one solid guy with me."

"Oh, I would expect nothing less. This has nothing to do with it. In matters of the heart, he has some healing to do. I don't think either of us is ready to jump into anything long term, despite what it looked like. But it was a fun wedding. And Stephanie looked radiant."

"Thanks. So who is this guy you didn't want to be alone with."

"The father of a student I'm having difficulty with. He's a little high strung. I should never meet him alone, and now I've fixed that. But yesterday I needed him to know I had allies. Those guys bailed on me, who were supposed to be at the meeting. Like I said, I've fixed it, Colin. It won't happen again."

"You sure?"

"Of course I'm sure. I'm good at what I do, just like

you are."

"Maybe Luke can run protection for you."

"No. I'm afraid I have to distance myself from Luke for the foreseeable future. He wants nothing to do with me, trust me."

"I'm sorry to hear it. I thought you two were perfect for each other."

"Like I said, matters of the heart are different from knocking down a few beers at the local bar or surfing together."

"Guess so. But we've had some heart-to-hearts. I consider him the brother I never had. That close."

"I'm happy for you. But you have to stop thinking of Luke and me as a couple. I've moved on. I'm sure he has too."

"So this father is your new guy? You're dating?"

"Are you kidding? I just said I didn't want to be alone with him. Absolutely not. He's an overbearing parent. I'm going on a trip to Vegas with my girlfriend during summer break. Then I'll see about dating. But right now I'm focused on getting ready for the summer session."

"Gotcha. Well, I'm still glad I called. Stephanie and I were very worried, Sis."

"Thanks. How's the Caribbean?"

"God, I could live here. Love to get a little turquoise house down by the beach somewhere here. Just a place to go to relax and forget the world. We met this guy who does these cottage vacation rentals. Next time, no tourist packages, even though the bridal suite at the Grand Caribbean is outstanding. They have this huge aquarium which takes up the whole lobby, and another beautiful saltwater tank in our room. Unbelievable place."

"Sounds nice."

"You'd love it."

"I'm sure I would. Well, don't want to run up your cell phone charges. Have a safe journey back."

"Thanks. Wish it wasn't nearly over. We'll have you over to the house when we get back."

"Sounds great."

They hung up, and she made herself a cup of tea and slipped into bed with one of her favorite romance novels. She fell asleep seeing a white beach somewhere and feeling Luke's kisses on her flesh. In her dream state, she saw their fingers entwined, saw him lift her fingers to his lips and kiss them. She asked him all the same questions she'd had before and he smiled and nodded, as if he'd answered them just with his gaze.

Just before she fell asleep she heard him say those words he'd spoken to her just five short days ago.

"I love you, Julie."

JULIE DIALED ANNALISE first thing in the morning.

She'd finished her classroom setup yesterday, and she was feeling restless and a bit bored. She had four days until the summer session began and wondered if they could work in a trip to Las Vegas earlier than planned.

"I'm at work now. Perhaps I could come down with the flu. We'd have to drive."

"Exactly what I was thinking. Annalise, I'm so glad you're able to do it with me. For some reason, I just need this."

"I got your back, Jules. You know that," Annalise sighed. "Okay, now I gotta do sick. Meet you at your house in, say, an hour? I'll text you when I'm on my way."

JULIE DROVE THE two of them the four hours to Las Vegas. They'd gotten a complimentary room at one of the large casinos thanks to Annalise's club points from previous gambling trips. The room was huge.

"They love you here Anna." The strip looked dusty, but would ignite the area with neon at dusk.

"I usually make money every time I come."

Julie knew it wasn't true, but let it slide for now. They went downstairs and wandered along the slot machines until they found their favorites. They drank watered-down drinks and then decided to check out some of the local shops. At one of the sports bars, Annalise stopped.

"This place has great burgers and seems to attract all the cute guys," she said. "You hungry?"

"Kinda starved."

They went inside, having to let their eyes adjust before trying to find a table. Big screen monitors covered the walls. No matter where a person sat, they could watch horse racing with tabletop features for online betting. Several basketball and baseball games were on the monitors, and the bar mostly filled with men.

Boisterous whooping and hollering were coming from the corner where about ten muscled guys appeared to be celebrating a basketball game. Someone tossed a basket of popcorn over someone else's head.

A head that looked familiar.

Luke!

Julie noted how different the men were. Some were dark and tanned, others red-headed and light-skinned. But they were all built. Huge shoulders, relatively the same age, and all extremely attractive. They had the full attention of a group of girls at a nearby table, but the SEALs seemed not to notice.

What am I going to do?

Annalise was quick to look over where Julie's attention had gone. "Whoa! I get your drift. Nice! I think we should make a trip to the ladies' and take a closer look. What do you say?"

"No. I'll watch your things. I'm staying here."

"You crazy?" Annalise asked her.

"No. I'll hold the table down. You go on ahead."

Julie decided not to tell her who she'd seen. She wasn't sure what would happen if he discovered her. She decided to just avoid looking in that direction.

She ordered a burger for both of them and two beers. She considered switching places so she wouldn't risk another of those furtive glances in his direction she couldn't seem to help, telling herself each time it was some action she'd seen out of the corner of her eye on the monitor which made her look up. But her eyes always landed on the back of Luke's head and the curly hair she had loved sifting her fingers through.

In spite of what her head said, her body responded to the sight of this warrior and his strong shoulders and the brotherhood of the men around him who loved him better than she probably ever could. The ache in her chest was more than just missing the steamy sex, it was because she knew if he gave her half a chance, which was a big if, she could heal him. Or better said, she'd be able to find a way to help him heal. Because the healing had to come from him. She also knew that unless he was willing he would not get better, and she would not be able to do more than be a distant bystander.

And yes, she wanted more. She believed she would never find another man who affected her so positively, as though they had some ancient chemistry. Once she'd tasted him she was dead for any other.

The room got blurry, and she realized she'd teared up.

Damn.

So no one would see streaks on her face, she turned to stare down at the tabletop and let the droplets land there. And then she wiped them away.

Another burst of easy laughter came from the table in front of her. Suddenly she was too close. Was she somehow smelling his scent? That was just crazy. She tried to look out the window at the ridiculous display of odd tourists walking past the large windows. Such a collection of humanity, it could almost be a bar scene from a science fiction movie. Every excess, both beautiful and depraved, paraded past. Her life seemed so ordinary and dull in comparison.

Another wave of laughter filled the room, and this time she recognized Annalise's voice in the middle of it. She looked up and, with horror, saw her talking to the seated men. She had her palms pressed onto the table in front of them. She was leaning, squeezing herself together the way she liked to do, giving them a hefty dose of her womanly gifts. It was something Julie used to laugh about, but right now, the thought of her friend attracting the young men drove her into a panic. What if she got Luke to come over to their table or,

God forbid, made him turn around?

Frowning, she and Annalise made eye contact and Annalise motioned for her to come over and join her.

Julie felt sweat prickle across her back while her palms got clammy and her throat dried. She tried to deliver a terrified look to Annalise, who was laughing, talking, and flirting, and not paying much attention to her reaction. It took her some seconds before she realized what Julie had been trying to communicate.

"Don't know what's gotten into my friend. Hey! Julie, these guys are from San Diego too!" she yelled over the three or four tables between them.

Julie closed her eyes and squeezed her fists. She would have strangled her friend if she could have.

No. No. No! This is all wrong, Annalise. Don't do this to me!

She repeated the words several times and then released herself to the inevitable. Opening her eyes slowly, she got a good look at Luke, who had turned to stare at her, and then swallowed hard. The sight of his face sent an electric jolt up her spine. His eyes seemed to envelop her in the blue gaze she'd lost herself in so many times. And then he stood up. The noise level behind him rose while he made his way toward her, past his buddies. His shoulders were swaying above the loose easy gait of his packed torso and thighs.

The air seemed to leave the room. He'd stopped so

close to her his knee lightly touched her thigh. She could feel his heat. Her cheeks flushed when she stole a look at Annalise and saw they had an audience of more than just the ten at the table, everyone hanging on every tiny movement. The space between her breasts got damp, and the hair on her forearms stood on end amid goose bumps.

But worse, a jumble of nerves and emotions came flooding in, hitching her breath and making her ache—the dull ache reminding her she missed him so much she could, really could, debase herself and ignore all the warning signs. Her will was dissolving more every second he waited for her to respond.

Though she knew it was a mistake, she looked up at him. He was examining her lips so she looked back down quickly.

"Julie, I—" He stopped himself, but the damage had been done. Hearing her name roll of his tongue stimulated every cell. Her body had never needed someone so much while her head was screaming she had to ignore it.

She knew what side was going to win. No question about it.

"May I sit down, Julie?" His gravelly voice was all man. All tender man, which was the biggest turn-on of all.

She could barely talk, so managed to squeak "Sure,"

and moved to the side. She didn't dare look up at her friend or the men who were still observing with great interest.

Luke did what he had no right to do. He put his huge muscled arm up on the top of the booth, so it just barely touched her shoulders and the top of her spine. His fingers were idle, not forcing themselves on her. But she so needed his touch, especially in the special places now coming to life. His thigh pressed against hers made something in her abdomen vibrate.

Inhaling, it was impossible not let the deliciousness of his scent fill her lungs, breathing life back into her, though logic was screaming, alarms were buzzing in the background. Being in his proximity was making all things possible again, promising he'd be focused on her and not wanting to run from her. In a terrible mixture of confusing wonderfulness, she dared to look back at him.

Big mistake. Huge mistake.

Their hungry eyes searched the other's briefly before studying each other's mouths, before she involuntarily licked her lips, and he bent so slightly it might not have been perceptible to the outside world, and she fell into the fantasy of meeting him halfway. As their lips touched, a little squeal burst from the back of her throat, followed by his low, rolling growl. His tongue requested entry and she opened to him, to all of him, drinking in his taste and the scent and heat coming from his body.

He adjusted his body to squirm slightly on the burgundy leatherette seat, turning his torso into her, gently kissing down the back of her jawbone, under her chin, and up the other side.

"Baby, we need to talk," he whispered.

Her wary look made his eyes dance. She could see he liked that thought.

"Okay, whatever you want, then," he whispered as his lips caressed hers and he sucked on her lower lip. "I've been thinking of nothing else but you for these past long days. Trust me, I've missed you."

Her steely resolve had turned to tin foil in spite of what she was telling herself, what her rational self was jumping up and down screaming. But she couldn't resist him, wondering how long he would stay this way. Not sure where it was leading, but holding out hope. Somehow hoping she was coursing in the right direction even without the words. Those would have to come later.

She rolled her head to the side, and he covered her neck with kisses she now realized she was more than willing to get naked for.

"Come on, baby."

He slid out of the seat, checked out his buddies with a quick mock salute, and made a grateful bow to

Annalise with a hand over his heart. With his other hand he linked their fingers, slipping them together as comfortably as old friends. He squeezed her hand and helped her stand.

He stood behind her, placing his hands on her hips, palms down, gently pulling her back against him so she could feel his erection.

As if she didn't already know.

She knew she should stop him. But it wasn't what she was going to do. Though it was probably the dumbest thing she'd done in her life, she'd go with him wherever he wanted her to.

She just hoped to God she had the strength to stop at her own personal boundaries. His illness she knew somehow she could handle. If he ever stopped wanting her, *that* she probably would not be able to handle.

CHAPTER 28

LUKE HOPED THE guys entertained Julie's girlfriend in a respectful manner, giving him time to clear things with Julie. Well, not exactly clear things, because he wanted his body pressed against hers so much he'd do anything to get it. Including tell himself he was well enough to handle all this.

He didn't know how he felt about it, had avoided feeling anything, just focusing on his job and the guys. Putting thoughts of Julie out of his mind. But when he saw her sitting across the room, those eyes needed him. He suddenly felt like the guy who could do it, could give her the love and devotion she so deserved. He saw her need of him. But he also saw her strength. He needed that too.

He didn't ask her where they were going. He just followed her through the crowd. Cigarette smoke was getting to his eyes. He had her hand so tight he wondered if it was too tight, so he loosened it to check out her temperature. She squeezed him back so hard it nearly hurt.

He was going to go for it. The whole enchilada. She was what he'd always wanted. Trick was to convince her of something he wasn't entirely sure he understood. The doc had told him to be careful, but to follow his gut. And to tell her when he was feeling rocky so she had some advance warning. It was only fair. And to go on with meetings, support groups. Connect with other elite warriors who were dealing with the same issues. At least he didn't have to deal with a physical injury like some of the guys he'd met.

Dr. Brownlee had been hopeful on their last visit. Took it as a good sign he decided to come in early and not wait. He had so much he wanted to tell her. He hoped to God she wanted to hear it.

He'd been afraid to look at her until they got to the elevator.

"You good with this, honey? Because I can stop now, but I won't be able to later. Honest, sweetheart," he said with his palms on either side of her sweet pink cheeks. The sight of her face, begging him to kiss her, made his chest rise, blood pumping all over, especially in his lower abdomen. Her soft kiss was something he could sink himself into and spend the whole day, just there. If she'd let him, and if her friend didn't interrupt them, he'd spend every second pleasuring her enough so neither one of them would be able to walk afterward.

But first they'd have to talk. Painful as it would be, they had to clear the air. Say the things which should be said, whether or not either of them wanted to hear it. It should happen in a certain order, and just screwing her didn't show her the respect she deserved.

The elevator door pinged open to a gathering of Chinese tourists packed so tight it took them a minute to un-wedge the first passengers off.

A couple was starting to walk on, following Luke and Julie inside, but he barred the way. "Sorry, folks. You'll have to take the next one."

She chuckled and leaned into him, fostering in him the need to wrap his arm around her, protecting her from the space in the elevator. He'd never felt so fuckin' hard or big. "Missed you, baby."

The doors opened on her floor, and in seconds they were standing alone in a room just now being warmed by the bright lights of the strip. He thought he'd like to say what he wanted to say while he watched the shimmer of those lights on her beautiful face.

"Baby, I'm getting better. I want to get better for you. I want to be a whole man. I'm not there, but I'm going to work on it."

She nodded and said the words he'd dreamed about every night for the past few days. "I'm not going anywhere."

"This isn't just a hookup for a few hours and then we go our separate ways, Julie. I can't propose to you until I got all my shit together—"

"Shhh, Luke. There is no hurry. You know we have time. There is no race."

But of course there was a fuckin' race. He needed to be inside her. He needed to touch the gateway to her soul while he filled her with all the power and love he possessed. He was grounded with her, found, seated on a solid foundation that could withstand any earthquake or tidal wave.

He pulled her onto his lap when he sat on the edge of the bed. "I've got one more tour, and then I'm thinking I'll get out. I don't want to do anything that sets me back into the dark ages, but I don't have to think about it for a while. I've got a few weeks, maybe a few months, to decide. But I'm promising you right now, I'm going to make getting healthy a priority, to work on it."

"I don't want you to change anything for me. I want you to do and be what you would do and be if I wasn't around."

She was fiddling with the hair at his temples, toying with him, making his ears buzz. The way her heaving breast leaned into his bicep, the little nipple teasing his grateful body part, made the blood in his veins pound.

He looked up at her, rubbing a palm over the top of her thigh, needing to see her close her eyes while his fingers pressed between her legs. "Not possible, baby. I am who I am because of you. You make me the man I want to be by loving me in return."

"I want you to teach me what I need to do to assist, Luke. There's so much I don't understand. But I'm willing to try. Teach me."

"With pleasure, baby. I just wanted you to know. I just didn't want you to think—"

She pressed her lips so hard against his he almost bit her. "Take me, Luke. Please take me. Love away all the doubts. We'll figure it all out later. I promise. But I need you now or I'll go insane."

Well, hell, if that wasn't the biggest fuckin' green light of the century.

He kicked off his shoes and quickly dropped his pants, while she slipped off her top and did the same with her pants. She arched to unhook her bra and he stopped her. "My rules. My job."

She lifted his T-shirt off his head, folded her fingers behind his ears and then traced a finger down his jaw to his lips. He accepted her forefinger, pulled her whole hand up to his face and sucked two fingers loudly. Her other hand found the tent in his pants and had slipped inside the elastic of his red, white and blue boxers, finding his cock, squeezing it, and then squeezing his balls.

He quickly shucked the boxers and brought her to the bed. She lay back, her knees apart, lacy cream panties barely covering the slit of her opening. When he reached under her to remove her bra, she arched toward him, bit his neck and wrapped her legs around his waist.

Her body was warm and friendly. It was like coming home after being scared shitless in some of those desolate places where he'd been deployed. She was all apple pie and parades and everything he loved about what normal people did. In his mind's eye, he saw children in the streets and dogs sleeping on the lawn. He saw the pleasure of a future with her.

He carefully pressed her knees apart and slipped his tongue under the lace to dip into her opening. The first taste of her almost made him weep. He'd been so sure they would never again have this kind of afternoon together, but the grieving he'd done for this relationship was suddenly over. The long winter, the cold which had gripped the strange parts of his emotions, was lit by the fire burning within her. He would be her love slave for as long as she'd have him.

When his ministrations made her arch and writhe, her lovely, soft belly got concave. His hands smoothed over the cream of her thighs, moving along the backside to fondle the cleft in her butt cheeks. He used his forefinger to touch the dimples at the top of her ass and then snaked up her spine to hold her up to him.

Wet from her juices, he reached her mouth, and she sucked his tongue while pressing her pubic bone against his thigh and rubbing hard with a groan. He decided he wouldn't take off the panties. His cock was in need of immediate satisfaction. There would be time to explore that delicious pink pussy of hers later. Right now it was all about the feel of her pulsing around him while he came.

Then he remembered the protection he didn't have.

"Honey, I don't have anything."

She examined his face. "Then we'll have to risk it," she whispered.

"No, baby. That isn't smart. I can probably get—"

"Shhh." She lifted her head, and he placed his hand under the base of her skull, helping her to reach his ear to tell him something. With a moan and a whisper, "Fuck me, Luke."

Well, okay.

He moved her panties to the side, letting his fore-finger slip up and down her slick channel. He pressed her nub with his thumb, allowing his fingers to lightly penetrate her one at a time, and she was going wild. At last he pressed himself at her opening and allowed just the head of his cock to enter.

He cupped her lovely face, his fingers massaging

her scalp, his thumbs rubbing across her lips. He looked into those chocolate eyes, gently kissed her lips and thrust deep, watching the little worry lines crinkle at the top of her nose even as he filled her.

Her face was filled with pain and it scared him. Tears shimmered. He stopped. "Baby, are you okay?"

"Are you going to leave me again, Luke?"

"Oh, honey," he said, he tucking his head under her chin while he pumped her deep, in and out. Then he lifted and gazed into her eyes again.

"Never." His own eyes had gotten moist. "Never leaving you, Julie. Never."

"Your promise is your bond. I take you at your word. I love you, Luke. I don't want to have to learn how to live without you."

He moved himself in then out, then deep again, knowing they would have to have "the SEAL wives' talk." The one where she learns what to do in case he didn't come home. She'd have to understand, if she was going to love him, it was always possible he would not return. Not likely, but possible. She had to understand what they shared was precious, but perhaps short-lived. And that he'd strive with every fiber of his being to come home to her, but it was never guaranteed.

But it was also what would make their life together more precious.

CHAPTER 29

LAZING IN THE colorful lights of the strip and the noise of laughter, vehicles and music, she watched the colors move across his chest. She'd never felt so wrung out or so satisfied. She kissed his left nipple and felt him stir, and then he rolled to his side and covered her hip with his thigh. The sheets were all over the place, but one hid the powerful thighs and hips which had loved her into oblivion. She knew it would always be like this. She'd always feel this way in his arms. She was safe. The world was right. Nothing could shake her belief that somehow they'd make it.

His eyes were open, and he had on his sexy smile. The Luke who had loved her was still here, had fallen asleep and woke up being the same Luke who had pleasured her just an hour ago.

She reached down and stroked him. He pushed his hips into her palm, so she tucked her shoulder under his thigh, moving down on the bed and put her lips on his cock. Sucking and swirling her tongue over his crown, she was rewarded by feeling him stiffen and rise to life again. Then she slid her tongue down to his balls. She took them in her mouth and sucked, rolling them around, pressing with her tongue, then rolling them with her fingers while she licked her way back up to his tip.

He flipped her onto the mattress, pressing down her upper arms with his knees, holding on to the headboard of the bed while she sucked and pulled at his member. His hips worked in a fluid circular motion while she worked the length of him, up and down, then held still while he came. She wanted to wait, prolong their play, but his control was slipping.

"Baby," he groaned, his hips jerking.

She reached around between his legs and pulled at his ball sack, and he lost it. His warm sperm spurted, coating her throat as she held him deep and absorbed him all the way to the hilt while he came. She sucked every drop he had to give, slowly and lovingly allowing him to sink back into the bed.

With his head resting on his forearm, his knees splayed to the sides, he looked at her and smiled. "I was saving it for you, sweetheart."

"Oh, yes, and I thank you."

She was following the line from his belly button up between his nipples when a buzzing sound alerted them.

"What's that?" she asked.

"My cell." He leapt up, standing at the lighted window, his broad shoulders and small butt just visible to her in the bright lights of the strip.

"When?" he asked. He had gone serious.

"Roger that. We'll be right down."

He set the phone on the bedside table and sat back down on the bed, rubbing a palm from her jawline, down over one breast and then the other. Her nipples perked under his touch, then he palmed her sex and traveled along one thigh.

"We gotta go, sweetheart," he said. "I'm so sorry, but we have to return to base."

She sat up, her breasts calling to him. He squeezed them and bent down for a last-minute kiss. "I'd planned on staying in this room as long as you'd have me," he finally said.

"I thought you didn't deploy for a few weeks."

"That was the plan. But we have been called to duty for something special. I can't talk about it, but it's special."

"Okay."

"And sweetheart, you can't talk about it. Not to anyone."

"Well, Annalise will know."

"Not the details."

"You haven't told me any details, Luke."

He smiled the warm smile she craved. "Just tell her we've been called back to base for a meeting."

"When will you be back, then?"

He continued stroking and squeezing her nipple, then cupped her jaw. "Just as soon as we can. We never know." He stood and began putting his clothes back on.

"Come on, Miss Julie. I've got to get you downstairs so we can check out and get ourselves over to the airport."

"Airport?"

"We're taking a military transport which will pick us up in less than an hour. You'll be okay?"

She stood in her nakedness. He wrapped an arm around her waist and pulled her to him. He was shirtless, and she loved the feel of his powerful shoulders as he tensed, squeezing her in his delicious man-scent. He ended the hug with a brief kiss signaling they were done.

A short time later they had assembled in the hotel lobby. She and Annalise were saying goodbye while the guys loaded Luke's dark blue Hummer and headed for the airport.

"Damn," said Annalise. "I was in love, there, for a minute."

"Not hard to do, Annie. Not hard to do."

They both sighed.

They walked along the strip, back to their hotel room. Despite how Annalise tried to worm the information out of her, Julie basically told her the truth. She knew nothing more than they had to go back to San Diego for a meeting. She tried her hardest not to make it sound top-secret, but in the end she wasn't a very good liar.

Julie hoped she'd be able to wait the day or two Luke thought they'd be separated. He promised he'd call to give her an update.

But when morning dawned and there was no text message, she began to worry. She and Annalise tried to stay busy, but Julie's mind was not there. She wanted to go back to San Diego, in case Luke had a stolen hour or two. Being four hours away was too far. Annalise resigned herself to having their girl's weekend cut short. But Julie noticed she wasn't too disappointed. Must have had her eye on a couple of Luke's buddies.

CHAPTER 30

Luke arranged for a new Team 3 guy to go pick up his Hummer. Sanouk and a couple others would drive the guy up to Las Vegas, where Sanouk was interested in trying his hand at some bigger stakes. He made the new guys promise Sanouk would not be allowed to touch the Hummer, no matter what the circumstances and no matter how much money the Thai threw at him.

Kyle and Senior Chief Powers were waiting for them at the Team Briefing Room. It was a room no one other than a Team 3 SEAL or their Senior Chiefs or Commanders could enter. Pictures of past missions, maps and memorabilia of highly classified operations were pinned to the wall. Cell phones were left outside.

Luke sat down next to Tyler, who gave him a thumbs up. Which meant their relationship had completely healed.

Powers began. "The Azim Khan Primary School in

the Ghorak district of Kandahar has received night letters recently." Night letters were what local militia leaders were using to instill fear in the local population, as well as warn them of an impending attack. It was used mainly as a way to close schools without having to fire a shot. "As you know, after the bombing last year a number of churches pooled their resources and had the school rebuilt. It was open for about a month without incident until now."

Members of the Team—Kyle, Cooper, Rory, Luke, Jones, Tyler, Fredo, Armando, and three others—shifted and shared glances. It had been a difficult tour, mostly because the school had been targeted and one two of the teachers, along with several children, were killed. Both teachers were women. They weren't allowed a public burial, their village was so afraid of Taliban retaliation.

Eventually all eyes were on Luke. He was the one who had wrapped the stump of the pretty schoolteacher who had lost a hand in the explosion. He'd wrapped it with her Hijab, having to argue with her before she'd let him use it to keep her from bleeding to death. He had saved her life.

Right after the blast they'd been pinned down by snipers, which gave the mastermind, Mohammed Hamid, time to get away. Luke had sent three of the snipers "back to the source" as their unit was fond of saying. The one he was unable to get was taken out within seconds of his Team's arrival.

They'd nearly caught this warlord several times, and he'd been on the high-value target and shoot to kill lists since the last rotation. But word had it he was popular with the locals, which Luke doubted.

It had weighed on Luke especially, because he'd been alone with the Marine contingent sent to protect the school. He had lost the young would-be medic to the first sniper. Luke's kill was done with easy precision.

Seeing the carnage, trying to find survivors lying amid the school's dead and dying children and teachers, had given him nightmares on top of what he was already having.

Senior continued. "While it isn't our place to second-guess the judgment of the Powers That Be to rebuild a school for girls, it is our job to protect innocent lives. We have reason to believe this warning, which is tantamount to a kill order, is also the work of Mohammed Hamid. And we have pretty good intel saying he's staying nearby. In fact, we know which three houses he is staying in."

The warlords and other militia leaders had a habit of moving from house to house so they were usually impossible to capture. Often their own lieutenants didn't know from one night to the next where they were staying.

"What kind of intel?" Everyone looked at Luke.

"The brother of the school teacher whose life you saved, Luke. He's a terp for us."

Luke nodded. But then he'd had some time to get to know the family.

"They look upon it as a debt they owe in gratitude for her life."

I saved them once. I can do it again. I knew this could happen. That's why I'm here.

"They have temporarily closed the school. We had originally hoped this would call off their planned attack, but apparently this is not the case. And we have reason to believe the families of several teachers and children who attended the school are next."

Grunts and groans were abundant. Several shook their heads and swore under their breath. It was the worst thing a SEAL could hear: innocents were being targeted, just for being innocent. It was one thing for a fighting man to die because he signed up for it. But quite another to attack the families of children who just wanted an education.

"This would be volunteer only. Out of rotation. And, sorry, there will not be anything but hazard pay bonus, nothing big. We'll fill anybody who can't go with others from Team 3, but you've been requested." Senior Chief Powers nodded to Luke. "They trust you."

Which meant he couldn't say no.

There were no holdouts. Everyone was in, which Luke had expected. Luke's previous deployments with the East Coast team had taken him to that village, and when he returned with Team 3 he'd been greeted with friendship. But it quickly changed. Events moved swiftly, and a series of suicide bombings scared the entire community. The invites to homes suddenly dried up. While no one showed outright hostility to them, they didn't show any kindness which might be detected—and misinterpreted—by a sharp lookout or spy.

Why the school had been permitted to rebuild was a mystery to most American observers. And because things seemed calm, the Team had been called elsewhere and had left Luke in charge, with the Marines to guard and him to run a small medical and first aid clinic due to his medic training. Coop was the senior medic and could not be spared on their other deployments. So Luke had been chosen to stay behind.

"Our intel says Hamid is planning to blow up the school when it is chock full of students, and he'll wait it out until they return, which is supposed to be this week. We've alerted them, and they refuse to stay shut down. But they have requested our assistance, and we've been cleared for the mission."

They spent the next hour going over plans Kyle and

the Senior Chief had roughed out. There wasn't anything about the mission they hadn't done before. It was about getting in, getting their guy, and getting out without alerting any of the defending militia or local authorities. Something they'd done hundreds of times. What was different was this time, if they failed, a lot of kids and teachers were going to die.

He managed to give Julie a call just before they took off. Other Team members were doing the same.

"We aren't sure how long we'll be gone. It could be for a few months, Julie." He wanted to overestimate the time. He suspected it would only take a week, maybe two, but couldn't let on about this for fear of jeopardizing the mission.

In his mind, he could see her face and hear the slight quaver in her voice, though he could tell she was trying to be brave. He was proud of her effort.

"Will I be able to call you?"

"No."

"Will you be able to call me?"

"I'll try, but not promising anything. You might get a funny, scrambled-looking call you normally wouldn't pick up. You'll want to answer those for a while, because one of them could be me."

She laughed.

"And if it's not, you can have a nice conversation with a telemarketer."

"Funny. Yours is the only voice I want to hear."

"I got you, baby. Believe me, nothing would make me happier."

The space was awkward. This was the first time he'd needed to say goodbye to someone he cared so much about before a deployment. Now he knew what the other guys meant. And he had new respect and admiration for them, especially the married guys with kids.

"Come home to me, Luke."

"Roger that. Get ready, because when I come home there's going to be fireworks."

"I'm counting on it."

"Love you, sweetheart."

"Love you too, Luke. Remember, you promised."

"Yes, I did, and my promise is my bond. Soon, Julie. And then nothing will keep us apart. Nothing."

HALF A DAY later and a whole world apart they touched down at the military terminal at Kandahar. After being delivered to their base, they checked with their contacts on the ground.

Luke recognized the skinny eighteen-year-old interpreter, a good-looking kid they called Jack Daniels so they could talk to or about him without giving the bad guys a clue to his identity. Luke had met him the day he tended the kid's sister at the school. Luke didn't even know his real name or his sister's.

Today the kid looked ten years older, and yet it had only been a year. He realized what a toll the war was taking on the country's younger people, who basically didn't have a coming-of-age anything like the Americans did. From the time they were old enough to be useful, they spent the entirety of their time trying to survive.

Working for the American forces had been this kid's way to put food on his parents' table. Luke went over to tell him the Marine units and the SEAL community were committed to getting his sister a mechanical hand, and arrangements were being made
"Thank you. I am glad it is you who has come, Luke."

"How *is* your sister?"

"Grateful to be alive. But she feels worthless."

"We'll get her a hand. She'll enjoy doing the things she loved to do before. You'll see. They have amazing technology."

"Not all. There is no need for teachers now. She is collecting firewood, helping my father with the deliveries. It is dangerous for her. But now you are here. You have been sent by the Prophet."

"Well, I'm here, true. Ask your prophet to protect me. I have a girl at home now, okay?"

"You will be favored. You'll see. You will be favored. For the good work you do."

"Thank you Jackie. So tell me, is this intel coming from you?"

"Yes. I am a friend of a woman, a girl, actually, who is to be his third wife. She is barely old enough, and I do not think she can bear him children yet. She does not want to do this, but you must not tell anyone," Jack said.

Luke had a hunch there was more Jack wasn't saying. He suspected there was a personal angle to it, but decided not to pry.

"He comes to their house to try to convince her parents to let him carry her away with him. Her parents are afraid and do not know what to do."

"Ah." So it was as Luke suspected. Like many things in the Afghan culture, allegiances and balances of power were very important. What Hamid hadn't realized was, although he could get away with bombing a school, killing innocent teachers and children…coming between a boy and his love interest was a mistake he might have to pay for with his life.

It was smart they hadn't told the U.S. Government this part of the story. Although they had a good enough reason on the surface. He knew the school had been teaching a modified Christian message, funded by some powerful groups in Washington. He knew there had been some twelve hundred schools laid waste or shut down in the past three years. One more wouldn't amount to much, yet they were here. And that was all there was to it. He never questioned the why of it all.

And in the past year, young Jack Daniels had learned to do something his country's government was still learning: how to summon the most powerful strike force in the world. And he'd get men who knew what Hamid looked like, knew the village, and wanted to get even for all those dead kids. He looked at the kid with renewed respect. Another man who would do anything for the woman he loved.

Deal done. Just another day at the office.

CHAPTER 31

JULIE BEGAN HER week of the summer session without incident. Her mother delivered Corey the first two days. Julie tried to engage the woman in conversation.

"I understand she has a fondness for chickens and rabbits."

"I am not aware of any such thing," Mrs. Miller had answered. She seemed afraid to reveal anything personal about her daughter and quickly turned to go.

"Your husband told me this. Your older daughter raised them, he says."

She stiffened. "She was not my daughter."

"I'm sorry." Julie had made the slip on purpose. "She's gone to live with her mother, then?"

"I believe so. Why are you asking me all these questions?"

"Like I told your husband last week, it will be easier for me to engage Corey if I do it through things she already likes. It will make it more fun."

Mrs. Miller stopped briefly at the doorway. The bell rang, and Julie knew the students would be filing in any second. "She used to like her dolls."

"Does she still have them?"

"No. Look, I'd like to help, but I'm afraid I can be of no use. You're on your own, Miss Christensen."

The strange woman departed quietly when the room started to fill with students. Corey stood by the window and watched her mother drive off. Julie wondered why the woman hadn't said goodbye to her.

ON THE THIRD day, she got a call from Luke. The phone call was scratchy, and she could barely make out his voice. But hearing he was alive and out of immediate harm's way was reassuring.

"Love you, baby," she could hear.

"Come home to me, Luke."

"I plan to. Take care."

JULIE THOUGHT SHE was coming down with the flu and opted to stay home. They found a sub for her and she went back to bed, feeling dizzy and sick to her stomach. When she woke up a couple of hours later she barely was able to make it to the bathroom to be sick. She spent most of the day trying to drink broth and bland cottage cheese and toast, but everything she ate made her sick. Even the smell of coffee turned her stomach.

Later in the day Noreen called her.

"Sorry you're sick."

"How did you know about it, Noreen?"

"I spoke to Carl. He told me you weren't there when he dropped Corey off."

"Carl?"

"Carl Miller."

"No, Noreen. I meant you are calling him by his first name now?"

Noreen laughed on the other end of the phone. "He's not a creep, Julie. Honestly I think he's a pretty good guy." After a pause, she added. "He's stopped by and brought me lunch a couple of times."

"You're dating?"

"Not allowed and not smart under the circumstances. But I have to admit, Julie, I have a fondness for him. I think he's pleased with the progress you're making with Corey."

"What progress? She still won't talk in class. And she gets angry if I make her read. That's new, but I would not call it progress."

"Well, he's told me you're working hard and he appreciates it."

"Good to hear."

"So, kiddo, you feeling better?"

"I'm just tired. I guess all the stress of starting the summer program and Luke shipping out has gotten to me a bit. I never know when he'll call. I worry."

"Of course you do. How long—"

"I'm not on the list to get the information. He'll tell me when he's back in country. I'll have no warning."

"Exciting."

"Not when you're sick to your stomach."

Noreen chuckled. "Maybe you're pregnant."

Julie was going to laugh it off…until it hit her they'd not used any protection more times than they had. She mentally counted the days and, yes, her period was late.

Holy Mother of God.

"Jules? Did I just strike a nerve?"

"Don't be silly."

"Is it possible? Could you be pregnant?"

SHE PURCHASED A home test kit, and the results were negative. But she decided to have a blood test done, and did so on her way into work the next day. Friday dragged on slowly, but she thought the kids were beginning to trust her. Her nausea subsided and she finally began to feel normal again. Maybe she wasn't pregnant after all. The test had been negative. It was foolish to worry about it.

At the end of the day, when the clinic number came

up on her cell phone, she excused herself to the hallway. The kids were working on their first test for the week.

"Julie Christensen?"

"This is she."

"The results of the pregnancy test are in, and you are indeed pregnant. We recommend repeating the test in another two weeks."

The caller kept talking, but Julie was staring off at the large oak trees bordering the school grounds. A gentle breeze made their boughs wave from side to side. She was carrying Luke's child. She was going to have a baby. She'd never even considered the possibility. How was he going to take this? Would he pressure her to—want to—she couldn't bear to even contemplate the choices. What if he didn't come home? What if he got angry and broke off their…could this even be called a relationship?

The buzzing in her ears came back. Then she realized the clinic person was still talking, asking questions.

"Thank you," she said, and hung up while the person was mid-sentence.

Her life had suddenly changed. She couldn't even decide if she was happy about it or not. Pregnant and not married. Not even engaged, although Luke did love her, she was certain.

What would her mother say? Here Colin and Stephanie had gotten married, yet she was the one who was going to have the baby. Everything was backwards and inside out. She and Luke had never had time to sit down and really discuss a future, she'd been so selfishly caught up in the sex. She felt sure they had one, but to bring a baby into the world before all of this was nailed down just seemed wrong.

She was filled with regret, because she remembered they'd had the opportunity in Vegas, and she'd been too greedy for him to allow them time to talk. And the next wave of emotion coursing over her was shame. Shouldn't she be happy about this? After all, she did love Luke. But had her lapse in good judgment cost them the chance they needed?

Like a zombie, she returned to class. She studied the bowed heads of little minds while she began working out future study plans. Her eyes filled with tears, until suddenly she felt the warmth of Luke's love flooding through her. A little part of him, of them, was growing inside her, using the nourishment her body provided, growing, becoming a child.

Then she realized that, regardless of what Luke did about it, she would love this child. She'd do everything in her power to bring him or her into the world in a loving household, hopefully with Luke at her side.

So, yes, she was happy. Very, very happy.

Corey sat staring at the same page in her workbook. Julie was filled with compassion for the little girl.

She took Corey outside the classroom while the other students were quietly occupied.

The two of them walked slowly down the hall to a concrete bench. She sat and asked Corey to join her.

"Anything you want to tell me?" she asked the youngster.

Corey looked up at her, and that's when Julie noticed the child's pallor and the dark circles under her eyes.

"Honey, are you feeling okay?" A sudden wave of nausea hit her, and she had to swallow hard to keep it at bay, because this was Corey's time. She wanted to show some tenderness to the girl, perhaps pat her on the top of her head, but knew it wasn't wise, so kept her hands to herself.

"What do you mean?" Corey asked.

Julie saw fear and dread, two things she'd hoped never to see on the face of a second grader. But could this be her own maternal instincts kicking in? Without thinking, her hand went to the top of Corey's head, and when she made contact with the youngster's hair, the child flinched. Which allowed Julie to see a two-inch-long bruise that had been partially obscured by a large barrette.

"What happened to your head, Corey?"

"Nothing."

"You have a bruise there."

Corey pulled away, and then stood up. "You're not supposed to touch me!" Her eyes were wide in her pale face, and her little mouth was turned down into a frown, her lower lip quivering. She was about to burst into tears.

Julie knew she finally had the evidence she needed. The confirmation of the feeling she'd had about Mr. Miller and Corey's family was physically evident right in front of her. Although heartened by the realization her gut instinct had been correct, she now had to decide whether to call CPS.

"Who did this to you, Corey? Did someone hit you?"

The girl looked confused for a second, as though she didn't understand the question. The anger was gone. Her words slurred, she said, "My dad. I was bad."

Had Corey also been *drugged*?

Oh my God!

Julie knelt in front of her student, placing her hands on the youngster's upper arms, and gently squeezed, keeping a safe distance between them.

"Don't you worry about anything, Corey, sweetheart. I'm going to fix this."

"Fix what?" Mr. Miller's voice barked behind her. Julie jumped to her feet as Corey fell into her skirt, hugging her knees and hiding her face. Her young arms clutched Julie's legs while she shook in fear.

Julie turned, keeping an arm on the child. Miller's cold, hard eyes stared back at her, smoldering in anger, his fists tightening at his sides like he was barely able to hold back a display of temper. He looked wild and dangerous.

"You're a monster," Julie spat at him.

"Not. And this is none of your business," he said, yanking his daughter's arm, jerking her away from Julie's protection. He turned to storm away.

"You can't get away with this."

Little Corey gave her a look Julie knew she'd remember for the rest of her life. The girl had tried to hold onto her skirts but Julie had let Miller yank her away. The girl's face was full of betrayal, and fear of what was coming next.

"Help!" Julie shouted. "Help me please!" she yelled at the top of her lungs. At first no one came, but then a couple of doors opened and heads peered out into the hallway. "Someone please call the police."

She wasn't sure what to do, but she couldn't let Miller take Corey off the school grounds. Behind her, the classroom she'd been teaching piled out into the hallway. The kids were agitated. She shouted to another teacher, "Please, watch them. I have to go after him. He's been abusing that child. I have to stop him."

She ran after Miller and the girl. Corey had been strapped into the front seat of Mrs. Miller's minivan, but when Julie tried to open the door, she found it locked. She banged on the glass. Corey's terrified stare switched to something on Julie's left.

Next to her, Miller whispered, "You couldn't stay out of it, could you?" just before he raised a cloth soaked with something that smelled like lighter fluid, and her vision tunneled.

And then nothing.

CHAPTER 32

KYLE, LUKE, TYLER and Armando had been sleeping on top of the large two-story building down the block from the target house. Jack Daniels had brought them food to supplement their rations as well as fresh water. They'd found shade in the makeshift cover installed by the owner, which was just large enough for a couple of folding chairs to fit under it. But it still was hot as hell.

The rest of the Team waited on the ground floor. Rory and Jones were waiting behind the hulk of a destroyed Russian tank which lay on its side and which gave them shade as well as cover. The crew downstairs rotated, taking turns moving so they stayed sharp and ready to roll on a moment's notice.

Two black SUVs pulled up to the front door of the target house. Luke recognized the swagger of the dangerous militia leader. He felt Jack tense up beside him.

They counted four men entering the building, all dressed in white robes. The SUVs barreled out of sight. Kyle spoke into his Invisio. "Have them, and I count two, repeat two black SUVs to be followed discreetly once they've left the city proper." They were working in tandem with a Marine unit who had been stationed in this part of the city for several months. Luke knew the Marines would pick them up and conduct a thorough interrogation.

Showtime.

Normally entering the home of a person of interest didn't involve a firefight. They would allow the SEALs to remove the insurgent. In some cases, the insurgents' families seemed relieved. At first, Luke had been surprised about their cooperation. But then he learned people who didn't care about killing innocent women and children often mistreated their own.

But today would be different. The entire family of the young girl Hamid wanted was being held hostage. Hamid wouldn't even have to pay them a bride price. He was just going to steal their most precious cargo for his own evil designs.

Which meant there would be no peaceful snatch and grab today.

They surrounded the building. Armando stayed back but still within sniper range, also on the lookout for other bad guys or accomplices from other homes nearby.

Sure as shit, when Kyle banged on the front door and shouted, "United States military, permission to enter," Luke observed a scramble, and two white-robed figures climbed out on the roof through a hatch in the second floor. Armando took care of them quietly.

Luke was second to enter the house behind Kyle, followed by Tyler, who touched him on the leg to let Luke know he had his back. The family of the girl huddled off to the side, leaving room for the SEALs to maneuver. Luke put a finger to his lips for them to be quiet. The Team needed to hear what was going on upstairs to avoid any of their own from being injured. Except for minor sniffles and muffled cries from a baby, the downstairs was relatively quiet. A television program was playing Arabic music somewhere upstairs.

Jones and Rory were watching the back door. Luke wished they had more men inside, but he followed Kyle while they trained their guns on anything that moved. Kyle motioned for Tyler to stay downstairs and got a thumbs-up. Tyler gave another thumbs-up to Luke, who returned it.

On the second floor, they found their person of interest holding the young girl, a pistol jammed into the side of her face. She was in a white cotton nightdress, her head uncovered, her hair wildly twisted around in all directions. Luke knew they were just in time to prevent a rape.

He recognized Hamid, because Luke himself had knocked one of the asshole's two front teeth out with a swift kick during the fight just before the insurgent had escaped. The Afghani shouted something in Arabic which didn't require translation. Hamid had one arm under her chin, cutting off her circulation, while the gun remained steady at her temple. Hamid pulled his face away from her wild hair and it was all Luke needed. He aimed for the vacant spot between his teeth and fired. The man's head exploded like a watermelon.

The fourth intruder surrendered without a fight and was turned over to the Marine unit for questioning off-site.

Jack came running up the stairs calling a name. Horrified at the bloody scene, he fell at the feet of the girl, who hurriedly reached for a headscarf and blanket to cover herself. Jack shouted something downstairs, and they could hear the happy acknowledgement from her relatives who had anxiously waited to learn the results of the mission.

AN HOUR LATER they mounted a transport to Norfolk, and then they'd take the bird back to San Diego. It would be another twenty hours or so before he arrived. He tried calling Julie's number and there was no answer, so he left a message.

Thinking she might be teaching or in a meeting, he texted her the news.

Headed in country. Home in twenty. Love, L

Kyle moved to take up the seat next to Luke. Across from them sat Tyler, who was listening to music with ear buds.

"I'd have you covering my fuckin' ass any day, man." Kyle extended his hand, and Luke shook it.

"Honor. Just like shooting fuckin' clowns at the fair back home."

"You knew for sure he was the motherfucker?"

"No question about it." Luke pointed to his two front teeth. "I did that to him two years ago. He was a mean motherfucker. You keep screwing over your own people, sooner or later you run out of fuckin' places to hide."

"Yup. Fuckin' died on his wedding day."

"Fucker."

"One thing I liked about today, though," Kyle said.

"What?"

"You didn't fuckin' hesitate."

Luke thought about it while he watched Tyler rock out to his music. Nothing had come between him and the mission. Even his hatred of the men who did evil things to innocents had stayed between the lines and remained calculated.

"I don't want to hear any more stuff about not being ready, unless you go home and pee on your own couch or some dumb shit like that."

Yeah. Luke knew he'd done good. The good guys had prevailed. He liked that.

He leaned back and closed his eyes.

Just another fuckin' day at the office.

CHAPTER 33

LUKE AND TYLER ate first then showered on the base at Norfolk and changed clothes, glad to shuck the desert gear. It always felt like he was finally home when he could get into his cargoes and flip-flops. He couldn't wait to talk to Julie. Actually, he didn't want to talk at all. He wanted her up close and personal for his own private form of snatch and grab, where the surrender was a jackpot for both of them.

But he couldn't reach her. He double-checked his phone, and his message had not been returned. He wondered if she somehow couldn't figure out how to do it or had some sort of scrubber on her phone blocking certain things.

He left her another message, "Hey, Miss Julie. I'm really missing you something fierce. I just wish I could listen to your voice before I hop on this next bird. Never been so glad to be back in the old U.S. of A. And as soon as—"

A man's voice broke into his conversation. "Who is this, please?"

"Who is this?"

"This is Detective Stanfield of the San Diego P.D."

Oh, no!

"What's happened? I've been overseas on deployment. Is Julie okay? I'm flying home to see her, leaving any minute."

"Well, son, we are trying to locate Julie right now. Seems she was abducted from her classroom yesterday afternoon. She's been gone for nearly twenty-four hours."

"Shit!" Luke paused to adjust his tone. "Sorry, sir. Julie is my…my…fiancée." There, he'd said it. Now he needed to say it to her. It was going to be the first thing out of his mouth when he saw her pretty face. He remembered her speaking about the parent she was having difficulty with. "Julie told me she was having trouble with some guy whose daughter was in her class—"

"We know all about it, son. Looking for him now."

Luke and the detective exchanged numbers, and then he boarded the plane.

"You call Colin yet?" Tyler asked him.

"Shit, no. Maybe he knows something. Do you think?"

"Probably not, but maybe the police have been talking to him. Worth a shot."

Luke tried his phone, but there wasn't any reception. "I'll wait and call him when I land."

"I know it's going to turn out okay, man. You two are fuckin' made for each other."

"How the hell do you know? Did you ever take her out?"

"Shit, no, Luke. You know that. I told you. It's just that Colin—"

"Tyler, that shit's not helping me right now."

Tyler rolled his shoulder and cracked his neck. "I feel you. My bad."

Luke waited a minute before he added, "She *is* fuckin' made for me, Tyler. The sweetest little thing you ever *didn't* have. And that's a fuckin' fact."

Tyler gave him a grin and punched his arm. Hard.

But Luke wasn't lured into the false hope everything would be fine when he landed, and worked to prepare himself mentally. Kidnappers of women usually made good on threats of violence. He recalled Julie saying the guy was wound up a bit tight. If anything happened to her, he'd risk his career to get even with the guy, exact his pound of flesh. If he—

He stopped his thoughts. They weren't productive and, amazingly, he was able to control his emotions immediately. He called Colin the minute they landed and left a message that he was back in town and asking about Julie.

"Not sure my sister and Colin are back yet," he told Tyler. "Maybe he doesn't know."

"Yea, good idea not to panic the guy by leaving a strange message then," Tyler answered.

Tyler drove him home, and Luke was relieved to see his Hummer there. He took the key out from under the bumper and fired it up.

"You want company?"

"Sure."

"Really?"

"Fuckin' get in the truck, Tyler, and stop it."

"Should we leave the duty bags in your apartment?"

"Nah, I want my gear."

"Okay. This will be fun."

"Not sure we can do anything, but we might think of something." Luke was amazingly calm. His damaged self would have been filled with remorse, guilt at having left her alone, which was ridiculous. She *had* to be okay. Had to be.

They went by the school, which was taped off as a crime scene. He asked for the detective he'd talked to last night, and he was shown to a short, portly man and introduced himself and Tyler.

"What can we do, Detective?" Tyler added.

"Not a damned thing. We have her cell phone, as you know. I noticed your two messages, but no one else called her except some clinic in town."

"A clinic?"

"Yeah, the Women's Reproductive and Fertility Clinic." Stanfield stumbled a bit on his words, hesitating. "You know anything about that?"

Stanfield watched carefully while he answered.

"No."

"Having a hard time believing they'd be involved in her disappearance. No, everything is pointing to the kid's father, a Mr. Miller. Several of the kids recognized him with his daughter, and saw Miss Christensen chasing after the guy. You ever meet the man, son?"

"I know someone who has, her union rep. You get hold of the principal yet?" Luke asked.

"Yes, he came over yesterday and gave us the Miller file."

Luke had some choice words he wanted to leave for the principal himself, so was glad.

"You been to her apartment?" Detective Stanfield asked.

"Nope. Actually, I've never been there."

"So you want to 'splain this to me? How can you two be engaged and you've never seen the inside of her apartment?"

Luke didn't feel like he was being treated as a suspect, but he didn't like the questions. Of course, he definitely didn't like the answers he was going to have to give. God he'd been such a dumb fuck. "I met her here, but not at the apartment. A couple of months ago. Then we re-kindled our friendship at the wedding of her brother and my sister two weekends ago, up in Sonoma County."

"You move fast, son."

"Fuckin' A, he does. Beat me to it," Tyler whispered and looked off to the side.

"I'm getting the impression you're military, Spec Ops?" Stanfield asked.

"Yessir."

"One of *those* guys?"

"Yessir."

"You think it has anything to do with her disappearance? I mean, Miller have a thing against the military or something else she might have mentioned?"

"No. She did tell me she was afraid of him."

"Well it sounds like her instincts were right on in that department. I don't know why she would chase after the guy, though, if she thought he was dangerous."

Luke knew she took her job seriously. Just like he did. But he was trained to deal with sociopaths and psychos, and she was not. She loved being a teacher. Just like the one he'd saved in Afghanistan. Maybe he'd have to tell her the story someday. About how he'd almost sacrificed his life for a teacher.

No, that was work. This was the rest of his life. This was the woman he was going to love and honor and cherish for the rest of his life.

Dr. Connors arrived, racing in from his car. Luke took a good, long look at him and decided he needed his clock cleaned. Tyler quickly stepped between them.

The guy looked white as a ghost. Luke wasn't sure if he was worried about Julie or his job. He definitely didn't trust him.

The man kept walking around with his palm to his forehead, as if he couldn't believe the situation. He was barely paying attention to Stanfield's questions.

"Sir!" Stanfield finally got impatient. "I'm going to need you to pay attention and answer my questions."

Connors looked at Luke and Tyler and grimaced. "You got undercovers going after her now?" he demanded with a scowl.

Stanfield rolled his eyes behind Connors's back. "Close. Okay, sir, let's step into your office, shall we?"

Later, Luke and Tyler followed Detective Stanfield over to Julie's apartment. Stepping through the door, he saw a warm, picture-filled apartment which was just like her classroom. Color everywhere. Pictures of trips she'd taken, friends. She had posters made by some of the students in her classes. Thank you cards penned by little hands. He was asked not to touch anything, and he didn't.

Outside again, Luke and Tyler waited by the Hummer. The waiting was the hard part. There had been no ransom demand. All of them were gone, including little Corey and her mother, too.

Then they caught a break. A motorist was flagged down by a mother and her child about ten miles east of the City limits in a rural area used for hunting and dirt bike riding. She was brought to the sheriff's office, and they told tales of being held captive by her husband, along with two other women. The message said one of the women was dead and the other one was still alive. She had managed to untie little Corey and her mother, and they were able to escape. Luke produced a map of the area, and they all studied it.

"Looks like they picked them up about here," Stanfield said.

"It's got to be Julie," Luke said. He refused to believe she was harmed.

"Look, much as I'd appreciate your help, this isn't your fight."

"The hell it's not. I'm all the way in."

"No, this is a police matter. You have to let us handle it."

Luke knew he had to convince the detective he was going to cooperate and leave, but had no real intention of doing it. And something told him Stanfield was also pretending and perhaps secretly grateful for the assistance.

The detective promised to keep Luke informed.

Taking advantage of the Hummer's off-road capabilities, Luke and Tyler combed back and forth across the rough terrain, searching the area with binoculars.

"God, I wish I had one of Coop's drones."

They drew a circle around the pickup point and estimated how fast the mother and daughter had been able to move to estimate how far out they had to search. On their second sweep of the southwest quadrant, he spotted a cabin with a gray van parked in front.

Luke pulled the Hummer under some trees and they both geared up, including his MP4 and a few miniature explosive devices, their sigs, some body armor and extra clips. Their night gear they left in the truck. There was no sense bringing any food or water, since it wasn't going to be a stakeout. This would be a quick rescue operation.

Using small trees and shrubs as cover, they first made their way over to the van and touched the hood. It was still warm. Luke got out his KA-BAR and sliced a three-inch hole in each of the right tires, the ones furthest from the front door, disabling the vehicle.

They listened for any signs of movement and heard nothing.

The cabin had a back door and a front door. A high

electrical line connected the house to a pole. Luke considered shooting out the power, but didn't want to give up the element of surprise.

"I'm thinking we blast both doors simultaneously," he said to Tyler.

"Roger that, boss."

Luke gave him a look.

"Old man," Tyler corrected himself.

"Thanks, man. I'm glad you tagged along, Tyler," he said while he handed him an Invisio.

"Hell, if you get shot, I get the girl. I'm fuckin' in it for *me* you asshole," Tyler whispered. Then he grinned, and they quickly got on with their mission.

"We go in two." They both checked their watches. Tyler went around the backside of the cabin.

Windows were boarded up, so Luke couldn't see anything while he made his way to the front door. He was careful not to cast a shadow, since there was a crack big enough for something to show through to what he figured must be a darkened interior. He placed the explosive, hanging from the door latch, and checked his watch. He set the thirty-second fuse and retreated around the corner of the house.

Tyler's IED went off a full two seconds before Luke's did. Immediately he heard automatic gunfire and hoped for the best. His device had only partially split the door, which must have been reinforced from the inside. He kicked in the rest.

Dust and smoke were everywhere, along with the unmistakable smell of death.

He caught sight of something moving and was relieved to see it was a thigh, more particularly, one thigh he knew very well.

Julie's alive!

Then, *Jesus!* He was hit in the chest with several rounds which nearly knocked him through the doorway into the dirt. His body armor held, though. Thank God the guy didn't have armor-piercing bullets.

More gunfire came from the back, and he heard a muffled scream just before someone hit the floor.

Miller was on Luke in a flash, using a wicked hunting knife a little smaller than his KA-BAR but with a nasty blade. Luke barely had enough time to deflect the man's crazed lunge. Luke grabbed the man's forearm and quickly broke the two bones between his elbow and wrist with a quick snap like shortening sticks for a campfire. Miller howled, so Luke kicked him in the balls for good measure, which doubled him over on his knees. He gave the man's head a kick with his steel-toed boots and he collapsed, immobile.

Tyler came limping out from the shadows. "Caught one in the leg, man, but I'm fine." Luke check the blood staining the man's dark green pants and knew he could wait briefly for first aid.

Which meant he could follow his instincts and release the woman writhing on the dirty mattress. Julie was bound hand and foot, with a large, dirty rag around her mouth. She'd sustained some bruising, mostly on her wrists and ankles from the restraints, with a scratch here and there which had bled shut, but otherwise looked pretty fucking incredible to Luke. He would have to say beautiful.

Her eyes widened when she realized who he was. He dropped to his knees and cradled her head in his arms, whispering sweet messages and reassuring her he was here, and everything was going to be okay.

"Are you hurt, baby? Did he hurt you?"

She shook her head until the gag was removed. "Oh, God, Luke. He was going to kill me. You got here just in time. Corey—"

"All safe, baby. It's how we found you. They're both safe." He followed her gaze to another mattress on the opposite wall. A decomposing woman's body lay splayed out, naked, her blonde hair caked with blood from the slit in her throat. Her hands were still bound, but not her feet.

"Noreen," she sobbed into his chest.

"It's all over, baby. Nothing to worry about now. You're safe. I've got you."

Her pungent body odor after nearly two days in the dirty cabin was still the sweetest perfume he'd ever smelled.

CHAPTER 34

LUKE HAD A long discussion in the morning with his psychiatrist, Dr. Brownlee. He'd wanted to stay with Julie at the hospital, where she had been kept for observation. But he told her he needed to keep an appointment, and he wanted to talk to his professional like he would talk to an expert in his field before planning a mission.

What he had in mind was a lifelong mission. His old self would have made fun of wanting to get permission from his doctor to marry Julie, but this was a new phase in his recovery. He would seek out every tool in his arsenal so he would continue to heal, to become the best husband a girl could want. Asking for help was a good sign, he thought, and he decided to follow his instincts.

"I'm happy for you, Luke," Dr. Brownlee said. "But you understand these symptoms are not going to go away just because you've found the right girl? We're talking about a process here, and it takes years."

"I know."

"How long since the dreams?"

"A week…fuck, no, ten days. And not since I've been back. Sorry about the language."

"I'm used to it." He paused and examined Luke carefully before continuing. "It's good your mission didn't trigger anything. It also doesn't mean your next mission won't. Have you thought about that?"

"I have."

"You taking meds?"

"I don't f—like the way they make me feel."

"You're going to have to be honest with me, Luke. Far better to take them to avoid a return to the depression and deep black holes of those places you go than to walk around dangerously untreated. But, I don't think your PTSD is as severe as some I've seen. If I insisted you stay on your meds, even with all the side effects, would you stay on them?"

Luke looked down at his folded hands. "Will I ever be 'cured'?"

"We don't talk like that. We talk about recovery. Peeling the onion. Making strides. But the frank answer to your question is—no. But with therapy and possibly the use of drugs, if necessary, you will recover if you put the time in."

"Okay, I get that."

"All up to you. There are tools you have which you didn't have a month ago. The meditation, the sessions, possibly some couples sessions—all these things will help. And we prepare for the dark times to come."

Luke stared at his hands. He knew the doctor was right. He sighed heavily.

"What's the sigh about?"

Looking up, he could see Brownlee wasn't going to miss a beat. The doctor's own daughter had married one of Luke's best buddies on the Team, Coop. Which was why he'd chosen to work with Dr. Brownlee, because he considered him part of the family of the brotherhood. And he'd been doing some free group sessions for the Teams on his own time. The man was an expert in his field, just like Luke was. Like they all were.

"I don't like thinking about the dark times. I just don't," he said, and shrugged.

"Who would? But tell me what's going on with you right now."

"From where I sit today—I mean, I feel good, really good. Solid. I don't want to think those dreams might come back. But I know you're right."

"Think of all the things you'll be dealing with, like the things that came up before, except now you'll have a wife, someday a family. Suppose one day something happened to them?"

Luke thought about Camilla. He tried to visualize her dying in his arms, but he couldn't. He wondered if it would change. He wondered if this ghost, this vision would ever come between him and Julie.

"You're talking about other stress, picking at a scab."

"You're about to merge your life with another person, someone you barely know. I'm not saying your decision is a bad one, just that it's very quick. But then, I know you guys, and this is what you do, don't you?"

"Yessir."

"You feel the pain of what you've endured, the loss of life both here and abroad, and it means you're human, Luke. You'd be a psychopath if you enjoyed the killing or the danger—"

"Honestly, doc? I love the fuckin' danger."

Brownlee chuckled. "I get it."

"I mean I hate it when we go over there and just hang around doing nothing, waiting for something. I'd rather be in the middle of—"

There it was again, the niggling doubt. Did it make him good husband material, because he actually liked putting his life on the line? Like it was something he was chosen, called to do? It wasn't the killing he loved. That would make him a monster. It was providing protection he loved, and the brotherhood of the Teams. He knew some day he'd have to get by without it. Was he weak for thinking—no, knowing—he still needed his buds around him? Did it make him weak?

He asked the doctor. He could see Brownlee felt emotional about Luke's explanation of what he felt.

"This is what an elite warrior must face every day. Not sure the world understands this. I didn't realize it about my brother until years after he was gone. One of the biggest regrets of my life is I didn't understand him."

"I'm sorry, sir."

"No, this is about you, not Will. This is what makes you human, questioning all these things. We need to keep talking about all of it. It's healthy for you to question yourself. Examine everything. It's what we work on. When we put a label on it and say, 'I'm good,' then I start to be concerned. You understand what I'm saying?"

"Yes."

"Huge congrats for reaching out to me today. Huge, Luke. An excellent indication you are fully participating in your own self-care and recovery. Facing your demons. But they won't go away. They don't go away. They fade a bit. And you learn tools to deal with them when they come up, because they will."

"I got you. So you think marrying Julie is one of those tools?"

Brownlee chuckled again. "Fucking no."

Luke was surprised when he swore. But then he saw the wide grin on the face of a man he trusted, truly trusted with these intense, personal issues of his soul.

"Marrying Julie is your prize. You get to have your prize if you continue the work, Luke. You get to have a life in living color if you handle the paperwork, so to speak. If you do the advance planning, you reach the goal, right?"

"Right."

"So you haven't answered my question, Luke."

Luke knew what he was referring to. It wasn't an easy thing to answer, but he knew he had to.

"Yes, Doc, if I need to, I'll go on the meds. Just not today."

CHAPTER 35

LUKE SAT ON the hospital bed with Julie, his huge arm draped over her shoulder. He asked questions about everything the staff did. What her blood pressure was, her temperature. He wanted to see when they added lab work orders to the electronic chart. They finally gave up withholding information and showed him everything without him needing to ask first.

When he left to call Kyle, the large nurse who took her blood pressure, Adele, gave her a wink.

"That's some kind of fiancé you got yourself there."

"Fiancé?"

The nurse took a step away from the bedrail and put her hands on her hips, the stethoscope draped around her neck. "Girl, you mean, you're just finding out about it? He's been telling everyone around here you guys are engaged."

She peered down at Julie's hand. "No ring," she said, and sighed.

Julie linked her hands together, rubbing over the spot on her left hand where a ring would have gone. Would go some day. And smiled. It was lovely to know Luke was telling everyone. But she would rather have heard it from him first.

"I have a question, Adele." "Can you re-run a pregnancy test, you know, to make sure everything's okay? I'd just found out, and it's very early. You know. I don't want to tell him if something happened."

"Glad you mentioned it. Wasn't ordered on the routine panel when you were admitted." She leaned into her and whispered, "I'll get it added right now so they don't have to redraw."

"Thank you. Will I get the results quickly? Or do I have to wait for all the other lab work to come in?"

The nurse winked at her, "Let me see what I can do, hon. Are we going to be happy about this?"

"Are you kidding?"

"That's what I thought. I'll go make the call right now."

She nearly collided with Luke at the doorway.

Luke pulled up the leather lounge chair and grabbed Julie's hands, giving them a kiss. "How're you feeling?"

"I'm fine. A little tired. Hungry. Starving, actually."

"All you had was the bar I gave you in the truck. As soon as they say it's okay, you'll be eating wonderful hospital food."

"I don't want to stay here. I want to go back to my place tonight."

"I think they just want to finish checking you out. The school's liability carrier might require it. We'll just let them do their job. Besides, we have to talk."

A little electric jolt sizzled through her.

He stood, then sat on the corner of the bed, and cupped her hands between his. "Jules, I want to make this a permanent arrangement. I want you to marry me."

She was about to throw herself on him when the nurse poked her head around the doorway and gave Julie a double thumbs up.

I am pregnant!

"Let me tell you something first, just in case it makes a difference, Luke." She stuffed down the emotion bubbling to the surface. His warrior face, peering down at her, the blue gaze which had mesmerized her the first time she saw him in daylight, his gentleness, the restraint and control, and the powerful arms and shoulders that had held her, could carry the world with, was what she loved about him. But his heart, the tender spot inside this elite warrior he had shared so intimately and privately with her…that was what she loved best. She hoped he'd be good with the news. Maybe even more than good. But she'd be okay with just good.

He'd wrinkled his brow, and he squinted. "Is there something wrong, Julie? You don't want to—"

"I'm pregnant, Luke. Very early pregnant, so, you know how these things go, you're a medic, and—" she was going to babble on, but his kiss interrupted her.

"Then we get married right away," he whispered to her lips afterward. "Think your folks could handle another backyard wedding, but on a much smaller scale? Or we could go to Vegas—"

"No. I'd love to get married in the Airstream if we could, but I'll call Mom. But no Vegas wedding, please."

His palm stroked her cheek, his thumb lightly skimming across her lower lip. "I love you so much, Julie. I've learned a lot about myself in the past few weeks. The deployment only made me realize I'm doing what I love to do. Are you sure you're okay with it? Because I'd give it up if that's what you want."

"No. It's who you are, Luke. It's not *what* you are that I love, it's *who* you are. You are the man who does those dangerous things others can't. Or won't. I understand. And I already know it comes with a whole other set of challenges. I'm in for the long haul."

She knew there would be rough patches in the road ahead, but she would be vigilant. She wasn't going to turn her back on him, even at his worst.

CHAPTER 36

THE GARDEN FLOWERS were just as beautiful—he'd have to say even more beautiful. Luke walked in his tux through the rock-walled patio area. The collection of white chairs, arranged in rows, was much smaller. Everything about this wedding was on a much smaller scale. No DJ, no dance floor. It was what Julie wanted. He'd have been okay with whatever she wanted.

Kyle, Cooper, Fredo and Tyler walked out into the yard to join him. Kyle handed Luke a beer. Julie's brother, Colin, was his best man but remained inside.

"You nervous?" his LPO asked.

"Fuckin' no, Kyle. I'm petrified." It was the truth. He hadn't slept a wink last night, and he wasn't sure if it was nerves about the wedding or something from his dark side creeping in. He didn't like that Julie had chosen to spend her last night as a single woman with her girlfriends. He'd needed her something fierce.

"Well, just like over there, we got your back. You pass out, you're all Cooper's. You run, you're fuckin' mine.

Tyler punched his arm. "Go ahead, run, you prick. I'll console the bride."

"You're not even allowed a peck on the cheek, you asshole."

"I say leave it up to Julie, my man. She want to plant something on me, I'm definitely all in."

The group groaned. "Watch it, Tyler. That mouth is going to get you into trouble," Cooper said.

Reverend Dobson joined them on the patio, accompanied by Colin. "I'd like a private moment with the groom, if you gents don't mind?"

The group retreated to the house, and Dobson motioned for Luke to walk over near Mrs. Christensen's garden.

"I've known Julie her whole life, son. Not sure if you knew this."

"Yessir, she told me."

"I was present at her dedication when she was a baby. She attended my new members' class when she was a teen. I wrote a recommendation letter for her college application. Julie always has been one of my favorites, I don't mind telling you."

"I can see that, sir."

"She had concerns about jumping into this marriage too soon. And she's told me she is with child."

"Yessir."

"You will not have months or years to get to know one another like a lot of couples do. You are going to have to work on it, kind of speed up the process."

"We already tend to work at that speed, Reverend. We've sort of established it as our pace. Not that it will continue, but we both make our minds up rather quickly, sir. I've thought a lot about it. I asked her to marry me before I knew she was pregnant. Wanted you to know."

"Yes, son, I am aware of it. I'm sure your intentions are pure."

Luke wasn't so sure. He'd been sporting the biggest hard-on in creation all night *and* this morning. It was hard not to let it distract him, but he tried to listen to the Reverend.

"Love heals all things, son. It isn't forced. I'll be talking about it just for a little today, if you don't mind."

"Do your thing."

"No, Luke, this is your thing. This is the day you step through the doorway and join another brotherhood. You become a husband and father. You become protector and guardian of a new family. It will be your most important mission in life."

THE LUTE PLAYER began while Julie's mother and father began their procession down the row between chairs. Dr. Brownlee and his wife and Libby, Coop's wife, were escorted to the front row on Luke's side. Libby was looking radiant and extremely pregnant.

Luke took up his spot next to Reverend Dobson, and his groomsmen entered, each with one of Julie's girlfriends on their arm. Stephanie, Luke's sister, was the last to come down the aisle, walking with Fredo.

Luke saw his future father-in-law at the entrance to the Christensen kitchen waiting for Julie to make her way to his side. The audience rose and, for a few seconds, she was cut off to him. But when she rounded the corner onto the patio pathway, his eyes burned and he could scarcely breathe.

She had never looked so beautiful, so pink and lovely, all covered in white crinkly fabric which made quite a noise, even from this distance. Bowing to tradition, he hadn't seen the dress, but he knew she would have made sure whatever she wore underneath created that sexy chiffon on chiffon sound when she walked toward him. And he'd never needed to tell her what the sound of that fabric did to his libido.

But there were so many things he wanted to tell her, whisper to her. He just wanted to spend as much time with her as humanly possible. She'd be with him every waking minute of the day. She'd be his reason for coming home, his reason for leaving, too. She'd be his anchor, his lighthouse. His rock.

His love.

REVEREND DOBSON WAS concluding his short sermon with a chapter from Corinthians:

"Love is patient, love is kind. It does not envy, it does not boast, it is not proud. It does not dishonor others, it is not self-seeking, it is not easily angered, it keeps no record of wrongs. Love does not delight in evil, but rejoices with the truth. It always protects, always trusts, always hopes, always perseveres."

IT WAS TRUE, Luke thought. At the pronouncement of their joining, Luke lifted Julie's veil and spoke to her just before their lips met. "For ever and ever, Julie. I'm here forever."

As their lips parted she whispered back, "And when you come back to me, I'll always be here, waiting for you. Always. I love you, Luke."

The intimate moment had most of the audience in tears. Unlike Colin and Stephanie's wedding, Luke could hear sniffling and saw people wipe their eyes.

He grabbed Julie's hand, just the way they'd done at his sister's wedding, and walked down the aisle, stopping at Dr. Brownlee and his wife. Brownlee gave him a hug and pat on the back. "Good luck, son," he whispered in his ear. "Pulling for you."

He and Julie continued their exit, shaking hands and hugging people they knew along the way. He noted Christy, Kyle's wife, holding a fidgeting Brandon in her arms.

The simple party was elegant…and way too long, Luke decided. He was impatient to start his new life with Julie, and the party was almost an imposition. But the Christensens had been gracious, and if they felt an ounce of regret they hadn't gotten to give a lavish party for their own daughter, it didn't show. He attributed it to Julie's handling, especially of her mother.

He caught her arm when she walked past him to deliver a glass of champagne to a guest.

"You've been swishing around, making that dress tease me something fierce, Miss Julie. I'm in desperate need, here."

"It's only fair. Soon, Luke. Remember the 'all good things come to those who wait' part?" She leaned in and gave him a long, languid kiss. He didn't want to let her go, but she held up the champagne flutes. "Let me do my job, and then later I'll let you do yours."

He was thinking about it long and hard when Tyler came up behind him. "Totally, completely happy for you, man. You fuckin' hit the jackpot, Luke."

He examined Tyler's face. He'd die for this man, for all of them, if he had to. But he still was going to give Tyler hell for that comment.

"And don't you forget it. Hands off. No kissing my lady. Don't even think about it."

"Can't you take a fuckin' joke at your fuckin' wedding, you asshole?"

"There you are, Tyler," said the dark-haired bridesmaid who'd walked down the aisle with him. She slipped an arm under his and pressed her body against him.

"Careful, Tyler," Luke said as he winked and went to retrieve Julie.

He'd left instructions for her to keep on her wedding dress when it was time to go. Mrs. Christensen had intervened, suggesting she'd be more comfortable for the trip in her street clothes, but Luke overruled firmly but with a smile.

With fond farewells and a shower of birdseed, the two of them jumped into Luke's Hummer, which was towing the Christensen's Airstream.

CHAPTER 37

THEY HAD RESERVATIONS at Yosemite for tomorrow, but Luke had refused to tell her where they were going tonight. Julie was sure it wouldn't be far, knowing Luke. He drove West, toward Highway 1 and the coast.

"Where are we going?" she shouted over the rumble of the Hummer's powerful engine.

"The beach."

"Thought we had reservations at Yosemite."

"Not until tomorrow. Tonight it's all about us and the beach, okay?"

"Not a problem here," she smiled. One of the things she didn't like about the Hummer were the bucket seats in front. But somehow, rather than going off in a chauffeured limo like Colin and Stephanie did, this seemed more fitting. The Hummer bounced, and she jounced along with it. Her bulging bodice, which she couldn't wait to get out of, was getting so much attention from Luke she was halfway worried it was too much of a distraction for him.

"Eyes on the road, Mr. Paulsen."

"Yes, Mrs. Paulsen."

They pulled into the campground at Bodega Dunes about a half hour later. He'd secured a private campsite tucked away by itself with easy access to the beach.

After setting the trailer in place, he escorted Julie inside, flounces and petticoats flying everywhere. He locked the door behind them.

She threw herself in his arms and reveled in the way he lifted her up and carried her back to the bed at the rear of the trailer. The sun was setting outside, and a bright orange glow permeated the sky. They could hear seabirds and the muffled boom and hiss of waves crashing on the beach on the other side of the dunes.

Amid the orange light she watched his face while he lay her down and peeled her petticoats back one by one until he found her white stockings and garter belt. He snapped one and then smoothed over the back of her thigh with his palm.

"So sweet, Julie. You are the most beautiful woman I've ever known. You skin is so…" He kissed her along the garter, unclipping and removing the stocking while he did. He peeled down her right and then her left stockings until she was bare.

"Oh, my," he said when he discovered she'd not

worn panties. She loved motivating him with her own bit of risqué behavior.

"I just figured I'd be making you work so hard to excavate through those petticoats, I'd give you a little surprise."

"I love surprises, Miss Julie."

His mouth was on her sex so fast it made her hitch in her breath. The dull ache in her core snaked up her spine while he sucked and tasted the lips which were full and ripe with lust for him. It had been an agonizing evening without him. The excitement and anticipation of their joining today was almost too much for her to bear. All night she had dreamed about his taste, the feel of his tongue *there*, just like right now, and how full his cock would feel while he rode her.

Spreading his thumb over her nub, he kissed the little organ to a peak, rolled it around with his tongue. He lapped down her further, searching and rooting deeper. Lusty excitement sizzled through her, and her channel craved his tongue, his fingers, craved the moment he'd fill her with his powerful cock.

"I want you inside me," she moaned.

Her bodice made her breasts press deliciously tight, plumping pillows of flesh above the sequined and beaded top. He got to his feet, removing his shirt, but all the while looking down on her face as she scooted up the bed in a cloud of organza and chiffon.

"I just about come whenever I hear that swish. My buds are going to give me hell if you ever tell them."

"Only one way you can secure the secret."

"What's that, dear Julie?" he said while he slipped down his slacks and underwear.

"You come right now and fuck me silly in my wedding dress."

"All the material gets in the way,"

"Yes, and I love it."

"But I want to feel your flesh against mine."

"But I need to feel you inside me, right now, on my wedding day. Just today. Humor me, my love."

"Nothing would give me greater pleasure!"

Luke's bare knees pressed against the underside of her after he climbed the bed. He brought one of her knees up and over his shoulder. He angled himself to enter her.

"You are mine, Julie," he said as he arched and slowly slid into her wet channel. "Mine, baby," he said as he lazily pumped her. Each time he was in all the way to the hilt, she moaned at the incredible feel of him filling her.

She heated up rapidly, feeling the dull coil of arousal take over her body while he maneuvered his hips in fluid motions, holding tight to the knee up and over his shoulder to help him penetrate deep. Her anticipation brought her quickly to the edge. She quickly fell into the erotic throes of a woman desperate to be consumed by her man, needing to be filled and stretched by his girth. His demanding thrusts took her breath away, and finally she began to spasm out of control.

He began lurching against her internal muscles which had clamped down on him hard. She heard his whispers calling her name, the deep growl vibrating from his chest as he repeated his urgent need over and over again. When he climaxed at last, she was at the height of her orgasm. They both shuddered, gasping for air while their slick bodies at first hardened against each other and then softened. The dress swooshed when they slowly disentangled and he nestled against her, resting his torso in the pile of organza and beading. The sound almost kept time to the dull pounding of the waves outside the window.

Their combined breathing slowed at last while the sounds of the ocean became more and more prominent. She loved the feel of being completely spent, yet feeling the arousing, wet kisses he planted on the back of her neck. Wrung out and sweaty, she would gladly give even more if he demanded it of her. She drifted off into a lover's sleep, fully content.

She awoke some time later feeling hemmed in by her dress, along with a need to feel his warm chest pressing against her breasts. Shifting beneath him and running her fingers through his hair, she kissed his ear and brought him awake with the undulation of her body.

"I'm ready to get naked now," she whispered.

"Ah, there's my girl. Oh, boy, I get to remove all this," he said, holding up a handful of her skirts in one fist.

"Thank you."

He unzipped the side of her bodice, kissing the newly exposed flesh. "Thank you, Mrs. Julie."

"Ever since I was a teenager I had a daydream of fucking in my wedding dress." He was watching the smile she couldn't suppress. "It was even lovelier than I'd imagined."

"I aim to please, Julie. I want to fulfill all your fantasies. Every one of them," he said, prying open the dress and lifting it over her head, leaving her completely naked. "So lovely," he kissed her ear, pressing the words warmly against her, making her ears buzz.

He hesitated, as if in a private thought about something deep.

"What is it, Luke?"

"I was just thinking about that first night. On the beach, when we met."

"Completely random and chance encounter resulting in this." She turned in his arms, placing her hands onto his chest and then up over his mountainous shoulders to his neck. She urged him forward and when their lips touched she whispered, "And now we have forever."

"Yes, we do, baby." He nibbled on her lips, extending kisses under her chin, under her ears, and then further down to the space between her breasts. He lifted his head and they stared into what they could see of each other's eyes illuminated by a distant outdoor lamppost. "Let's take a blanket down the beach. I want to do what I wanted to do the first night, Mrs. Paulsen."

He wrapped the bedspread around her and begged off sharing it, instead walking with his arm around her shoulder, his fingers massaging her spine at the back of her neck. The evening sky was filled with stars, undiminished by the occasional trail lamp and a handful of tall light standards. She couldn't remember it being so peaceful.

But the ocean roared while they walked over the dunes to the beach below. The sea birds were quiet. Distant lights along the bay's edge twinkled. There were no sounds of man and, except for the lights, there was no evidence of civilization. The powerful waves hitting the shore shook the ground in tempo with her heart. Her body heat began to rise inside the bedspread when they neared a stretch of smooth sand still warm from the afternoon sun and he stopped her.

She knew the ocean was important to him. Knew

they'd always live by the ocean, even when, some day, he'd no longer go on missions as an active SEAL. She knew he would never cease to be an elite warrior in everything he did. And right now this warrior was focused on her body, unwrapping her, exploring her skin with his intentional kisses, because it was how he was, how he would be forever.

Her temperature continued to rise until she dropped the spread and stood in front of his warm body, touching from thigh to chest, arms extended and fingers entwined behind his head, pressing against her rock of a man. Her forever man. Her sometimes-broken man, whom she would love until the day she died.

The night air made the skin on her backside tingle, but the warmth of his arms, the growing bulge in his groin area emanating the heat of his desire, made her insides quiver. It would always be like this. There would be the cold reality of the world, when she'd be separated from him for weeks or months at a time, and then he'd come back, holding only her body in his powerful arms. He'd chosen to share his life with her. This honorable man would forever make her feel safe, would shelter her from whatever cruelty and coldness the world could dish out.

She'd support him in his healing and only hoped she could give him all he deserved. It would have to be enough, because she would give her all for him.

He knelt in front of her and she felt worshiped. She held his head to her abdomen. The soft kisses he placed there were not intended for her, but for their child. He was whispering something to their baby. His flesh and blood was growing within her. It was her honor. It was her future.

She saw his eyes sparkle when he looked back up at her face. The smile was pure heaven, illuminated in the moonlight. “I’m going to love being a father,” he said loud enough to be heard over the waves. “And you’re gonna love your mamma,” he said to their baby.

She ran her fingers through the hair on top of his head while his kisses got more inquisitive, while they drifted lower. Like a homing beacon, he maintained a relentless aim for the juncture between her legs, smoothing his callused palms along the insides of her thighs and parting them to allow him entry. She heard him moan when he saw the gaping hunger of her sex. His fingers played in her labia. She sank to her knees, holding his jaw in her palms, smoothing over his lips with her thumbs. “You are so precious to me, Luke. I love that what you give me is delicate and at the same time fierce. Thank you for not giving up on us. For giving me the chance to be part of your life.”

He kissed her. Their bodies remained connected from thighs to upper torsos.

"I'm far from perfect. I'm flawed, Julie. I make no pretense."

"I don't need your perfection. I just need you."

"I'm here."

"I need you to come back to me. Always come back to me."

"Which I will do, Mrs. Julie. With every ounce of my being."

THEIR LOVEMAKING HAD been soft and gentle, not frantic. He relished how she matched his rhythm, how she let him know what she liked and how he could please her. She'd kissed the frog-print tats on his forearm, the scars on his back, and the large Centurion helmet he'd put there when he was only twenty-two. If he had to do it today, he'd choose a Latin saying or a different symbol, not the battle dress of an ancient warrior.

But it's what he was. And now he was off on another adventure, this time with Julie by his side. As Reverend Dobson had said, through a doorway to another brotherhood, that of father, husband and protector of a dynasty, the family they created. A family who would grow up knowing the intense love he felt for this woman, and knowing how, no matter how strong and brave he knew he was, he needed her like the air he breathed.

He would fight, for now. And then he'd come home to Julie, and the baby who was the best part of both of them.

* * *

Did you enjoy this book? Some of you have read the previous 5 books in this series. Others are reading this series for the first time! Before I tempt you with Book #7 in the SEAL Brotherhood Series, here's an excerpt from Sharon's latest book, SEALed Forever, Book 3 in the Bone Frog Brotherhood, which releases 4-16-19. It's available to order here.

sharonhamiltonauthor.com/sealed-forever

Here's the first chapter for your reading pleasure!

Chapter 1 excerpt, SEALed Forever, Book 3 of the Bone Frog Brotherhood Series:

NAVY SEAL TUCKER Hudson squinted across the beach bonfire that roared taller than any of the men on his SEAL Team 3. He was back—at least in all the ways he could be. He was now forty years of age—a retread. He'd survived the landmines of past deployments, the vacancy of those years off the teams, as well as the grueling BUD/S training re-qualifying for his spot. He was ready for his first mission as a new *silver* SEAL, as the ladies called him. He was a Bone Frog, one of the old guys on SEAL Team 3.

He was ready for the do-over. Told himself he deserved it. But just to add a little gasoline to the fire in his soul, his childhood best friend, Brawley Hanks, was failing. And that's what ate at him.

Brawley had just spent six months in rehab while Tucker completed his SQT, SEAL Qualification Training. His Chief, Kyle Lansdowne, had misgivings about allowing Brawley to go on the next mission to Africa, but since Tucker would be there, he'd overruled a suggestion from higher up to sit him out. This didn't help Tucker's nerves any. He knew it was his job to cover all that up and make those jitters disappear.

He watched the ladies dancing around the bonfire and looked for his wife of two months. Brandy cooed over Dorie and Brawley's little pink daughter while Dorie showed her off. The toddler was fast asleep. Several of the Team's kids jumped to get a look at the child until Dorie knelt and let them stand in a circle and check her out.

Their particular SEAL platoon tradition made them gather at the beach before a new deployment. All the wives, the kids, the close girlfriends and occasionally parents were there. But only those on the inside, in the know. Some had lost loved ones. Some had been injured. Some had suffered too much. But these were the people who held them all together—who would hold Brandy together while he was gone.

The past two years with Brandy had been the hardest but most rewarding years of his life. When he was a younger SEAL, sometimes the ladies made him nervous since he didn't have anyone to come home to. But now that he did, now that he could actually lose something dear to him, it made this little celebration all the more special. He'd missed those evenings under the stars in Coronado, surrounded by life and the promise of living forever.

No one would understand this kind of SEAL brotherhood, Tucker thought. You had to live it to know how it felt to be part of this family. You had to cry and celebrate with these people, tell them things would turn out, somehow. The miraculous would happen, because it always did. That's who they were. There wasn't any other group in the whole world he'd rather be a part of, and he'd tried doing without before. He knew better.

Tucker studied the beautiful, round face of his new bride, and all her other curves that enticingly called to him by firelight. It seemed she grew more and more stunning every day. Her eyes met his, and he glanced down quickly, embarrassed that he might look like a teenage boy. But that's the way he felt. He was back to being the big quiet kid the Homecoming Queen or head cheerleader came over to tease. It used to happen a lot in high school and he'd never gotten used to it.

Chief Petty Officer Kyle Lansdowne took up a seat next to him. His Chief was the most respected man on the team, even more than some of the officers, who were never invited to these events. Kyle had worked hard to make sure Tucker came to his squad. Although slightly younger than Tucker or Brawley, Kyle's experience leading successful campaigns through sticky assignments made him one of Team 3's most valuable assets.

"You nervous?" his LPO asked.

"You asked me that the day of my wedding, remember?"

Kyle nodded.

"I was nervous then." Tucker took a pull on his long-necked beer. "I know what I'm getting into this time." He smiled, which was reflected back to him.

"Well, you know what they say about leading men. Don't ask a question you don't know the answer to first." Kyle clinked his bottle against Tucker's.

They both watched the children fawning over Brawley's daughter, still sleeping by the firelight, tucked in Dorie's arms. Kyle's two were right in the middle of them. Brandy gave Tucker a sexy wave.

"You got a good one, Tucker. I'm really happy for you," Kyle whispered, continuing to follow the ladies.

"You bet I did." Tucker meant every word he uttered. He'd always liked women he could grab onto and squeeze without breaking half her ribs. Brandy had the heart he did and that fierce joy of living, which also matched his own. And she'd earned that because of how she'd fought for every ounce of respect she so richly deserved. She spoke her mind. She loved with abandon, and he was damned lucky to have her in his corner. He was also grateful she let him go off and be a warrior again, just when most friends his age had wives ragged on them to quit.

And that was okay too. The SEAL teams were a revolving door of fresh and old faces, and internal dramas played out every day all over the world. It was sometimes hardest on the families. Men had to consider all of that when they played Varsity.

Kyle searched the crowd.

"I haven't seen him in about twenty minutes," Tucker mumbled. It worried him, too, that Brawley wasn't nearby. "I think he might have gone to get more beer, but that's just a rumor."

He knew Kyle suspected he was making up a safe story, which is why he didn't say a word. Then his Chief slowly turned, facing him. "You let me know if he gets shaky, and I thoroughly suspect he will." Kyle's voice was low, avoiding anyone else's ears.

The two men stared at each other for a few long seconds.

"I got it, Kyle. He's not on his own."

"And you only risk a little. Don't let that go over the edge."

"We don't leave men behind." Tucker knew Kyle

understood what he meant.

"No, we don't. I want you both upright. Both of you, Tucker."

"Roger that."

They gripped hands. Then Kyle broke it off and punched him in the arm.

"Dayam, Tucker. You can stop drinking those protein shakes anytime now."

Tucker liked that thought but dished some trash talk back. "Lannie, it ain't protein shakes. It's her," he said, aiming his beer bottle at Brandy. "You should see how she works me out."

Kyle stood up and then murmured, "I can't unsee that, dammit," and disappeared into the crowd.

Tucker hoped Brawley would show himself soon. His "ghosting" wasn't a good sign. He should be at Dorie's side. Tucker kept searching and then finally spotted Brawley pissing into the surf, which meant he was drunker than he should be.

Come on, Brawley. You're gonna get us both killed.

Brandy was still occupied with the women, and Kyle was having a little nuzzle time with Christy while carrying one of his two on his shoulders. Tucker scrambled to his feet and strolled toward his best friend, who was now throwing rocks into the ocean. His jeans were wet, and he was barefoot.

Brawley Hanks grew up alongside Tucker's family

in Oregon. He couldn't ever remember a time when they weren't best friends. Always competitors when it came to sports and girls, even enlisting in the Navy the same day, they attended the same BUD/S class. They'd planned on getting out after their ten years, but close to the end, Brawley met Dorie, and, well, the poor guy couldn't help himself and got hitched up. She had pushed for the re-signing bonus so they could buy a nice house in Coronado. A beautiful, classy girl with all the wildness Brawley had, Dorie was missing his self-destructive bend.

Tucker wondered at first if their marriage would survive, but as Brawley showed all the signs of getting seriously embroiled in a lusty kind of full-tilt love that made him go stupid and do dumb things like buy flowers, he became convinced his friend had finally been tamed and had given up his wandering ways.

Except that after his last two deployments, Brawley was back to being the bad boy he'd always been before he met Dorie. He drank and chased too much. And although they had high hopes for his rehab, he wasn't as convinced as Brandy or Dorie that his bad days were behind him.

"Hit any fish yet?" he asked Brawley.

"Fuck no," Hanks replied, slurring his words and letting go of another smooth, flat stone. It didn't skip like he'd been aiming to do.

"You know the more you hit the ocean, that ocean is gonna get you back, Brawley."

"I'm registering my complaint."

Tucker had to proceed with caution. He was at one of those turning points. But if Brawley lost it, at least he'd lose it here and save Kyle the trouble of having him sent home in shame. It sucked to be thinking this way just a day from deployment, but it was what it was. No sense sugar-coating it.

"I think your registration is going to the wrong department. Got your branches of service mixed up, Brawley. You should take it up with the man upstairs. Have you had that conversation recently?"

Brawley squinted back at him, as if the moonlight hurt his eyes. He did look like a big teenager, albeit a lethal one.

"I wear the Trident. Poseidon and Davy Jones are my buds. The man upstairs has given up on me."

His challenge hit Tucker in his stomach. *You dumb fuck. Where are you goin?*

He walked to within inches of Brawley's hulking form. Inhaling deeply, he worked to calm himself down so it would be effective. He knew he only could say this once, so he made sure Brawley didn't misunderstand his steely stare.

"I'm going to remind you that you just brought a daughter into the world. What kind of a world do you want her to grow up in, you old fart? You want her to grow up with an angry son-of-a-bitch for a father, like you did, Brawley?"

His best friend started to interrupt him, and Tucker grabbed his ears and spit out his message.

"Or were you thinkin' you'd check out over there in that shit African red clay, making Dorie a widow and your daughter fatherless? Maybe causing the death of one or more of your friends who have pledged their lives to save your dumb ass. You willing to take us all with you? You want to be that kind of best friend to me, Brawley? Or, are you gonna man-up?"

Tucker released Brawley's ears and pivoted like a Color Guard. He thanked his lucky stars he hadn't gotten clobbered with that delivery and called it good. Whatever Brawley did next was up to him.

It was just something that had to be delivered *before* they left for Africa. After they were there, it would be too late.

Tucker had done all he could.

If you enjoyed that excerpt, you can order your book here.

sharonhamiltonauthor.com/sealed-forever

But Wait!! There's more. Did you know Sharon bundles all her series books so you can enjoy binge reading? And, all these bundled books have audio books (which you can get at a discount if you have the digital copy by some retailers). If you already know you want to read more about the Brotherhood, Sharon's original SEAL series, here's how you can get bundled up!

Ultimate SEAL Collection #1 (Books 1-4 with 2 novellas) Order here. sharonhamiltonauthor.com/Ultimate1

Ultimate SEAL Collection #2 (3 novels) Order here. sharonhamiltonauthor.com/Ultimate2

Or, for those of you who just want to read one book at a time, in order, here's the next one. And don't forget to leave a review!

Continue reading the first chapter of the next book in the SEAL Brotherhood Series…

SEAL Of My Heart (Book #7), available here. sharonhamiltonauthor.com/SEALBro7

Book 7 in the SEAL Brotherhood Series: SEAL Of My Heart

Chapter 1

AIRPORTS WERE MOSTLY happy places for Kate. She pretended she was going on an exotic vacation, a tour of lands where everything from the smells to the language and customs of the people was foreign. In her fantasy, she'd meet a gorgeous, mysterious man and they'd spend a romantic week together exploring, indulging in glamorous restaurants and glittering casinos and sensual delights.

And even though she was engaged to be married to the most eligible bachelor in Sonoma County, the favorite son of the favorite first family of wine, she couldn't help it. The fantasy lurked just around the corner in her psyche, waiting to wrap her in a sensual blanket and whisk her away from the reality of her humdrum future.

It worried her some that she wasn't happier about her upcoming wedding or that she was even considering escape. Why didn't she feel more like a blushing bride-to-be? Something seemed...wrong, uncomfortable, but she forced herself not to think about it, writing the whole thing off as stress-related panic over the big day.

Her airport fantasy persisted though, and was kicking in big time this afternoon. She felt like having an adventure, something far away from everyone she knew, perhaps something far different from what she'd ever imagined for herself and her life. And as she examined the crowded terminal in San Francisco, she couldn't quell her quickening excitement while she boarded the plane, even though Portland was not even close to being an exotic land, and her sister was a poor substitute for a dark, handsome man who would sweep her off her feet.

It was going to be a fairly full flight, and she wasn't lucky enough to have an early boarding ticket. She preferred to sit by a window, but figured it was unlikely. Scanning down the rows ahead of the slowly shuffling line of passengers, she only saw one open window spot on the left, with someone occupying the middle one. When she came upon it, a briefcase lay on the cushion at the aisle. The young man in the middle seat was fully occupied in reading a book.

He looked up as if he'd heard her silent plea for the window position. His warm blue eyes lit on her face casually. She knew he wanted to scan her figure but stopped himself, and then he smiled.

What was it about handsome men who smiled easily? Did the smile mean he would like permission to engage? Did it mean he liked what he saw? Did it mean he was hiding something? He didn't look like the type to feel awkward, certainly not as awkward as she felt.

Her eyes darted to the open position next to him, and his glance followed hers.

"You want the window?" he asked.

She didn't say anything, stuck in place as if her feet were encased in concrete. A passenger from behind pushed into her back, reminding her she was holding up a line of travelers yet to be seated.

"It's yours if you want it," he whispered in a bedroom voice.

Damn.

These sorts of attractions to strange men weren't supposed to happen to a happily engaged young woman whose life was planned out nearly moment-by-moment. In spite of her fantasy life, which was *not* planned out and definitely *not* scripted, she decided to allow herself to get dangerously close to this stranger.

He was dangerous because he was perfect in enough ways to upset her ordered life. And he matched her fantasy man to a T.

"Thank you. That's very kind of you," she said.

Kate saw he was not only good-looking, he also revealed himself as tall, very fit, and muscular as he eased gingerly across the aisle seat and slowly uncoiled the muscle and sinews in his upper torso. And, boy, did she react…enough for him to hear her heartbeat probably, or see the slight involuntary shaking of her knees or the quiver of her lower lip. She caught his scent with a hint of lemon from an aftershave applied earlier in the day. She loved lemon on a man.

She actually heard a low growl of approval, and that made her traitorous panties go wet. It was all the right and oh-so-wrong kind of chemistry in front of impatient strangers. Over two hundred of them.

And she didn't care.

Kate turned a shoulder, crouching to sidle in front of him, her butt grazing the tent in his pants with interesting discoveries. She didn't dare say she was sorry. Just best to pretend it never happened. She settled at the window, placing her Kindle and her slim briefcase on the seat next to her and stashing her purse on the floor. Then she watched out of the corner of her eye as he settled himself back into place and then connected his seatbelt with long, strong fingers.

So far, so good. No harm, no foul.

She became extremely interested in the loading of bags into the cargo hold, the position of the little vehicles servicing the plane, the weather, other planes taking off in the distance, all the while willing her breathing and her heartbeat to return to normal. When she thought sufficient time had passed, she let her eyes drop to her lap, and then she shot a furtive look at the stranger at her side without turning her head.

He was reading his book again, not paying the least bit of attention to her. She told herself it shouldn't matter what kind of book it was, but she was *dying* to know in spite of herself.

She could tell he knew she was watching him, because his eyes scanned the pages, and his lips stayed pressed together but began to quirk up in a smile. The laugh lines at the corners of his eyes were deliciously short. His shiny, dark hair was slightly curly, a little longer than it should be, which made her think maybe he was an older college student. A retread.

She faced forward while the cabin doors closed. Then she sighed, and it did seem to let out some of the tension.

He brought out a small set of expensive ear buds and plugged them in, adjusting the pieces into his ears before resuming his reading.

Kate closed her eyes and told the fantasy in her head to chill, explaining to herself and the cast of fantasy characters who wanted argue about it that she wasn't in any danger of doing anything inappropriate and that today's trip was going along a normal, well-worn path. She told them it was going to be a boring day.

Until he tapped her on the shoulder. He was smiling again and holding his book out to her.

"You read romance?" he asked.

"Y-yes." How hard was it to admit the truth?

"Well, I've just finished my sister's book, and she said to give it away to someone else who might like to read it, so it's yours if you want it."

Of their own volition, her fingers snatched the book. Did he notice how quickly she'd made up her mind?

Be With Me. The title was familiar. She'd read about this particular book on one of the blogs she followed. A time travel romance, by Linda Gray. It was exactly what she needed to get her mind off the handsome stranger to her left.

"Thank you." She smiled in spite of herself. Trying to play it cool.

She glanced back down at the book, flipped open to the title page and found a signature.

"My sister," he said, nodding at the page. "In case you were thinking I read romance as a regular thing."

"I've known some men who read romance," she lied.

"Really?" His eyebrows scrunched atop his nose. "I've never known any."

"You just said you read this book."

"That's different."

After a short pause, she asked, "You don't think they're manly?" She was enjoying this a bit too much. A fall was coming. She knew it just as surely as she knew the plane had started to move and announcements were being made over the loudspeaker.

Mr. Gorgeous had to lean in closer to her to be heard, and she found herself meeting him halfway—involuntarily, of course, just so they could hear each other over the blaring intercom.

"Kinda embarrassing about all the sex scenes," he said. "I mean reading them in public, with a cover like this." He ran his finger over the front cover and touched the back of her hand in the process. The male torso on the cover looked oddly familiar.

She looked back up at him. "That's you on the book?"

He wiggled his eyebrows. "She says she uses me as her inspiration. My sister. My sister wrote the book."

"She *writes* romance?"

"Yes. Does quite well, I guess."

This was definitely not the twist she'd expected. She examined the shirtless torso on the cover again, the ripples of muscle, the huge arms, veins that snaked out along his shoulders and forearms, and one dangerous vein that disappeared into the top of a pair of jeans hung almost low enough to—to—He was hotness personified. And as handsome as he was on the cover, all wet, dark and brooding, in the flesh he was even more impressive.

She didn't know where her next comment came from. "Your girlfriend must be jealous of all the women who fantasize—"

"Don't have a girlfriend. So does your fiancé get jealous of you reading romance?"

Fiancé? Oh, yes…there was that huge two-carat diamond on her left hand that people practically had to wear sunglasses to admire properly. How could she have forgotten? But still, it meant he'd checked her hand out. Not like she'd waved it in his face to draw attention to it, but the thing was hard to miss, all the same.

"My fiancé—my fiancé—" That's when she realized the answer to his query. She was about to marry a man who knew nothing of her tastes in romance. As a matter of fact, she wasn't entirely sure he'd approve of her reading them. And how was that going to work? "He's never said anything. I doubt he notices."

"Really?" The guy gave a puzzled smirk. "Lets you wander around, reading about strange men and the things—" Now it was time for him to stop. He leaned back into his headrest, his eyes straight ahead as if fascinated by the texture and pattern of the fabric on the seat in front of him. He adjusted his pants discreetly. Rested his hands palm-down on his massive thighs. A circle of thorns was tattooed onto his forearm. His chest expanded with each inhale, expanding a good two inches, then his upper body relaxed back into the seat, his abdomen going concave. His jeans were loose-fitting, and she was busy figuring out they were loose for a reason when he suddenly opened his eyes and caught her examining his package.

Oh shit.

She darted a peek back out to the little window to her right and blushed in spite of herself.

"I'm sorry," she said out of the side of her mouth, knowing he was still looking at her.

"Don't be sorry, darlin'." It was a deep, luscious rumble. "That just made my day."

They were interrupted as the plane accelerated to takeoff speed. She felt the pressure of the G-force against her chest as they were lifted into the air, swinging around San Francisco Bay below until everything began to resemble a miniature scale model of Silicon Valley.

After they leveled off, the stranger extended his huge, callused hand, flexing the tat on his forearm, and said, "Hi. My name is Tyler Gray."

"Kate Morgan," She lay her palm against his and enjoyed the warm squeeze he gave her. She could feel what those fingers were capable of.

He was the first to withdraw his hand. He clutched his right thigh as he cleared his throat, licked his lips, and began speaking with a croak until he paused to clear his throat again. "Having a sister who writes romance is kind of embarrassing. I don't normally tell people about it."

"I'll bet."

"Most of the time on her covers, they cut off my head, so all you see is, well, my chest and a little below."

"I noticed."

Where in the hell did that comment come from?

"I'm happy to do it for her."

"For her. Sure. Nice of you to do it for your sister." It was her time to tease. Was he blushing? "You're actually blushing, Tyler Gray. Do cover models blush?"

"When we're affected."

That one was going to have to hang in the air a bit until she could figure out what it meant. *Affected?*

"Sometimes I do a shoot with a model. Things can heat up even though I don't know the girl."

Did she want to hear this?

"I imagine it can affect her too." *The girl would have to be blind!*

"Well, sometimes funny things happen. I'm sure you can imagine."

She could. She really could. And her mind shouldn't be going there at all. Not. At. All.

The pause between them felt a little awkward. "What brings you to Portland, or are you going on further north?" she asked.

"I'm going home to spend some time with the folks before—" he hesitated. "I'm in the military and I deploy in ten days."

"Ah." So that hard body was beginning to make sense. And his longer hair triggered a realization. She'd read enough romances to peg him as a Special Forces guy. "I'm guessing you do something dangerous."

He seemed to like that statement. "Some would say so." He was studying her reaction like his life depended on it. Without her meaning to, her eyelids fluttered and she found herself looking at his smooth, full lower lip, the clenched jaw muscles bunching under a day's stubble, and the swallow that moved his Adam's apple down his powerful neck. He had exactly the body parts she loved to see in a man. The soft lips that could give pleasure, the eyes that wouldn't waver from her face. Honest and relentless. Full of courage and unflinching. She liked men who would look back and not hide their attraction.

Because that meant she didn't have to hide hers.

And there it was, like a dragon coming to life, the danger and the power of getting swept away. The fantasy coming to life again, transporting her from where she sat on a plane to visit her sister before her upcoming wedding, to the edge of an adventure next to a man, God help her, she wished she could get naked with.

SEAL Of My Heart (Book #7) is available here.
sharonhamiltonauthor.com/SEALBro7

ABOUT THE AUTHOR

NYT and USA Today best-selling author Sharon Hamilton's award-winning Navy SEAL Brotherhood series have been a fan favorite from the day the first one was released. They've earned her the coveted Amazon author ranking of #1 in Romantic Suspense, Military Romance and Contemporary Romance categories, as well as in Gothic Romance for her Vampires of Tuscany and Guardian Angels. Her characters follow a sometimes rocky road to redemption through passion and true love.

Now that he's out of the Navy, Sharon can share with her readers that her son spent a decade as a Navy SEAL, and he's the inspiration for her books.

Her Golden Vampires of Tuscany are not like any vamps you've read about before, since they don't go to ground and can walk around in the full light of the sun.

Her Guardian Angels struggle with the human charges they are sent to save, often escaping their vanilla world of Heaven for the brief human one. You won't find any of these beings in any Sunday school class.

She lives in Sonoma County, California with her husband and her Doberman, Tucker. A lifelong organic gardener, when she's not writing, she's getting *verra verra* dirty in the mud, or wandering Farmers Markets looking for new Heirloom varieties of vegetables and flowers. She and her husband plan to cure their wanderlust (or make it worse) by traveling in their Diesel Class A Pusher, Romance Rider. Starting with this book, all her writing will be done on the road.

She loves hearing from her fans:
Sharonhamilton2001@gmail.com

Her website is:
sharonhamiltonauthor.com

Find out more about Sharon, her upcoming releases, appearances and news from her newsletter, **AND receive a free book** when you sign up for Sharon's newsletter.

Facebook:
facebook.com/SharonHamiltonAuthor

Twitter:
twitter.com/sharonlhamilton

Pinterest:
pinterest.com/AuthorSharonH

Google Plus:
plus.google.com/u/1/+SharonHamiltonAuthor/posts

BookBub:
bookbub.com/authors/sharon-hamilton

Youtube:
youtube.com/channel/UCDInkxXFpXp_4Vnq08ZxMBQ

Soundcloud:
soundcloud.com/sharon-hamilton-1

Sharon Hamilton's Rockin' Romance Readers:
facebook.com/groups/sealteamromance

Sharon Hamilton's Goodreads Group:
goodreads.com/group/show/199125-sharon-hamilton-readers-group

Visit Sharon's Online Store:
sharon-hamilton-author.myshopify.com

Join Sharon's Review Teams:

eBook Reviews:
sharonhamiltonassistant@gmail.com

Audio Reviews:
sharonhamiltonassistant@gmail.com

***Life** is one fool thing after another.*

***Love** is two fool things after each other.*

REVIEWS

PRAISE FOR THE GOLDEN VAMPIRES OF TUSCANY SERIES

"Well to say the least I was thoroughly surprise. I have read many Vampire books, from Ann Rice to Kym Grosso and few other Authors, so yes I do like Vampires, not the super scary ones from the old days, but the new ones are far more interesting far more human then one can remember. I found Honeymoon Bite a totally engrossing book, I was not able to put it down, page after page I found delight, love, understanding, well that is until the bad bad Vamp started being really bad. But seeing someone love another person so much that they would do anything to protect them, well that had me going, then well there was more and for a while I thought it was the end of a beautiful love story that spanned not only time but, spanned Italy and California. Won't divulge how it ended, but I did shed a few tears after screaming but Sharon Hamilton did not let me down, she took me on amazing trip that I loved, look forward to reading another Vampire book of hers."

"An excellent paranormal romance that was exciting,

romantic, entertaining and very satisfying to read. It had me anticipating what would happen next many times over, so much so I could not put it down and even finished it up in a day. The vampires in this book were different from your average vampire, but I enjoy different variations and changes to the same old stuff. It made for a more unpredictable read and more adventurous to explore! Vampire lovers, any paranormal readers and even those who love the romance genre will enjoy Honeymoon Bite."

"This is the first non-Seal book of this author's I have read and I loved it. There is a cast-like hierarchy in this vampire community with humans at the very bottom and Golden vampires at the top. Lionel is a dark vampire who are servants of the Goldens. Phoebe is a Golden who has not decided if she will remain human or accept the turning to become a vampire. Either way she and Lionel can never be together since it is forbidden.

I enjoyed this story and I am looking forward to the next installment."

"A hauntingly romantic read. Old love lost and new love found. Family, heart, intrigue and vampires. Grabbed my attention and couldn't put down. Would definitely recommend."

PRAISE FOR THE SEAL BROTHERHOOD SERIES

"Fans of Navy SEAL romance, I found a new author to feed your addiction. Finely written and loaded delicious with moments, Sharon Hamilton's storytelling satisfies like a thick bar of chocolate." —Marliss Melton, bestselling author of the *Team Twelve* Navy SEALs series

"Sharon Hamilton does an EXCELLENT job of fitting all the characters into a brotherhood of SEALS that may not be real but sure makes you feel that you have entered the circle and security of their world. The stories intertwine with each book before…and each book after and THAT is what makes Sharon Hamilton's SEAL Brotherhood Series so very interesting. You won't want to put down ANY of her books and they will keep you reading into the night when you should be sleeping. Start with this book…and you will not want to stop until you've read the whole series and then…you will be waiting for Sharon to write the next one." (5 Star Review)

"Kyle and Christy explode all over the pages in this first book, *[Accidental SEAL]*, in a whole new series of SEALs. If the twist and turns don't get your heart jumping, then maybe the suspense will. This is a must read for those that are looking for love and adventure with a little sloppy love thrown in for good measure." (5 Star Review)

PRAISE FOR THE BAD BOYS OF SEAL TEAM 3 SERIES

"I love reading this series! Once you start these books, you can hardly put them down. The mix of romance and suspense keeps you turning the pages one right after another! Can't wait until the next book!" (5 Star Review)

"I love all of Sharon's Seal books, but *[SEAL's Code]* may just be her best to date. Danny and Luci's journey is filled with a wonderful insight into the Native American life. It is a love story that will fill you with warmth and contentment. You will enjoy Danny's journey to become a SEAL and his reasons for it. Good job Sharon!" (5 Star Review)

PRAISE FOR THE BAND OF BACHELORS SERIES

"*[Lucas]* was the first book in the Band of Bachelors series and it was a phenomenal start. I loved how we got to see the other SEALs we all love and we got a look at Lucas and Marcy. They had an instant attraction, and their love was very intense. This book had it all, suspense, steamy romance, humor, everything you want in a riveting, outstanding read. I can't wait to read the next book in this series." (5 Star Review)

PRAISE FOR THE TRUE BLUE SEALS SERIES

"Keep the tissues box nearby as you read *True Blue SEALs: Zak* by Sharon Hamilton. I imagine more than I wish to that the circumstances surrounding Zak and Amy are all too real for returning military personnel and their families. Ms. Hamilton has put us right in the middle of struggles and successes that these two high school sweethearts endure. I have read several of Sharon Hamilton's military romances but will say this is the most emotionally intense of the ones that I have read. This is a well-written, realistic story with authentic characters that will have you rooting for them and proud of those who serve to keep us safe. This is an author who writes amazing stories that you love and cry with the characters. Fans of Jessica Scott and Marliss Melton will want to add Sharon Hamilton to their list of realistic military romance writers." (5 Star Review)

Made in United States
Orlando, FL
05 August 2022

20581802R00205